UNLEASHED

ALSO BY SOPHIE JORDAN
Uninvited

The Firelight Series
Firelight
Vanish
Hidden
Breathless (a digital original novella)

UNLEASHED

SOPHIE JORDAN

HARPER TEEN

An Imprint of HarperCollinsPublishers

HarperTeen is an imprint of HarperCollins Publishers.

Unleashed

Copyright © 2015 by Sharie Kohler

All rights reserved. Printed in the United States of America. No part of this book may be used or reproduced in any manner whatsoever without written permission except in the case of brief quotations embodied in critical articles and reviews. For information address HarperCollins Children's Books, a division of HarperCollins Publishers, 195 Broadway, New York, NY 10007.

www.epicreads.com

ISBN 978-0-06-223371-4 (trade bdg.)

Typography by Torborg Davern

15 16 17 18 19   PC/RRDH   10 9 8 7 6 5 4 3 2 1

First Edition

To Kari Sutherland —
for getting me through five books
and teaching me so much in the process.
Thank you doesn't come close to covering it.

PART ONE
RESISTANCE

Presidential Proclamation
Section 1. Funding for Detention Camps

a) Within forty-eight hours of the issuance date of this memorandum, and in conjunction with the Department of Treasury and the Office of Management of Budget, a sum of $1.27 billion shall be released to the Wainwright Agency for the express purpose of the administration and expansion of all detention camps for the continued harmony and protection of this country against the threat of HTS carriers, whose genetic mutation prc disposes them to commit violence. . . .

ONE

THE MAN I KILLED WON'T LEAVE ME ALONE.

He comes to me at night. The first time he intruded on my dreams I thought it was an isolated thing. A sudden troublesome nightmare that would fade with the night, never to return.

But it does. *He* does. And I begin to realize he's never going away. Brown eyes. Bullet hole. Black-red blood. He will always be there.

The knowledge sinks slowly, awfully, like an animal's teeth biting down and holding deep and hard into my muscle. I can't pull away. Can't shake it. I'm caught. Pinned in its jaws.

Strangely, I thought being labeled a killer and losing everything—my future, family, boyfriend, friends—was the worst thing that could ever happen to me. It's not. Finding out they were right? Finding out that's exactly what I am?

That's worse.

He's just a shadow in the corner of the room tonight. A dark, motionless shape, the edges of him blurred like smudges on paper.

I sit up in the bed, drawing my knees to my chest. Sean lies beside me, chest rising and falling softly, unaware of our late-night visitor. And I guess he's only *my* visitor really. Nothing haunts Sean. For him the past is just that. Something left behind, and I envy his ability to move on. To accept himself. To simply accept what is.

My gaze slides back to the dead man. I feel his familiar eyes crawling over me. Watch him watching me while cicadas drone a steady lullaby outside the trailer. Looking at him, I remember everything. That moment when the director of Mount Haven forced my hand and demanded that I kill. Oh, Harris gave me a choice. I guess. If letting him kill Sean was a choice. Either I killed a stranger—an anonymous carrier—or Sean died. That was my choice. No matter what, someone would have died. Either way, my fate was decided.

Sean sleeps on, blissfully unaware, his body like something sculpted from marble, the dark ink tattoos on his arm and neck standing out starkly against his lighter skin. I try to use this—the familiar, comforting sight of him—to make me feel better. He's why I killed that man, after all. So Sean could live. But it doesn't work. Unable to look at him, unable to bear the reminder, I turn away.

And that's what Sean has come to be. A reminder of the most horrible moment of my life. I don't regret saving him, but it doesn't change the fact that I'm a killer now.

When we first fled Mount Haven and arrived at this trailer practically sitting on the US-Mexican border, everything was great. Sean. Me. *We* were great. Holding hands, touching, kissing. Like two teenagers who had just discovered each other. In a way, I guess we were that. We curled around each other every night, our bodies like two spoons. There was no pressure beyond whispered words and lingering kisses. Just the scent of him, his skin warm and solid next to mine, was enough. Being with him filled me with a giddy sense of hope—a belief that everything was going to be all right. Was that only days ago? How quickly things disintegrated and dissolved to dust.

My nails dig into my palms, indenting the flesh with tiny half-moons. I embrace the pain, taking the punishment. Rolling on my side, I pretend that the figure in the corner isn't there anymore, watching me. Brown eyes. Bullet hole. Black-red blood.

I pretend Sean hasn't become someone I can't bear to see or touch or love.

Closing my eyes, I tell myself pretending will eventually work. That it will become real.

* * *

I'm the first one up. I feel achy and tired all over, and I take an extra-long shower, bowing my head and letting the water beat down on my neck. It doesn't help that I never really went back to sleep, too afraid of a repeat visit from Brown Eyes himself. I used to treasure my eight hours of sleep every night.

Back home, Mom had to shake me awake two or three times every morning. I loved my bed. The down-filled comforter. The surplus of pillows and stuffed animals from my youth. The way the morning sunlight would filter through my pink-and-green diaphanous curtains. It's strange how much you miss all those little things. What I wouldn't do to hug one of my old stuffed animals. To be that girl again. Sometimes on Saturdays Mom would make French toast and sausages. The savory aroma would fill the house and lure me from bed. It's hard to accept that those days are gone. Even lunches at my old private school, Everton, had been delicious. Not that I appreciated it at the time. I miss the salad bar and the made-to-order stir-fry.

Gil pops up on the couch, his hair sticking out in every direction. He rubs his eyes as I pour cereal into a bowl. No milk, but I'm already used to eating it dry.

A book slides to the floor. He must have fallen asleep reading it. It's an old, yellowed, dog-eared copy of *The Hobbit*. Last night he told Sabine the general plotline. She sat before him like a little girl, holding her knees and rocking in place, her eyes wide as he painted a picture of hobbits, dragons, and all manner of fantastical creatures. Sean had listened, too, his smile rueful as his eyes slid from them to me.

"Sorry." I wince as I set the box back down on the table. "Didn't mean to wake you."

Blinking, Gil reaches for his glasses sitting on the upside-down crate serving as a coffee table. No longer blind, he zeroes in on me. "Nah, I needed to get up anyway."

I resist asking why. It's not as though we have that much to do. Sean monitors the comings and goings at the river below. Gil occasionally joins him or relieves him. Right now we're just waiting until Sunday, when we'll make our crossing. Along with a copy of *The Hobbit*, we discovered a box of checkers on the dusty shelf in the corner of the trailer. We play that a lot, even though Gil always wins. There's the challenge, the hope that we might beat him, that keeps bringing us back. That and boredom.

I munch noisily as Gil removes a stale bagel from a bag and takes a huge bite. Our food choices are limited. The place was supplied with minimal groceries when we first arrived. Nothing fresh. Mostly items that won't expire or grow mold anytime soon.

"Didn't think I could miss anything about Mount Haven," he mutters, dry crumbs falling from his lips.

I nod, understanding. "The food."

"I never ate that well before. Unless you count jumbo slushies and bags of Cheetos from the gas station."

I nod like I agree. Like I didn't eat well in my old life, too. Except I did. We ate out at the best restaurants. Sushi. Chinese. Italian. And Mom was a good cook, even if she only bothered once, maybe twice, a week. She made a lasagna so deep you could lose a fork in it. Dad would groan at the sight of it. My chest tightens, an uncomfortable ball forming in the center. I wonder if I'll ever see them again.

Sean and Sabine join us. We all move around in companionable silence, preparing our unappetizing breakfasts.

Sabine isn't a morning person. You're lucky to get a word out of her before ten a.m. She rips the foil packaging off a Pop-Tart and sits across from me at the table. Shaking long brown hair back from her face, she manages a smile, biting into the pastry. Crumbs fall to the table, and she brushes them onto the floor.

Sean uses one of the jugs of water to make some coffee, and soon the rich aroma fills the trailer. He offers me a mug and I accept. After the first bitter swallow, I reach for the sugar and add a generous spoonful. Then a second. Maybe someday I'll enjoy a latte again. Maybe they have those where we're going. Maybe. My life is full of maybes. Even more than the maybes are the "never happening agains."

I sigh against the ceramic rim, grateful for the surge of caffeine to my bloodstream.

"Good?" Sean asks.

"Yeah. Thanks."

Sabine's gaze darts between us. There's silent inquiry in her eyes. Speculation. I know she's wondering what's up with us. Well, with me.

Sean gathers up his well-worn map and binoculars and the spiral pad he's been using to take notes. The map in his hand crinkles as he says, "I'll be back later." His gaze sweeps the room, lingering on me the longest. "I wouldn't mind some company."

I nod, and the motion feels jerky, unnatural. "Sure. I'll be out in a little while." Like I have something keeping me inside the trailer.

The trailer door shuts quietly after him.

Gil rises. "Hope you don't mind, but I'm gonna borrow one of the beds and go back to sleep. That couch sucks."

He heads off, the weak linoleum creaking under his bare feet. I've been here almost a week and still can't stand walking barefoot over the gross floor.

"So what's up with you and Sean?"

My gaze whips up. Sabine has moved on to the second Pop-Tart. She chews primly.

Despite our less-than-stellar diet of Pop-Tarts and dry cereal, she looks good. Better than she did when I first met her at Mount Haven. There's color in her cheeks now and her gaze is bright.

"What do you mean?"

She rolls her eyes. "You can barely look at him."

Is it that obvious? We're all getting along. Smiling. I put on a good show. At least I thought so. "We're fine. Nothing's wrong," I deny. Because it can't be. Whatever this is, I'll fix it. We'll be fine. I'll be fine.

"Right." The corner of her mouth lifts. "When we first got here, you two couldn't keep your hands off each other. It was like being stuck with a couple of honeymooners."

My face warms. "It's nothing. I'm just focused on getting across. I'll relax once this is over and we've made it to the other side."

She shrugs a slim shoulder. "We'll either make it or we won't. I'd think you'd want to get in as much quality time with Sean as you can before we leave. Especially since we might be caught or killed. Carpe diem and all that." She says it so matter-of-factly. Our life has become this. The subject of our potential demise commonplace. *Caught or killed.* At this point, they're one and the same.

Her smile slips away and she stares at me evenly, a sharp glint in her eyes. Almost like she's annoyed with me. How can I explain to her what's going through my head? That since we settled in here, I'm having a hard time coming to terms with killing that guy. Being close to Sean is . . . difficult.

Rising from the table, I murmur something about making the bed and head to the back of the trailer. One thing about being stuck in an eight-hundred-square-foot space is that there is nowhere to hide. Not from one another. Not from ghosts.

I wake with a jolt again that night. Opening my eyes, I sit up and immediately look for him. The man I killed. He's not here. A relieved breath pushes past my lips.

"Davy?" Sean's there, sitting up beside me. I blink at the empty space surrounding us and lower my body back down on the bed, clutching the sheets to my chest in knotted fists. I gaze at the ceiling, focusing on the web of spidery cracks in the vinyl-covered ceiling.

Sean settles beside me. His hand curls around my arm in a loose touch.

"Bad dream?" His deep voice rumbles through the dark.

I nod. It's easier than explaining that I woke because I was afraid a manifestation of the guy I killed might have decided to come visit me again.

"Are you okay?"

My voice scratches across the air papery-thin. "Yes."

"Why do I feel like you're just telling me that because you think it's what I want to hear?"

It's what *I* want to hear, too. It's what I want to be true.

I face Sean in the dark. He's so close but feels far away from me. It's as if I left him in the past. Back at Mount Haven, where they were grooming us to be something more than the killer stamped onto our genetic code. Something worse. Except he isn't gone. He's here. "I don't want you to worry about me."

"I'm always going to worry about you, Davy. That's called caring."

"I know. I care about you, too." *I'm just not sure I can be with you anymore. Not like this. Not the way you want me to be. Not the way you deserve.*

After a moment, his hand slips from my arm and some of my tension whispers free, and I hate this. Hate that I've pulled away from him and he knows it. Sabine noticed. He'd be a fool not to notice. If it wouldn't be so awkward, I would move into Sabine's room across the hall. But that would only be like waving a red flag that something is wrong, that I'm broken.

"Good night, Davy."

"Good night," I return.

I'm going to be okay. We're going to be fine. Broken things get fixed all the time. I'll stop being so weird around Sean, and everything—the world included—will work itself out.

A beautiful eagle was gliding through the vast skies when he heard the hiss of an arrow. He screeched as the tip pierced his body. Mortally wounded, he plunged down to earth, his life-blood draining into the sand. Looking down at the arrow jutting from his side, the eagle discovered that the shaft had been feathered with one of his very own plumes—his destruction that of his own creation.

—*Aesop's Fables*, "The Eagle and the Arrow"

TWO

GIL HAS TAKEN TO PREPARING OUR DINNERS, AND IF I never eat another peanut butter sandwich again, that would be just fine with me. I long for a warm meal. French fries. God, *pizza*.

"I miss my mother's cooking," Sabine murmurs, tearing off bits of her sandwich and placing them in her mouth. "She made schnitzel and sauerbraten. Like the real deal, you know?" She cocks her head to the side. "Think I'll ever have German food again?"

"In Germany," Gil volunteers.

Sabine laughs without humor. "Yeah. My chances of going back home to Garden City, Idaho, to visit my family are better than me making it to Germany." Sabine hasn't said much about her family up to this point. I know she's one of six kids—the only one with HTS. Her father considered taking her and running away, but he couldn't abandon the rest of the family. Not just for her. I think she understands that, but it must sting nonetheless, knowing you're the sacrifice.

"Where we're headed?" Gil shakes his head. "I doubt you'll ever see bratwurst again. Your mom never taught you to cook?"

"She tried. I never paid attention. I was too into robotics."

"I never knew you were a tech geek." Gil's face brightens.

"I wasn't that great at it, but yeah. I was on my high school robotics team."

"You must have been good. They brought you to Mount Haven for some reason."

"Yeah, because I speak German and passable French. Not that that's gonna help me much in Mexico." She reaches for a pudding cup, tearing it apart from the others in the pack. It's like she feels the pressure of our gazes, though. She looks up and gives a small shrug. "And I had a nearly perfect GPA."

"Oh." Gil rolls his eyes. "That might have been another factor."

Tucking a long strand of brown hair behind her ear, she smiles at him, then glances at me and Sean.

"I miss my mom's lasagna," I volunteer, arriving at

something to contribute to the conversation, determined to shake off my funk and be as normal as possible with my friends. Because they are my friends. The only friends I have left. I need to make an effort.

"Enchiladas," Sean adds, taking a bite of his sandwich. Gil made him two. A good thing, considering he devours half a sandwich in one bite.

"I don't think that will be a problem where we're going. We should get some decent Mexican food at least." Sabine reaches for another pudding cup. She peels the foil top back and licks it clean.

"We can hope," I say.

"You kidding?" Gil shakes his head. "I'm expecting some serious Mexican food like what my *abuela* made. I can't wait for some *chicharrónes*."

I can't help smiling. "Or what? It's a deal breaker? We'll stay here and eat peanut butter and pudding cups forever?"

"Hello, Debbie Downer," Sabine teases, tossing empty pudding cups into the nearby trash can.

"Watch. In a month we'll be missing pudding cups and peanut butter." Sean nudges my shoulder lightly. I smile back at him, and it's not too hard.

Sabine wrinkles her nose. "Doubtful."

I try to imagine where we'll be in a month, but it's all gray. Just fuzzy static when I try to visualize the future. There's no clear image, and this is still strange to me. Months ago, I could picture my future down to the smallest detail. Prom. Graduation. Me with Zac in New York. Juilliard.

Gil gets up and takes his plate to the sink. "I'm going to try the radio again."

Sabine groans. "The reception is terrible."

He shrugs. "I caught something earlier today."

He sits on a stool at the short stretch of countertop and fiddles with the radio. Sabine starts on her third pudding cup. I don't know where she puts it, but at least she looks less gaunt than when we first met at Mount Haven.

Scratchy static fills the air as Gil hunts for a station.

I glance at Sean. "Do you think they're looking for us?" I don't have to elaborate. He knows I mean the people from Mount Haven. The fear has weighed on me—on all of us, I'm sure. It's like we consciously try not to voice it. I search Sean's face.

"I doubt they're giving up any staff or manpower to come after us. Someone will be keeping an eye out for us, but it's probably not anyone from Mount Haven. Just general Agency people and the Border Patrol."

"We're probably on some kind of list, though," Gil chimes in, his face screwed tight with concentration as he slowly turns the dial. "Probably got our faces plastered all over the internet and every gas station between here and Austin."

Sabine snorts as she scrapes at the inside of the cup. "Like a list of the government's most wanted carriers or something?"

Not "or something." There's probably just such a list, and we're on it. My stomach knots uncomfortably. I think about the fact that our faces are out there for every agent of the Wainwright Agency to commit to memory. We'll never be free to return to this country.

"We should think about altering our appearances," Sean suggests. "I mean, we're always going to be two guys and two girls . . . but maybe we can do something."

I nod, wondering how we could do that out here in the middle of nowhere. Tossing a knowing smile at us, Sabine gets up and moves down the hall to the bathroom.

Gil continues to work over the box, turning the dial, inching along. Every once in a while a snatch of Tejano music fills the air. I grimace. The world still plays music. For some reason that strikes me as odd. Wrong somehow. Which is really weird for me to think. Have I actually reached a point where hearing music feels so wrong?

"Hey." Sean nudges me. "Finish your sandwich. You need your strength."

I force a smile and take another bite, working the thickness of peanut butter around in my mouth.

Sean studies me, his eyebrows drawn tightly together in an expression of concern. He watches me like this all the time now. Like he's worried something he says or does might be the final straw that shatters me.

Sabine returns then, brandishing a few boxes in the air. "I just figured out why these are under the sink. This underground network thinks of everything."

"What are they?" Gil asks.

"Clairol." She reads each box. "Ebony Mocha, Nutmeg, and Midnight Black." She looks back at me and Sean with an arched eyebrow. "Who wants to go first?"

* * *

Sean and Gil watch in silence as Sabine cuts my hair with a pair of kitchen scissors. The blades saw sharply through the thick strands. Gil's eyes widen as the long pieces fall like dandelions dropping through air.

We all agreed cutting my hair would help alter my appearance, but the decision was mostly just to ensure we had enough dye. The instructions recommended two boxes for long hair, and since we only have one box of any given color, Sabine got to play barber.

Sean's expression is calmly neutral, but he watches me carefully, closely, staring at my face, not my rapidly diminishing hair. It's like he's waiting for me to crumble.

Over *hair*? Does he think I'm that fragile? I start to shake my head at the idea, but stop at Sabine's warning hiss.

Holding still, I face myself in the mirror as Sabine moves around to the back. I watch my transformation with a curious sense of detachment. Oddly enough, I feel lighter. Unburdened. Like with every lock of hair hitting the floor, a bit of the old me is left behind, too, making way for a new girl.

My hair now closely frames my face, ending just a little bit below my ears. My eyes pop, enormous in my face without my hair shrouding me. And my imprint pops, too. The dark band with the trademark H more pronounced than ever.

"I think it's pretty straight," Sabine murmurs, her forehead knitting with intent focus. She clamps the scissors between her teeth and squats before me, grabbing the ends of my hair dangling just below my ears and stretching them to see if they match.

"Doesn't matter," I say. "It's just hair."

"Oh, this looks hot." She grins at me.

I snort.

"Good?" She looks at Sean and Gil for confirmation.

Sean steps inside the bathroom and suddenly everything grows tighter, claustrophobic almost. He lightly tugs at a lock of hair brushing the back of my neck. "This piece here. It's still too long."

Sabine leans in and snips. "All right . . . now for the good part."

She shakes a plastic bottle holding the dark dye for several seconds, still grinning.

"You're having too much fun," I accuse.

She nods. "You know it. Maybe I have a future in this. When we get to where we're going, I can open a salon."

Setting the bottle down, she tugs on a pair of plastic gloves with surgical precision and squirts some of the dark goo into her palms. The strong aroma fills the space, stinging my nostrils and making my eyes tear up. She cuts me a glance. "This might hurt a little."

I laugh. "Quit it."

"You're not performing heart surgery," Gil utters from the door.

Sabine glances at Sean, who still fills the small bathroom, arching an eyebrow at him. "Gonna give me some room in here, big guy?"

He hesitates a moment, looking from the handful of dark glop to me.

I smile encouragingly. "It's just hair," I remind him.

And I'm not just saying that to make him feel better. It's true. A thing like cutting off my hair and dying it midnight black might have seemed reprehensible to the girl I used to be. But it didn't even register on the radar of things I care about now.

"That's right," Sabine agrees. "You're not in love with her hair, right?"

I glare at Sabine and bite back the impulse to argue that he's not in love with me at all. At least he's never said those words to me. It's a relief, actually. The words would only make me feel bound to him, responsible for him in a way that I can't deal with right now. I already care too much about him. About him and Gil and Sabine. I don't need to pile on more.

I hold my tongue in the strained silence that ensues. And that isn't awkward. No. Not awkward at all.

She rolls her eyes and with her one free hand adjusts the towel draping my shoulders. Leaning down, she says near my ear, "Lighten up."

That said, she smacks a handful of dye onto the top of my head and starts working it into the short mass of hair. It doesn't take long until my hair is a wet black helmet hugging my scalp.

Sabine glances at Gil. "Give me thirty minutes, then we'll check it. Might take longer."

He glances at his watch. "Okay."

Her gaze narrows on Sean. "Next."

"All right. Let's do this." He pulls off his shirt and tosses it down, revealing his well-muscled torso. Zac was a rugby player, and I spent a lot of time in the summer around rugby guys. I always thought they were big, but Sean makes me reconsider my definition of big.

Sabine's eyes widen like she's never seen a shirtless guy before, and I guess a shirtless Sean is a little gawk-worthy. It's like he takes up all the space in the small bathroom.

I sit on the toilet seat, lid down, and suffer the stink of dye soaking on my head. My scalp tingles and itches, and I have to resist digging my fingernails into the ink-dark mess piled on top of my head. The stench stings my nostrils, and I can only think of Mom right then. Her horror if she knew I was dying my hair. Then that thought dies. It wouldn't have been the most horrible thing to happen to her daughter in recent months.

Sitting on an upside-down bucket, Sean is stoic as Sabine makes quick work of his hair. He leans his back against the sink, looking as ridiculous as I do. Gil waves a hand in front of his face. "Sorry. Gotta bail before I pass out from the smell."

"Wimp!" Sabine calls, yanking off her gloves and tossing them in the trash. Taking a towel, she gives us both her attention, wiping at the skin edging our hairlines, cleaning off the brown ring so it doesn't stain our faces too much. "You're both going to be a pair of brunette beauties." I smile. It's hard not to.

She turns and washes her hands in the sink, scrubbing at

where some of the dye reached her forearms.

I glance at Sean. "It's good to see you smile," he says.

At his words, my smile threatens to slip away, but I fight to keep it in place.

"I'm sure when we get across we'll all have a lot more reason to smile," Sabine interjects, staring at both of us in the mirror's reflection.

I nod, hoping she's right.

ENTERTAINMENT Weekly

News Release

June 5, 2021

News out of Los Angeles, CA: The country is reeling from the news that forty-two-year-old beloved three-time Oscar winner Evangeline Alvares has stepped forward and announced that she carries the HTS gene. No word yet if she will be relocated to a detention camp. Agency spokespeople have refused comment. . . .

THREE

THAT NIGHT THE DEAD MAN LURKS IN THE CORNER
again. I sneak a glance at Sean, still asleep. Nothing disturbs
him. Not the girl slowly losing her mind beside him. Did I possess a mad gene, too, to go along with my kill gene? Because
clearly, I'm losing it.

I return my gaze to the figure in the corner. He's motionless in that I-could-spring-at-you-any-moment way.

"What do you want?" I demand, my voice whisper-soft,
fingers clutching the blanket, fearful that I might wake
Sean.

There is no reply. I bury my face in my hands and then

slide them up, pulling my hair back almost violently, eyes fixed unblinking on him.

"I'm sorry. Just go away. Leave me alone. Please leave me alone." The mantra trips from my lips, picking up speed.

His guttural, barely-there voice reaches me. I lock up, all of me freezing tight as I search his shadow, straining to hear that hoarse stretch of a single word. *"Never."*

The solitary word tears through me like a rusty wire. Of course he's never going away. I killed him. Took his life. Gazed into his eyes as he took his last breath. It's impossible to hide from this. He'll find me. Here. In Mexico. Wherever I go, he will go with me.

A sob strangles my throat and I look down unseeingly, rocking, staring into my lap, tugging my short hair back until my scalp stings. Gibberish, incoherent pleas flow from my lips, begging him to go, to leave me alone. I don't know who I'm talking to. God maybe. If God still listens to the prayers of someone like me.

I relax my grip on my skull and look up. The dark shape is gone. Shadows bleed over the walls with the oncoming dawn. *God.* I laugh softly. Maybe I am losing my mind. Hallucinating. Either that or a ghost really is visiting me. Whatever the case, I'm pretty much in a world of suck.

Sean still sleeps, lost in dreams. Or even better—that great oblivion of sleep where even dreams can't touch you. He's totally unmired in the past, and I envy him that. Maybe resent it, too. Even though it's not his fault.

I inhale, but the room feels too tight, the walls too close.

The odor of my freshly dyed hair sears my nostrils. I slip from the bed and make my way down the narrow hall, my sock-clad feet treading silently on the floor, my palms skimming along the wall as I walk. I step past the smaller bedroom where Sabine sleeps. Gil snores from the couch.

At the front door, I squeeze my feet into my shoes and turn the doorknob, desperate to taste air and feel open space all around me. Careful not to wake anyone, I ease outside.

Cool twilight greets me. The cicadas go at it, a hypnotic drone that drapes over a thicker layer of silence. It's this under-lying silence that unnerves me. It throbs like something alive, pulsing over my skin. Through me. The kind of quiet that you never hear in the city. Or in the suburbs. That indefinable thing, that electric *buzz*, is missing. *People.*

I tuck the choppy-short strands of hair behind my ears, exposing them to the bite of cold. I shiver, choosing my steps carefully over the broken and rutted ground as I make my way to the lookout. A quick glance behind reveals the hulk-ing shape of the trailer. It looks innocuous, grim, and desolate sitting on concrete blocks, the hardwood planks cracked and buckling in places. The harsh climate has taken its toll on the structure. It's as battered as the landscape.

A coyote yips in the distance. Months ago the sound would have startled me and sent me running back for shelter. I would have been terrified of coming face-to-face with a wild animal, but I don't worry anymore. There are worse things than beasts waiting in the dark. Things like me.

Wind tears at my hair as I lower myself down to the

outcropping overlooking the river far below. The rough scrape of rock abrades my palms as I settle my weight. Sean has spent hours out here, his skin turning brown from observing the comings and goings in the valley below.

The faintest color tinges the sky, casting the dawn a murky blue. I hug my knees to my chest, wishing I'd brought a blanket with me. It's cold in the mornings and at night.

I know that the temperature will spike once the sun rises and bakes the earth—and us inside the trailer. We have a couple of table fans, but they only seem to stir the hot air around. I should enjoy the chill while I have it.

The coyote is quiet now. It's only the purr of cicadas over the silence as I squint into the darkness below, detecting the barest glint of water there, waiting for us to cross.

Suddenly a blanket is draped over my shoulders. I start a little, glancing up sharply. Sean sinks down beside me.

"You should tell someone when you're leaving the trailer."

I nod. He's right, of course. We're fugitives. They're looking for us. Well, maybe not us specifically, but carriers. We can't be the only ones out here hiding. Hoping to get across.

"Thank you." I tighten my fingers around the edge of the blanket. The fabric helps ward off the chill, but I still shiver. Silence stretches between us as we stare out at the fading night.

Sean's voice strokes over me. "You ready to leave here?"

"As ready as I'll ever be." Maybe out there, on the other side, dead men won't haunt me.

I feel his gaze on me. "What's going on, Davy?"

I don't pretend that I don't understand his meaning. I tried that with Sabine, but I can't do that with Sean. Not after all we've been through. I owe him more than that. And yet I don't know how to explain it, either. Am I prepared to confess that I'm seeing ghosts? "I can't shake off Mount Haven. What I did there." It's as close as I can come to articulating the fact that I murdered someone in cold blood. He knows it, of course, but that doesn't mean I can say it aloud.

I turn and get caught up in his eyes. Their blue-gray glitters at me in the rising dawn, and I long for when those eyes used to make me feel all kinds of good. "It'll pass," he says.

I nod, wanting to believe that, wanting to find some happiness.

"Give it time," he adds. "Things happen. Things that you think you'll never get over. But you do. You move on. It gets better with time. You forget. Forgive. Whatever." A long pause follows, like he's thinking . . . remembering something. Probably that thing he's forgiven himself for. "Life goes on and you go on with it."

He sounds like he almost believes that. I study him, searching to see the crack in his expression that reveals he doesn't—that he's lying to himself. To me. It never comes. He's reached some kind of peace inside himself. Desperate longing for that same peace fills me, spreading in a bitter ache through my chest.

He catches me looking at him. "What?"

"You really believe that."

"Sure." A hint of a smile curves his lips. "I do."

"Then you mustn't have done anything really wrong."

Nothing like I did.

His jaw tenses and his gaze slides off me. In the emerging dawn I see a dimming in the light behind his eyes. "It was wrong."

"Tell me." My gaze flicks to his imprint—the dark band with the circled H. We're talking about this. Finally. About how he got the imprint. "How'd you get the tattoo?"

His eyes fall unerringly back on me, almost as though I compelled him. As though my voice forced him to look at me.

"Tell me," I repeat, needing to hear this. I've waited so long to learn what he did to deserve that—if he did really do anything at all. He had been a child when the Agency imprinted him. Hard to imagine he could have done anything too terrible. Especially then. As good, as honorable, as he is now, how could he have been worse as a boy?

"I was eleven," he begins, his voice drifting, curling into the brightening air washing over us. "It was before my foster mom took me in, and I was at a home for boys. We slept in a dormitory. I had a top bunk." He shrugs. "I thought it was cool. Bunk beds, you know."

I nod.

"I'd been there a few months. I'd moved from a different facility to this new one for older boys," he continues. "I was still fighting to find my place. Literally, every day. A bunch of us boys beating the piss out of each other."

"Sounds like a prison movie."

"Yeah. Not that different. Any time a new kid moved in, the hazing was brutal. Things had finally started to ease up for me, and then this new boy arrived. I can still remember his name. Branson." Sean expels the name with a heavy breath. "He was about the same age as me but a hell of a lot bigger."

"Bigger?" I feel my eyebrow wing high. Sean's no small guy.

"Yeah. I was pretty average for my age then. I shot up six inches the summer before freshman year. But Branson was like a grown man already. The guy had a beard by three p.m."

I smile a little.

He snorts. "His hazing was brief, of course. No one wanted to take him on. The second day he was there, he decided he wanted my top bunk." He laughs hoarsely. "He could have picked on one of the others with a top bunk, but no, I was the lucky one."

His hand moves to my hand resting on the rocky ground between us. His fingers trace a small pattern on the back of it. For once, I don't shrink from his touch. I'm too engrossed in his story. His words weave around me like a spell.

"I could feel everyone's eyes on me when he ordered me to switch bunks with him." His voice drops to a low rumble, and I know he's back in that moment, living it. "I knew if I let him have that bunk it would—" He shakes his head and makes a small grunt. "They would never let up on me. It would be hazing twenty-four/seven. It would be relentless. Hell."

"What then?" I prod, desperate to hear more. Desperate also for him to stop, fearful of where he's going with this.

"Neither one of us were going to back down. So stupid." He laughs dryly. I'm not sure if he means himself or Branson or the situation in general. "He was trying to drag me off the top bunk. He had me by the ankles, and I just hauled back and kicked him in the face. Hard. As hard as I could. I still had my shoes on, you know."

My hand turns beneath his, bringing our palms flush together. His skin is warm and solid. I give his fingers a squeeze. It's all I can do. Maybe just a futile attempt to give comfort. Except he doesn't need comforting. That's what he's saying, anyway. What he wants me to believe. Even if the way his hand clenches mine back says otherwise.

"What happened?" I press.

"He flew backward several feet. I heard the crack of his skull when he hit the floor." He leans back, dropping on the ground and staring up at the fading night. The stars are still visible, studding the sky. Still holding on to my hand, he drapes his other arm across his forehead. He studies the canopy of stars like it's a great canvas of art.

"Did he . . ."

"They took him to the hospital. He broke several vertebrae. Concussion. I didn't see him again after that. I think he was in the hospital for a long time, and he wore a brace afterward . . . at least that's what I heard."

"But he could still walk."

"Eventually." He nods. "Immediately after that I was imprinted and put in a home for boys with imprints. Met one of my foster brothers there. That's where Martha found us."

"It was an accident—" I start to say, and then stop. It's what he keeps telling me, and each time I never want to hear it. I wet my lips. He probably doesn't want to hear it, either.

"It was just normal boy stuff. Hardly deserving of getting imprinted."

"And slapping a boy because he was a jerk to you is?"

I flinch at this reminder of Zac. Slapping him had been immature of me, a thoughtless reaction to an ugly situation. A boyfriend turning out to be less than the prince I thought him to be was a crushing blow at the time. And yet slapping him shouldn't have been a crime. It shouldn't have gotten me marked for life.

"I don't kid myself. If Branson had been someone important—not another carrier—I would have ended up in jail. I'd probably still be there."

And I would never have met him.

I try to imagine this. I don't think I could have gotten through my time at Keller, once I was expelled from Everton, without him. Those weeks stuck in the Cage were awful. It was bad enough that we carriers were quarantined from the rest of the school in an old sports equipment room, complete with a lockable grate, but then to have that pervy sleazebag Brockman guarding the six of us . . . My nape prickles at the thought of what Brockman could have done to me. He'd already made life hell for Coco, the only other female carrier there. He would have tried to do the same to me. And again, at Mount Haven, Sean was always there to defend me, whether I wanted it or not.

"We're just doing our best to live in this world, Davy." Sean's voice stretches into the fading dark. "We're not perfect, but we're not monsters, either. We're just human."

"I know," I murmur. "I'm trying to get there." And I am. I really am.

I ease down beside him and join him in gazing at the stars. Eventually their light starts to diminish as day takes over.

Gradually I slide my hand away from his, still needing that distance, that space.

"So time is the answer?" I try not to sound so skeptical. Especially after everything he just revealed to me.

"You'll get there, Davy."

He sounds so certain. I wish I could be. After a while I prop myself up on my elbows and look out at the river again. That's all I need. Time and freedom. A life that isn't crippled with regret. Where brown eyes and bullet holes don't follow me everywhere. Then I'll be me again. Or at least some new version of me that isn't always looking behind her.

Our last night in the trailer I can't sleep. I don't let myself. Maybe it's because we'll be up in a few hours anyway, heading across the border. Once we cross, we'll meet with our contacts on the other side, sympathizers who help relocate carriers like us to refugee camps in Mexico. The driver who brought us here had given us the instructions. It could just be nerves, my anxiousness for the upcoming journey. That might be what keeps me awake. I know I should rest, store my energy for the trip ahead, but it's pointless. I can't sleep.

Sean shifts beside me, his arm draping over my waist, and I tense.

Lifting his arm from my waist, I slip silently from the bed

and ease from the bedroom. I take two steps down the hall before coming face-to-face with Sabine. I swallow back a gasp.

"Sorry," she whispers.

"Hey," I return. "What are you doing up?"

She lifts a glass. "Water. What are you doing up?"

I glance back to the shut door behind me, unsure how to reply, unwilling to lay it all out there. Especially since I'm fighting the truth within myself, determined to change it.

Instead I go with: "Couldn't sleep."

She nods as though understanding. "Nervous about tomorrow?"

I shake my head. "Not really. I'm ready." Ready and anxious.

She cocks her head, studying me, her gaze dark in the lightless hallway. She motions to her room. "Wanna talk for a while so we don't wake Gil?"

"Sure." I follow her into the smaller bedroom and sit on her mattress with my back propped against the wall.

She follows suit, sitting cross-legged and holding her glass in her lap, lightly tracing the rim. "What do you think it will be like when we get over there?"

I shrug. "Better than this, I'm sure. We won't be paranoid over the Agency showing up." At least I don't think they're following carriers into Mexico. And from what we've managed to hear on the radio, the Mexican government is too busy focusing their efforts on protecting the border. They're not chasing down fugitives inside their country.

We knew when we ran that there would be no going back

to Mount Haven. No second chances. If they catch us, we're dead. I rest my head against the wall and slide her a long glance. Forward is the only way to go. "At least over there we have a shot."

"You ever wonder if it's like Mount Haven over there, too?"

"What do you mean?"

"Well. A bunch of carriers cooped up together . . . we know how dangerous that can be."

"There won't be anyone forcing us to hurt each other. We won't be at anyone's mercy." My voice comes out sharper than I intended. I can't help it. It's always there. The fact that I'm just what they said I am—what my DNA proclaims me to be. A killer. "We'll be free to go or stay. That makes all the difference in the world. It's not a prison."

She takes a long drink from her glass. "But we'll still be trapped—"

"Not trapped," I quickly insert. "I'll never be trapped again. We can come and go—"

"And go where?" At my silence, she snorts, and the sound irks me, seeming to say, *I thought so.*

She shakes her head. "I'm just keeping things in perspective . . . and hoping you are, too."

"Me?" I blink. "Why wouldn't I be keeping things in perspective?" Whatever that means.

"I just don't think things will necessarily be better over there."

They have to be. I simply stare at her.

She continues, "We're different . . . all of us. You know

that, right? I mean this—" She waves in the direction of my neck and the imprint there. I resist the urge to touch it—like I can feel the brand on my skin. "Some of us are killers. It's in our blood . . . that ability. It doesn't mean we walk around killing without conscience, but we're just . . . better equipped to do it. Some people don't have it in them, but we do. You'll feel a lot better once you accept that."

I stare at her blankly, slowly processing her words. I refuse to agree. I can never agree. I don't want to be different in that way. I don't want to be *better equipped*. "I can't accept that."

"You killed—"

"I had to," I cut in swiftly, hating her a little right then for daring to throw that in my face. She's supposed to be my friend.

"Precisely." She nods. "For Sean. That's my point. Someone else maybe couldn't have even done that. But you're a carrier. . . ." Her voice trails off, her eyes gleaming at me suggestively. Encouragingly. Like a mother urging her baby to take its first step. *C'mon. You can do it . . . you can get there. Keep trying.*

I twist my shoulder in a semblance of a shrug.

She blows out a heavy breath. "You should be glad you're the way you are. Or Sean would be dead."

My lips part, impossible words hanging there, unformed, strangling way back in my throat.

"Think about it," she adds. "I'm not judging. I can understand it."

"You can?"

"When I was beating up Addy—"

"You didn't end her life," I remind sharply. Big. Difference.

"No, but it was easy. I didn't blink over hurting her."

I shake my head. "She brutalized you. She was trying to keep us from escaping."

"Exactly." Her eyes glint at me, satisfied that she has made her point.

"Maybe," I murmur, ready to quit talking about it and stick my head in a hole in true ostrich fashion. I scoot off the bed. "I'm going to try to get some sleep. Good night." Suddenly returning to bed and the room of my haunting isn't so unappealing. The conversation with her made my head hurt. Even after I make it back to my room and slide into bed beside Sean, I can still hear her words ringing in my ears. *You should be glad you're the way you are.*

NEWS RELEASE

For immediate release

Contact: Department of Justice—
          Office of the Attorney General

May 19, 2021

US Customs and Border Protection has announced its partnership with the Wainwright Agency in order to more effectively monitor and impede the passage of escaped HTS carriers from US detention facilities into Mexico. Already 180 agents have been dispatched to help with efforts to contain these violent individuals along the border of the United States and Mexico. . . .

FOUR

SEAN CHECKS OUR GEAR FOR THE THIRD TIME.

"C'mon, man, I think we're good." Gil shifts anxiously on his feet.

Sean straightens, staring down at our packs like he can see inside them. I know he must have the contents memorized by now. Still, he looks unconvinced. "You think we packed enough food?"

"We can't fit any more," I point out.

Sabine picks up a pack, wincing as she swings it over her shoulder. "I can't carry any more cans in this. I mean, not without tipping over."

Sean's lips quirk, his gaze sweeping her diminutive frame. "Yeah. Okay."

I pause over that smile. It's been days since Sean smiled. At least at me. Sure, he stares at me a lot. But not the kind of stare that used to make my stomach flutter. His stares are like the worried ones Mom gave me from the moment I was first declared a carrier. Like she didn't know quite what to say to me. Or how to act around me. That's Sean now. Unsure of me.

We depart the trailer into dark night. Or morning, I suppose. Three a.m. qualifies as morning. We trek down the mountain, careful with our steps, Sean leading the way. This isn't the time to turn an ankle. Sean scouted the trail several times over the last week and appears to know the best way down. Not that I'm surprised. He's capable that way. Of the four of us, he's the most fit. Gil can hack into any system and make a decent sandwich, but Sean can bench-press a Volkswagen. He's the one who needed the least amount of training at Mount Haven. Gil follows him, then I trail Gil. I can't hear Sabine behind me. Her steps fall without a whisper. Maybe Mount Haven taught her something. Or it could be that at five feet and a hundred pounds she moves with a natural stealth.

It's a slow descent. The incline isn't that steep, but there's so much brush and scrub that it's almost an hour before we reach the river. I can hear the rush of water as we approach.

Sean stops and faces us. His eyes glitter in the dark as he slips off his pack and drops it to the ground.

"Wait here," he instructs. "The boat should be nearby. Let me find it."

I hold my breath, watching as he disappears, his shadow merging with the night. I hold myself motionless, staring after him. Sabine fidgets nervously, her head swinging left and right. I can almost visualize her darting gaze, like prey scanning for danger. Although I don't quite consider her prey anymore. Not since I saw her take out Addy.

Not since talking to her last night.

Gil takes turns looking at the two of us and back to the spot where Sean disappeared. He's on edge as well, and it's reminder enough that we're toeing a dangerous line. Everything rides on chance tonight. The chance that we're not spotted. The chance that we make it across. The chance that the Mexican authorities don't grab us on the other side. The chance that the people we're supposed to meet are where they said they would be.

It's almost impossible to hear someone approaching with the cicadas so loud on the air. I don't know if that's a good thing. The din might cover our sounds, but then anything could creep up on us, too. We know the usual times the patrols run, but they could change their schedules. It's probably protocol for them to do so every now and then. They know we're out here, escaped carriers watching their patterns, hoping to make it across.

It seems like forever until Sean returns, his dark shape emerging, his bigger body separating from the night. A breath rushes from my lips, my shoulders sagging with relief.

Sean waves an arm, saying in hushed tones, "I found it. This way."

We follow him several yards to a narrow boat. I know nothing of boats. The only time I ever rode in one was the weekend Zac and his family took me to their lake house. They had one of those enormous pontoon boats that you hardly felt move as it purred down the lake. I remember I wore a bikini with green and pink polka dots. Every time his parents weren't looking, Zac would touch some part of me and I would swat at his hand playfully. It really was a lifetime ago.

This is no pontoon. It's barely long enough for the four of us. No engine, of course. The sound would attract too much attention. Two oars sit inside, and I wonder who besides Sean will row. I might be more adept at rowing than Gil. He could crack any code and broke through the Agency's firewall to make contact with carrier sympathizers right beneath their noses, but I've proven myself more physically capable. I may have started out as the girl who could barely keep up with the other carriers during training, but that changed. Like everything else.

The four of us all grab a side of the boat and heft it along the riverbank, hugging the tree line. A fingernail cracks from the pressure and my shoulder starts to burn, but I keep trudging along. I sigh in relief when Sean stops. Together we lower the boat to the ground, angling the nose into the water.

Sean faces the river, studying the wide expanse like he can see something within the black waters. My gaze skims his broad back before following his gaze. In the near darkness, I can't even see the other side.

"We cross here," he announces.

I squint at the water. In the daylight it looked brown, churned up with silt. Sean is moving again, situating his pack in the boat, shoving as much of it as he can fit under the seat so there will be room for us. Sabine and Gil follow suit, stowing their packs. I'm the last to move. For some reason my limbs feel sluggish, slow to act and follow the commands of my brain.

Sean holds out a hand for me. I stare down at the stretch of his fingers.

"C'mon." He beckons with an impatient wave.

Shaking off my hesitation, I place my hand in his warmer one and climb into the boat. I take up an oar, flexing my palms around the scratchy wood, letting the solidness of it fortify me as Gil and Sean push us into the water. Their feet slap on the bank, then splash when they meet with water. I wince at the sound. Even the noise of the cicadas can't cover that.

The boat sways as they jump inside at the last moment, joining us. We drift out on the slight swell of their final shove. My gaze strays to the shore we're leaving behind, my heart suddenly racing. I'm leaving for good. Leaving my country. Escaping to a new one. Will I ever see my parents again? My brother? *Oh God. Mitchell.* What will happen to him? How will he ever know what happened to me? I'm certain Mount Haven won't tell him the truth—that I escaped. If he knew that, he would hold out hope. They'll probably just tell my family I died in some training exercise.

My chest tightens as the shore grows farther and darker,

impossible to distinguish from the sky. The oar falls limp in my hands.

"Davy!"

The sound of my name snaps me to attention, unlocking me from the frozen moment I've been stuck in. The one where I can't wrap my head around the unknown I'm diving into and the familiar I'm leaving behind—even if that familiar is gone. A thing of the past. A life that doesn't exist anymore.

"C'mon, row, Davy," Sean's deep voice encourages.

Nodding, I tighten my hands around the wood and work faster, struggling to match Sean's even strokes. The oars cut through the water silently. It's still too dark to see anything, but I guess we're making progress, inching closer to the other side of the river. I visualize it in my head, letting the image motivate me.

Suddenly a low drone purrs over the river, distant but growing in volume. I still. My hands freeze. Sean turns his face in the direction of the sound. We all look that way, to the north.

Gil finally speaks, his voice the barest whisper but still somehow jarring out across the great expanse of water. "What is that?"

I shake my head, unable to say it. That something or some-one is out on the river with us. It can't be. It can't.

"Move! Move!" Sean's hoarse cry fires through me like a bullet. I tighten my grip and row, pushing my oar through the water savagely.

The boat lurches just as light flashes across the river. Water laps at the sides of our boat, splashing inside and soaking my pants.

"It's a patrol," Gil hisses.

"Keep going." This from Sean. And I obey. Because what choice do we have? We're sitting ducks out here. Once they see us—

The light spills over us, pulling away for an instant before jerking back and shining full on us. One giant spotlight. Bright and glaring and unremitting.

Indecipherable sounds choke loose from Sabine. Sean's movements become wild, his arms churning fiercely as he rows.

His eyes lash me. "Come on, Davy, keep going!"

I shake my head and push harder, muscles screaming in protest.

The spotlight fixes on us as a disembodied voice blares over the water. "Halt! This is the United States Border Patrol. You there, in the boat, halt!" The command follows in Spanish, although they can likely guess what language we speak by the direction we're fleeing. We're trying to get *into* Mexico. Like so many carriers are doing these days. I look over my shoulder and see another boat. Several figures crowd its deck, easily outnumbering us.

"Don't stop," Gil urges, grabbing onto the sides of his seat as he gawks at the bigger boat bearing down on us, pushing waves ahead of its hull and rocking our boat.

"Not a chance," Sean pants.

"What do we do? They're getting closer!" Sabine cries, her

shrill voice adding to the chaos of the moment. "We're not going to make it!"

"Don't panic," Gil warns, but there's an edge of hysteria to his voice that seems counter to his advice.

I swing back around and face forward, not looking anywhere except straight ahead. I refuse to look at the other boat. Sean is opposite me in his seat, and I lock on to his face as I row. His blue-gray eyes glow, caught in the harsh light ambushing us. The boat's motor is a loud, angry beast now, breathing down our necks.

He nods at me, communicating something. What precisely, I'm not sure, until he shouts, "We're going to have to jump!"

My chest clenches even as I acknowledge it's our only chance. I cast a grim glance at the water to my right, a frenzied froth now from the waves of the bigger boat behind us.

"What? Are you insane?" Sabine demands.

He looks at her. "Can you swim?"

"Yes." Even with her voice rising in panic, she looks mildly affronted.

"Then we're jumping. It's the only way."

I stare out at the swift waters. So dark and fathomless.

Sean points to his right. "That's the shoreline. Let's try to stay together—"

"What about our supplies?" Gil looks down to where our packs rest.

Sean shakes his head and grabs his pack, rifling through it. He tosses out a few heavy items. A can of green beans hits my foot. "I'll swim with this one."

"It's still too heavy," I protest, thinking of the rest of the things still inside it.

"I can manage." He grabs my bag and slides out the four-pack of flashlights. "These are waterproof." He thrusts one at each of us. "If we get separated, these can help us find one another on the other side."

I let the oar go and take the flashlight. It's slim and not much longer than my hand. I stick it into the pocket of my jacket where I stashed my knife, glad the pockets zipper shut.

"Ready?" Sean's eyes fasten on me as he asks this, searing and intent, and I realize I must not look ready.

I nod hard, just once. His hand clamps down around mine, and the clasp of his fingers feels good, reassuring. I'm glad for this. Glad that I can still feel some comfort from him. This hasn't been stolen from me entirely at least.

He jumps first, pulling me with him. The sudden plunge into water is a shock to the system. Briny, loamy water rushes into my mouth and nose. Still overly warm from the hot day, it's a far cry from the chilled swimming pools back home that I was used to.

Our heads all pop up close together. Gil and Sabine immediately start for shore. Sean still holds my hand, which makes swimming difficult. After a few strokes, we let go of each other to make better progress. Even with the burden of a bag strapped to his back, he quickly outswims me, even passing Gil and Sabine.

My shoulders burn as I try to catch up. Water slams into my face, filling my mouth. Choking, I keep going. The growl of the boat sounds like it's right above me. The water grows more turbulent, and I know without looking that the boat is closer now. Panicked, I plunge underwater and swim below the surface as long as I can hold my breath.

When I next pop up, I'm beside Sabine. Gil is just in front of us. Sean still leads, but his body is half-turned as he looks back at us, shouting for us to get moving. He could probably be to shore by now if he hadn't been stalling for us. This fills me with fury. I won't be responsible for his life. *Not again.* I can barely take care of myself.

Suddenly it's like I see myself from far above. A speck swimming for her life in a river with three other teenagers, men with guns behind us. How? How did I get from studying for my final exams and begging for an extra hour on my date with Zac to this?

"Go!" I shout as I cut my arms through water, pulling my body forward bit by bit.

He shouts something, but I can't understand him. The roar of the boat engine is louder now, muffling everything else. And then there's a pop, followed by a whistling hiss.

"They're shooting!" Sabine screams, and her movements become more frantic.

Of course they're shooting at us. They don't care about retrieving us. A dead carrier is probably preferred.

Sucking in a deep breath, I dive below, swimming as long

as I can, my arms pulling me. I stay under until my burning lungs can't take it anymore; then I fight my way back to the surface.

My head breaks free with a ragged gasp and I drink oxygen deep into my starving lungs. I keep moving, spotting Sabine and Gil far to my right now, just a little ahead of me. Sean is farther ahead, still idling, looking back to us, lingering. Holding back for us. Placing himself in jeopardy for us.

More bullets. Sharp pops that smack water inches from me. I surge and suck in another deep breath, preparing to go under yet again for another plunge. Hopefully the next one gets me closer to shore. I can't be far now. As I'm about to go down, my lungs gathering air to the point of bursting, pain punches me like a jackhammer, directly in the back of my shoulder. My breath expels from me in a screaming rush. I sink, swallowing a mouthful of river.

I come back up, sputtering, unable to move my left arm without agony. There's so much noise. The growl of the boat motor is deafening, on top of me now, churning the water into a stew of angry, lathering waves. The sound competes with the swish of water slapping over my face. More bullets whistle. Men's voices congest the air.

"Get the hook. Grab her!"

I fight to ignore the pain, my arms stroking, but I'm too slow, going nowhere. I dunk under and let the water take me. Too weak, too hurting.

When I come up again, the boat is farther away. I search for the others. For a moment I think I spot a head, a small dark smudge in the distance against the light from the patrol boat. The boat drifts in that direction, closing in on that person now.

I tread water for a moment, my legs working hard, unsure of my next move. My free arm swirls widely around me, helping keep me afloat. My other arm throbs, useless at my side.

I peer at the patrol boat in the distance, struggling to keep my chin above the waterline. They probably count me as gone now. Dead. Part of me yearns to head after the boat, knowing it's giving chase to one of my friends. But I can't. I have to seize my advantage and head for shore. I can try to find the others from there. That's what Sean would tell me to do. That's what he would do himself. Turning, I face the shore again and start swimming, using my legs and one good arm. It's slow going. And painful. I stop several times and float, tilting my face back against the water and storing my strength.

All of me aches with a bone-deep burn. Weariness nips at me, ready to sink in its teeth, but I refuse to let that happen. I know a watery grave will be my reward if I do.

Nausea rolls through me, and I fight that, too. Stopping, I take another moment to rest, dropping my head back. Water laps over my ears. My gaze blurs. Thousands of tiny stars dance against a blanket of dark night, and I rather deliriously wonder why they're moving like that. Are they all shooting stars? A smile curves my lips at the whimsical thought.

A buzzing fills my head, pulsing in rhythm to the throbbing pain in my shoulder. With my good hand, I try to reach there, to assess the damage. I feel only slick wetness. I can't distinguish water from blood. I lower my hand and shove away the fact that I've been shot. There's nothing I can do about it right now. Nothing. Nothing to be done about the fact that there's a bullet lodged in my shoulder and I'm hours from a hospital, stuck in a river. A fugitive. Alone.

If someone had posed this scenario to me before, I would have declared I didn't have a snowball's chance in hell of surviving. But that was before. Before I'd proven just how resilient I could be. And didn't people get shot in the old West and survive? I've seen enough of those spaghetti westerns with my dad on Sunday afternoons to know. They lived. I deliberately ignore the fact that that was television and I'm dealing with the real world. A world that has not been kind to me lately.

Gradually sound fades away. I don't hear anything anymore. No distant shouts. No growling boat. It's like someone hit the mute button and I'm alone in the world. Floating in endless space. Just me and dancing stars. Water crashing against my face.

I reach for the familiar music that so often fills my mind, remembering too late with a pang that it's abandoned me. Its absence heightens my loneliness, deepens the ache. I need a song. Crave it desperately. Just one song now more than ever.

Sputtering against the water, I sing a few verses, but my voice escapes broken and hoarse, terrible and off-pitch. I force myself to push through, waiting for the cadence to fill my ears, a six-string orchestra to sweep through and lift me.

It doesn't happen. My voice stops, quivers, and gives up on the lyrics. Darkness edges my vision.

"Please," I beg, but I'm unsure who, specifically, I'm pleading with. "Please," I ask no one again. *Help me.* "I need . . . please . . ."

Someone.

Water creeps over my head, and my vision blacks out.

Agency Interview

AGENT POLLOCK: Thank you for coming in to see us today, Mitchell. May I call you Mitchell?

MITCHELL HAMILTON: I didn't realize I had a choice. Your guys practically hauled me from my house. I guess you couldn't just interview me there? You had to drag me into this little room? Is this an intimidation tactic?

AGENT POLLOCK: Are you intimidated, Mitchell?

MITCHELL HAMILTON: What do you want?

AGENT POLLOCK: Your sister—

MITCHELL HAMILTON: You took my sister away.

AGENT POLLOCK: So you haven't heard from her? She hasn't tried to contact you?

MITCHELL HAMILTON: Why? Did you lose her? (laughter) God, I hope so. Because I'm not going to lie, that would be pretty great. I hope she runs far away and never looks back.

AGENT POLLOCK: You do understand aiding a carrier in any way is a crime under recently added statutes to the Wainwright Act? If you have any communication or contact with your sister and fail to report it, you face legal action.

MITCHELL HAMILTON: I understand that you can go to hell.

FIVE

I TASTE DIRT.

Grit coats my lips and lines my teeth in a grainy film. My tongue, the roof of my mouth—nothing is free from it. Coughing, I move my tongue, trying to work up some saliva. I shift my weight and then groan as my nerves wake to the pain.

My eyes crack open and wince at the blinding light. It only adds to my agony. Like needles stabbing into my corneas. I jam my eyes shut again and take slow sips of breath, as if that will somehow chase off the pain hammering into every pore.

I'm not dead. There's that. I focus on that. Cling to that. I didn't drown. After several more moments, I reopen my eyes and suffer the brightness. I have to get up. Get moving. Staying here, facedown in the dirt, equals death. If I don't get up now, I'm never getting up.

With a long groan that sounds more animal than human, I press down with my palms and push up. My shoulder screams out at the abuse, reminding me just how not okay I am. I swallow back a whimper, the thought skittering through my head that death might be preferable to this. I ease pressure off my left hand and use my right hand to push myself the rest of the way up. Sitting upright, I pant like I just wrestled an alligator.

As the haze of pain clears, I gingerly touch my shoulder. My fingers meet slick blood. Dropping my hand, I assess my surroundings. The river flows only a few feet away from me, the brown, sunlit waters swimming in a swift current. I made it across.

Looking left and right, I peer over weeds that reach past my waist, squinting at the horizon, hoping to see Sean, Gil, or Sabine. I'm desperate for a glimpse of them ... even as I know how unlikely that is. They wouldn't be standing out in the open. It's too risky. A hawk flies overhead, its screech echoing on the skies.

How am I going to find them?

Panic noses in, and I shove it back before I can swing into full-scale hysteria. That won't help. Sucking in a deep breath, I fill my lungs with warm air. Bracing for pain, I stand. And it's every bit as hard as I feared. With my good hand stretched out for balance, I secure my footing and exhale slowly. It's not so bad. I can do this.

I stagger a few steps and stop myself just short of falling over. Gasping, I stop, knees slightly bent to help steady me. *You got it. You got this!*

I start walking.

Progress is slow. I scan the horizon, holding a hand over my eyes as I search among the scrub and cacti, hoping the others are near. My pace drags to a crawl. Exhaustion weighs me down. It feels like lead weights encircle my ankles. I clutch my injured arm close, holding it at the elbow. Pain vibrates through me with each step.

Sweat trickles down my spine, and I'm unclear if it's just really hot or I'm feverish. My shoulder burns so much that I weep as I walk, silent tears trickling down my cheeks. Dully, I realize crying is probably a bad idea. Just a waste of fluids that I need. My lips are so dry. No matter how many times I lick at them, they stay chapped. It seems rather soon for me to be this dehydrated, and I know it must be a result of blood loss.

I don't know how long I walk, but the grim reality is there. I'm all alone. Still, I push, lifting one leg after another. To stop is to die.

I work on convincing myself that my shoulder isn't that bad. For all I know it's just a scrape and there isn't even a bullet lodged in there. Maybe the bullet grazed me. It's a faint hope, reed-thin, but I cling to it. I might just trick myself into believing that I'm not going to die out here.

My friends probably think I'm dead. My chest hollows out at this. I stop and gaze at the sparse brown terrain. That's why there's no sight of them. They moved on.

I know they made it across. They had to. At least Sean did. He's strong. A survivor. And he was so far ahead of the patrol boat, only holding himself back for us. They're probably all together now. They're probably halfway to the refuge by now.

This thought fills me with some comfort. I guess it's enough knowing they're okay out there. It will have to be. I can be at peace with that knowledge.

Still, I'm not going to stop. To quit. My legs keeping moving. I count my steps. Lift shuffling foot after shuffling foot. *Left. Right. Left. Right.* Fear drives me. Fear of dying out here alone. It's stronger than my pain. Stronger than the exhaustion.

For now anyway.

I realize that fear as a motivator isn't working anymore when I start to hear my brother's voice.

Davy. Davy. Come home. We miss you.

It's like he's right beside me, but when I turn to look for him, I see nothing. Just bleak, relentless horizon. *Is this the hallucination stage right before death?*

I laugh brokenly. Or maybe I'm already dead and caught up in some hell reserved just for killers.

Gnats buzz around me, attracted to the coppery-sweet scent of blood soaking through my shirt. I swat at them in frustration. One of my swipes is especially savage and throws me off balance. I stagger and fall, landing on my knees on the hard-packed earth. Pain jars through me. I hover there for a moment, swaying.

I press one palm down on the ground to see if I can get back to my feet again. No good. Even my uninjured arm isn't strong enough for the task.

Mitchell's voice is there again. *Get up, Davy. Keep moving.*

I moan, shaking my head. "I can't."

Groaning, I let myself sink, dropping to my side and rolling onto my back. Almost as if the thought of falling facedown is somehow reprehensible. Like I might get my cheeks dirty or something. The silly idea makes me giggle, and I know I've lost it. This battle I'm fighting is over.

Who knew it would end like this?

I think the part I regret the most is being alone. *Feeling* so very alone at the end.

Too late, I wish I hadn't shoved Sean away. Every time I cringed at his touch and winced at the sound of his voice— that is what he has left of me. I'll never see him again, and he'll have only that. Sadness swells through me.

"Mitchell?" I whisper, reaching for something. Even if it isn't real. "Are you there?"

I feel myself fading. Squinting against the harsh sunlight, I turn my face to the side, escaping the cruel glare.

"Mitchell?" I try moistening my hurting lips but can barely move my tongue. "Are you there?" My hand drops near my head, the backs of my fingers curling against my cheek. "I don't want to be . . . alone."

My lashes dip and darken my world for long moments before lifting to the sunlit earth again. I reach deep, hunting for the will to move on, to fight. Short tufts of straw-like grass dance before my vision as I stare out across the ground.

I take long blinks, the darkness easier to bear than the light. The next time I open my eyes, I know it's the last. Staying in the light, awake, conscious . . . it takes too much out of me. Every moment uses up energy from my rapidly depleting well.

Except I see something. Against the sun-bleached landscape. Something's out there, moving, coming toward me. A blurred shape a shade darker than everything else.

Ripples of heat undulate between me and the approaching figure. It grows bigger. Moves closer. Keeps coming. Boots. Dark boots. I know they're attached to legs, to a person—of course—but I can't lift my head to see the face. I glimpse only boots.

Is this the angel of death coming for me?

The well-worn pair of hiking boots stops directly before me. They're unfocused in my failing vision, but I can tell they belong to a man. Too big to be a woman.

The dry, parched flesh of my lips cracks as speech rumbles up from my chest. I don't know what I'm saying. My voice sounds so far away. Distant as if in a dream.

I pull from some reservoir of strength and turn my head. Look up. Just the slightest movement, but it costs me. For a split second my gaze slides up the long length of a body and locks on a face. Sunlight haloes him, blocking his features, giving him almost an angelic aura. Which kind of shoots down my angel of death suspicion and replaces it with the crazy hope that maybe he's a guardian angel here to save me. A bit of absurdity that mocks me. Not because guardian angels don't exist . . . but because I'm stupid enough to imagine one would waste his time with me. My head drops and my eyes fall shut.

I descend into the dark never.

Press Conference with Emily Rothchilde, Spokesperson for the Wainwright Agency

ROTHCHILDE: Rumors of resistance cells are highly exaggerated.

REPORTER: Then how do you respond to the partnership of US Customs and Border Protection with the Wainwright Agency? Such a measure doesn't indicate the government's belief that carriers lack organization.

ROTHCHILDE: We are talking about escaped carriers. They are no more than desperate, ragtag deviants who will soon be expunged from our country. The right of God is on our side.

SIX

WHEN I WAS FOURTEEN YEARS OLD, I DECIDED I
wanted to be more than a music prodigy. Well, maybe not
more but something else. I tried out for track. It didn't dawn
on me that my lack of athleticism might be an impediment.
For some reason I thought hurdles might be my thing. I
cleared the first jump. Unfortunately, not the second. I still
have the scar where I gashed my knee open. There was blood
everywhere. I actually lost consciousness, waking up with the
school nurse huddled over me, an ambulance and my parents
on the way. Friends surrounded me. Several of my teachers
heard what happened and hurried outside to check on me.

Everyone cared. My life was full like that.

Before one advance in science tracked me down in my perfect cocoon. Before a few laws changed everything. And now I have no one.

As I come to, it takes me several moments to realize that my eyes are even open. Darkness surrounds me so thickly, I feel like I'm buried under a blanket. I blink several times, testing that I'm right. That my eyes work properly and I am in fact awake. And alone. There are no familiar faces. No friends waiting for me, crowding around to see if I'm okay.

Only pain greets me, saying hello to every part of me. Every limb. Every nerve and pore. Nothing is overlooked. Especially my shoulder. The burn there is poker-hot, deep and incinerating. It drills through sinew and bone and spreads out like branches on a tree, eventually arcing down my spine into my toes.

I'm on my stomach, my face pressed into cool . . . rock, I think. There are sounds. A faint drip of water. The distant scurrying of a small animal. At least I hope it's a small animal and not something bigger. Like a person. My eyes flare wide.

Boots.

I remember the boots. I focus, trying to remember more. But there's nothing except those boots, which belonged to a man who was clearly no angel. He was flesh-and-blood real.

My relief at being alive flees as my situation sinks in. I passed out at the feet of some stranger. Clearly he moved me to someplace else. Where has he taken me? He must have seen my imprint. Will he turn me in?

A low glow begins to fill the space I occupy, growing in brightness as if the source of light is being carried toward me. Carried by someone. *Boots.* My gaze darts wildly, and I see more of my surroundings—which seem to be the walls of a cave. I can't see who approaches. Someone's coming from behind.

I hold still, listening carefully to every whisper of sound. Then I hear it. The barest scrape of a shoe inches from my head. I release a silent gasp and then bite my lip, take the dry flesh between my teeth until I taste the coppery tang of blood.

So close. I didn't realize how close he was. Apparently, Boots walks with a near-silent tread. My mind works, fighting against the panic, the hysteria that threatens to consume me right along with the fever raging through me, eating at my mind. So hot. I burn and know that can't be good. My decision making is probably impaired. I can think only of worst-case scenarios, imagining the kind of man who stumbled upon me. A criminal. Some drug runner. A carrier with a taste for killing. I almost snort at this—it seems the height of redundancy. A killer carrier. Isn't that what all carriers are?

Maybe he intends to amuse himself with me. I'm a marked carrier. I wear the imprint on my neck. I can expect no protection. No consideration. My life is forfeit.

The luminescence shifts, and I guess that he must hold some kind of electric lantern. I hear a soft clang as he sets it down. The light ceases to move and flicker over the cave walls.

My mind trips over my options and strategies to defend myself. With my sluggish thinking, it's a struggle. But then I remember the knife. My right hand twitches in front of me, working open the zipper of my jacket pocket. It's probably still there, right alongside my flashlight. I slip my hand under me, slightly lifting my hip as I ease inside the pocket, sliding two fingers inside, processing the small sounds behind me.

"How long are you going to pretend to be asleep?"

The deep voice fills the small cave. I freeze. My skin washes cold for one brief instant. Adrenaline fires through me as I hear movement, and I picture the faceless man bearing down on me, full of evil intent.

Deciding against waiting for him to make the next move, I pull the knife free and palm it, hiding it from sight as I roll onto my back, gasping at the shattering pain in my shoulder.

He's digging through a pack, not even looking at me. I frown, studying him. His dark hair, cut close at the sides, is only slightly longer on top. His forehead knits as he investigates the contents of his bag like he didn't just speak to me. Like I'm not even here. He's wearing the boots—the same ones that filled my vision before I passed out.

"W—" I stop at the croak of my voice and try to swallow, but my throat feels like sandpaper, raw and scratchy.

He flicks me a glance, and I'm pinned by his eyes. They're brown, but not as dark as his hair. No, they're more like the amber light dancing over the walls of the cave. I guess he's around my age, but his expression is so intense it's hard to know for sure.

And then I see it. The imprint around his neck. Everything in me seizes and locks up. He's a carrier. Like me. My already raspy breath catches.

That he's like me is no comfort. If anything, his carrier status pumps the adrenaline through me faster. The only carriers I ever trusted were Sean, Gil, and Sabine. The three of us had a connection forged in our past experiences.

Me and this guy? We have nothing. I can't even trust that he won't turn me in. What if he works for the Agency? What if they sent him out after carriers? A killer who hunts killers. Wasn't that the whole intention behind Mount Haven? Training carriers to follow orders?

One thing is certain. I can take no chances. In what I hope is a smooth move, I flip open the blade.

A corner of his mouth lifts. "What are you going to do with that?"

"Whatever I need to do."

"Huh." He angles his head like he's waiting for me to do it then. Whatever *it* is.

I don't consider my fate outside escaping this cave and him. Not where I'll go or what I'll do following that. And I guess that is the fever. Or the blood loss. Or fatigue. It could be all those things really.

I force myself up, using my leg muscles for support. My fingers clench tightly around my knife.

He watches me with detached curiosity. Like I'm some little rabbit caught in his snare. I scan the cave, looking for a way out. My gaze lands on a canteen, and my thirst slams into me almost as savagely as the pain.

With eyes fastened to his face, I inch a step closer and

snatch the water. Never looking away from his face, I drink. Water dribbles down my chin and neck, and it feels wonderful.

"Better?" he asks, like he isn't some killer. As if I'm not. I can hear the smirk in his voice over my labored breath and suddenly realize what a fool I am to think I can best him. I grimly calculate my chances of getting the jump on him. In my condition? Not good. My only chance is to outsmart him. Assuring myself that I'm smarter, that he has underestimated me, I bow my head and moan a little. As though the pain is too much. And then I drop. Fake losing consciousness.

I feel the uncomfortable bulge of a rock beneath my hip and loosen my grip on the knife. Because why kill if I don't have to? I can knock him out. Maybe it's the conversation with Sabine nipping at the back of my memory, insisting that we're equipped to kill. That we have a knack for it. I want to resist that logic and prove that I don't need to kill to save myself.

I slip my fingers under me and grasp the rock, its jagged peaks scraping my tender flesh. I hold on to it, taking comfort in its weight. If I learned anything during the weeks at Mount Haven, it's to take advantage of every opportunity that presents itself.

I wait, listening, straining for the slightest sound. And it's there. Just a breath. He's beside me. Sucking in a deep breath, I lurch upright and swing, trying to assess his shape—primarily the location of his head—so that I can do the most damage.

I make contact. A stinging curse rings out. His hand comes

up to cover his ear, and I see that I've just grazed him.

Grinding my teeth, I pull back, still clutching the rock, ready to try again. He guesses my intent. I see a flash of glittering eyes just as I'm tackled to the ground.

I cry out. Pain bursts through me as I'm pinned. Hands grab my wrists and trap them against the cave floor. I whimper and choke at the stretch of screaming muscle in my shoulder. The sound turns into a twisting sob that doesn't even sound like me but some wild animal.

I surge against him, trying to fling him off. Even if I wasn't so weak, it would be useless. His body is hard and strong over mine. Too late, I know I should have used the knife. I should have ignored that scrap of my old self that shied from killing.

"Do you normally brain people to death after they go to the trouble of saving your life?"

Panting, I eye him, appreciating the scrape of angry red skin on the side of his temple, courtesy of me.

"If you're such a Good Samaritan, get off me. You're hurting me."

He holds my gaze for a long moment, the amber-gold of his brown eyes crawling over my face and throat, missing nothing. Yeah. Even that. He knows what I am. My fingers itch to touch the flesh there. Still. After all this time, I still want to hide it. Still want it gone. I feel a stab of regret that I couldn't stick it out at Mount Haven. That I couldn't last there long enough to win their offer to remove my imprint. It's only a temporary regret, because then I remember how bad it was there—that they required me to kill a man. I had to leave. There was also the not-so-small incentive that Sean and Gil were leaving. With or without me. This reminder brings a fresh pang to my chest.

I lost them anyway. I'm alone and at the mercy of this guy.

He looks away, releasing my wrists. Plucking up the rock that I used to club him, he settles back down a few feet away from me, tossing it carefully between his hands.

"Pretty resourceful for someone with a bullet in her shoulder." He arches a dark eyebrow as though impressed.

Wincing, I sit back up, scooting into a secure position and holding my arm close to my side as if that might somehow control my pain. My movements don't do me any favors. Fresh blood trickles warmly down my back, soaking my shirt.

I glance down at my knife, which he left beside me, and back up at him, wondering at his game. He couldn't have forgotten about it.

He watches me in turn, his expression mild, unconcerned. "Are you going to use that on me?"

I stare, contemplating him as I pick the knife back up and stand with a grunt of discomfort. Looking down on him makes me feel somewhat better. "You want me to? Is that why you left it?"

"If it makes you feel better, keep it." Even as he says this, he doesn't fool me. He looks hard. Like something that belongs here, a part of the unforgiving landscape. A shadow of scruff brushes his jaw. He hasn't shaved in several days. A wide-brimmed hat hangs back behind his neck to protect him from the sun. And yet he's still sun-browned. He wears an earth-colored poncho. More protection from the sun. My gaze drops to his boots again. They're quality. Made for this type of living. If eking out an existence here could be called that. *But isn't that all I can hope for at this point?*

"What do you want with me?" I ask.

"I can't just want to help you?"

Maybe I could have believed that a few months ago. The inherent goodness of my fellow man. But not anymore. The world isn't the same. At least my world isn't. I'm not brimming with faith in the humanity of others. Especially carriers.

I nod to his pack. "Kick that over here."

He glances from it to me. Shaking his head, he starts to speak. "You have real trust issues."

"Just kick it over here." After a moment of hesitation, he moves, pausing when I sharply instruct, "Don't get too close. Keep your distance."

He kicks the bag, frowning, looking disappointed. And that annoys me. Why should he—a total *stranger*—act as though I disappointed him?

Sitting back down, he looks up at me. "You're not going to make it far. You've got a bullet in your shoulder."

"Yeah?" I snap. "I kind of noticed that, but thanks for the tip."

His gaze skims me. "You'll stand out like a hothouse rose there. There aren't too many girls traipsing up and down the border all alone. How do you expect to make it out there—"

"That's my problem."

His eyes narrow on me. "You've got a funny way of showing your thanks."

His words give me pause. Is that what he's truly doing? Helping me? I think of Tully then. And Jackson. Carriers I know. Guys who I would never want to be alone with. The things they would do to me . . .

Death would be easier than any of those scenarios.

How do I really know what this guy's intentions are with me? He brought me to this cave for what? So that I could recuperate?

The answer reverberates loud and clear in my head. *Don't trust him. You can't afford to be wrong.*

I slip one strap of the backpack over my good shoulder. I nod at him, and the motion makes my head spin. I stagger sideways one step before righting myself, reaching a hand to the cave wall for balance. "Thanks. No hard feelings."

"Nice," he says flatly as I inch around him, heading to where he entered, assuming the exit is that way. "I rescued you, and for that you're stealing my stuff and taking off. You're not going to make it. Just look at yourself. It's the hottest part of the day, and patrols are swarming out there. In greater force than usual." His amber eyes glint at me, sharp as a blade, cutting, probing. "Almost like they're looking for someone."

His words make my stomach clench. *Me.* They're looking for me. Maybe they already captured the others. *God.* Sean. Gil and Sabine.

He continues, "Apparently some carriers made it across the river into Mexico last night. It's all over the wire. I'm guessing you were with—"

Everything inside me locks up tight. "Wait . . . what? I'm not in Mexico?" I press a hand to my forehead as if this information just pinged me like a rock in the face. I'd been so close. I was almost to the shore.

He studies me a long moment, not responding right away. My heart thunders in my chest as I wait for an explanation. I lower my hand and demand hoarsely, "Tell me. Please."

My "please" does it. The rigid line of his shoulders seems to relax. "No. You're in the US." He snorts and drags a hand through his hair, sending the dark strands tumbling wildly. "And you think you can make it out there. You don't even know what country you're in."

This hits its mark. "You'd be surprised just what I'm capable of."

His gaze slides from my face to my neck and back again. "I bet."

"I was almost there," I continue, leaning back against the cave wall, suddenly unable to stand without some support. I just need a minute. I drag in a breath. "But then I got shot. Apparently I washed back ashore on the American side."

"Apparently." He nods. "You're still in the good old US of A. If I'd been leading you, you would have made it." My irrational brain interprets this as a slight against Sean. Sean, who might be dead. Annoyance flashes through me.

I stab the knife in his direction. "You'll never lead me anywhere."

He motions behind me, presumably to where the outside

world waits. "Fine. Then go." His voice drops lower. And he's speaking slower. Or it just seems like it. Like he's talking to me from somewhere far away. I squint, focusing on his lips. "I predict you'll be picked up in half an hour. Unless you pass out. Then the coyotes will find you and have a feast. Is that what you want, girl?"

I flex my hand around the knife, trying to let the solid feel of it reassure me. "I'll take my chances. And don't call me 'girl.' I have a name."

He unfolds himself slowly until he's standing. My neck angles back to hold his gaze. He's not as brawny as Sean but he's taller. Lean and rangy like a wolf. I blink once, hard, shaking off the comparison even though I suppose it's natural to compare every carrier I meet to Sean . . . Sean who has filled my world for the last several months. Sean who I killed for. Sean who is gone. Lost to me.

He holds up both hands, long fingers splayed wide. He waves them like I'm some wild animal he's trying to soothe and tame. "And what's that?" he asks gently.

I frown. The circular motion begins to make me dizzy. I focus back on his face, trying to get my gaze off the flurry of his hands. "Doesn't matter."

"Sure it does. Tell me your name."

He has a nice face, I think, and then blink, trying to snap back to myself and rein in my thoughts.

Is it just me or has he moved closer? I jab the knife in his direction. "Stay back." I cringe at the sluggish sound of my voice and press my other hand against my face. "Ahhh." I inhale a hissing breath against the heat of my skin and the sudden spin of my world.

My legs give out. I cry as I fall, tumbling in a graceless heap. The fall jars my shoulder and I moan. Boots loom over me. Squatting, he plucks the knife from my hand with embarrassing ease. Like taking candy from a baby.

"That. Hurt." I get the words out, each one punctuated with a pained exhale.

"How are you not dead?" he asks in a maddeningly even voice, but there's a gleam of amusement in his eyes. "You're a mess."

I laugh, the sound brittle and a little crazy even to my ears. My head spins. "Oh, but I'm special," I mock, not really knowing what I'm saying. I don't think my words through. They just fall from my lips. It's like being drunk with no filter. "One moment I was planning my dorm room at Juilliard, and then this . . ." I wave at my neck. "And then they wanted me . . ."

Closing my eyes, I search for the dark never that sheltered me earlier. Even a ghost couldn't find me there. I can feel it close, so very near, like warm breath at my neck.

"Who wanted you?"

His voice is insistent, like a buzzing gnat around my cotton-filled head. I crack open my eyes. Whatever flash of humor I thought I saw in his gaze is gone. I watch as he slips my knife away. It disappears beneath his poncho. He took it from me like I'm nothing. Definitely not someone to inspire fear. Even if I do have this stupid imprint on my neck.

I slowly roll my head side to side. "Funny, huh? They were

training me to be a really good killer. And I kind of suck at it."
My head dips to the side. My bangs fall in my eyes. "Don't I
look like a deadly assassin to you?"

"Who was training you?" His hand is there, brushing the
hair back. The contact is almost tender, and I resist leaning
into that touch, into the callused fingertips that graze my
forehead. They feel so cool on my overheated flesh. At least I
tell myself that's the reason behind the compulsion. He's not
tender in any way. He can't be. He's just trying to see my face
as I ramble incoherently. Even in my condition I know that.

"Who?" he repeats, capturing my gaze, those flame-
colored eyes drilling me for information.

"Same people who put that mark on your neck," I murmur, waving at him like I can see his imprint. I'm practically
under him. I can't see anything. "The Agency." I say this last
bit slowly, dragging out the words. "They put me in a special
camp . . . promised I could have my imprint removed."

"That so?"

"Believe it, baby." I laugh at this, highly amused with
myself.

"You're dehydrated," he announces, sounding grim.

My laughter ends on a sigh. "No. I'm dying."

He holds up a bottle to my lips. "Here. Drink."

I slap it away. "What for? Go ahead. Do your worst," I challenge, past caring, ready for the pain to end. The uncertainty.
"Kill a killer. I have. I did exactly what they wanted me to do."

The truth is always there. Even when his ghost leaves me
alone, I know it. And then I'm crying. Weeping uncontrollably

as I think of the man I killed. Those eyes that won't stop haunting me.

"Shh. You're not with them anymore," he murmurs, his hand back, the palm pressing cool and solid against my forehead. "Juilliard, huh? That's impressive." It's like he deliberately ignores all the other stuff I confessed about myself. "I bet you wanted to be an actress."

I don't bother correcting him. This gentleness from him is unexpected. I turn my head in the other direction, pulling away from him, hiding my weakness. It's embarrassing—that I can still cry and that I even care what a stranger thinks of me. His hand falls from my face.

He says nothing. The cave is silent, and I begin to wonder if he hasn't left me after all. If I'm alone again. Darkness thickens around me as a deep lethargy pulls at me.

His voice, when I hear it again, is a faint, faraway whisper. "I'm not going to hurt you. And you're not going to die." There's a long pause before he adds in a voice so distant I'm not sure if it's him or a figment of my imagination—of the part of me that wants to believe I'm still that fourteen-year-old surrounded by people who give a damn whether she's okay:

I won't let you die.

Conversation between Dr. Wainwright and the United States chief of staff:

WAINWRIGHT: The suggestion that carriers are organizing to any degree, that they pose a serious threat, is preposterous. They don't possess the discipline or levelheadedness needed—

SWITZER: I'm starting to think the same could be said of you and your staff, Wainwright. . . .

SEVEN

I'M MOVING.

The world jars around me like I'm on top of some lumbering beast. I have a flashback to my second-grade trip to the San Antonio zoo, when we still had class trips, before that part of the city became too dangerous to visit, and I got to ride on top of an elephant. It was just me and my best friend, Tori, laughing and screaming as the giant animal walked us in circles, its enormous ears flapping at flies inches from my tennis shoes. I actually feel my lips lift in a smile at the memory. That had been fun. This? Not so much. Not when my body feels like that elephant has stomped all over it. And my shoulder. *Oh*

God. My shoulder feels like blue-hot flames consume it.

My cheek rests against something firm and warm. My eyes open, and it's only slightly less dark than the backs of my eyelids.

The deep fold of night wraps around me. An owl hoots nearby. I hold still, trying to gauge precisely where I am. The beat of someone's heart thuds against my cheek, and I conclude that I'm being carried. Hands clasp me, one at my arm and the other at my thigh. I try to lift my head but end up moaning, the effort too much.

A voice sounds close to my ear. "Rest. We're almost there."

Where is there?

I think the question but can't get the words out. My throat feels like it's stuffed with cotton. I whimper. Shapes darker than the night are etched against the horizon. Shrubs and trees. The jagged outline of mountains.

He's moving quickly. No small feat in the near dark. The moon is just a sliver, softening the air the barest amount. His steps sketch over the ground rapidly, moving over the uneven rises and dips in the landscape like he knows exactly where to place his feet, like he has the terrain memorized . . . or is a part of it.

Another owl hoots nearby and he stops, holding himself rigidly as he listens. A few moments later the owl hoots again, and he resumes his swift pace.

I can do nothing but exist. Float through the night. Deadweight in his arms.

My eyelids sink back shut.

A voice emerges, softly at first, then louder, clearer, easing through the fog of my mind. Low and velvet smooth, like a wash of something warm going down. Spiced cider or hot chocolate, rolling through me, sinking into my pores, bleeding into my veins.

"You're the reason I'm travelin' on. Don't think twice, it's all right...."

Recognition flares inside me. I know these lyrics. I've heard them before. My eyes fight their way open, but only darkness greets me. Gray shadows on top of black night.

And that voice. It's there. Everywhere. Swirling, crooning somewhere just above my head. The words rumble up from the chest my cheek rests against.

The source becomes clear even in my pain-addled state. It's him. He's singing. *He's singing to me.* His voice is unlike anything I've ever heard, and I wonder if this is it. Have I died and gone on to wherever it is I'm supposed to go? I wouldn't have thought heaven waited for me, not after everything, but there's nothing in this voice that smacks of brimstone and ash. It's the complete opposite.

"Wha—" Speech cracks in my throat, and I try again. "What are you ... d-doing?"

He pauses long enough to shush me. Then he starts up again, singing low and deep. My eyes flutter back shut. I fall into the music like a child dropping into the arms of a protector.

My voice was strong and pure. Before I was a carrier, I was gifted in that way. And he is gifted, too. His voice shines like a ray of light in the darkness and brings me back to myself for a brief moment. Reminds me that I'm alive. That I *want* to be alive. That life is something I should fight for. I can't ever let myself stop fighting. His voice, in this moment, gives me all of that.

The will to live.

As his lyrics wrap around me, I sink back into the dark, reaching for the music, stretching both hands out, taking that voice with me. The last bit of sunshine in a world without light.

I wake to a world of sound and pain. Unfortunately, I can't simply dive back under the blanket of sleep. I wish I could. Wish I could escape the volume, the tiny hammers beating inside my body, fighting to burst out of my skin. No such luck.

The garbled voices build to an active rumble, separating into distinct words. And there are other sounds as well. The slap of running feet. A sharp clang. Countless small, identifiable noises that alert me to the fact that I'm in a place inhabited by people. It's not just Boots with me anymore.

Then the hands that hold me vanish. I'm on a bed, and even though it's soft and yielding, I whimper, missing that heartbeat against my ear. Cloth tears, an ugly rip. Cool air washes over me and I moan, curling my abused body inward, wanting desperately to ease the inferno raging inside me. More fabric rips, and hands move me. Roll me onto my back. Air crawls over my belly, and I dimly realize that my clothes are being cut off me.

Normally this would have fired all kinds of alarms to my system, but it seems like a secondary concern now. *If* even that. Funny how priorities shift. What would have seemed so important before, so critical, doesn't even register on my panic scale.

I keep my eyes shut, pretending to be asleep, listening, *feeling*, assessing what's happening around me as I push down the fear.

There are several people in the room. Multiple shoes sound, stepping and scuffing on the floor.

"She's lost a lot of blood."

"Who is she?" a second male voice demands. Instantly, I don't like this one. It's hard with a nasal quality. "Did you blindfold her before bringing her here?"

Silence meets this. Everything around me seems to go still.

The ugly voice again. "Damn it, answer me!"

"Look at her," Boots finally answers. I recognize the dry response, the velvet, low timbre. I really need to learn his name. "It's not a concern. She's in no condition to remember—"

"It's my concern!"

"I'll take responsibility—"

"Fat lot of good that does us if she's an Agency spy and we all end up captured."

"You're overreacting. I found her practically dead."

"Did she say anything . . . are there others? Where are—"

"She hasn't exactly been a wealth of information." If I didn't hurt so much—wasn't so scared—I might have smiled at his response. In another scenario. Another life.

That other guy keeps pressing, clearly unhappy to have me here. "Is she what all the commotion is about on the wire? And all that gunfire last night? Some of those other cells out there don't know their right from their left—"

"Well, since there's a bullet buried in her shoulder, I'm guessing yes." Again, I fight a smile. He's funny. "She's lucky to be alive."

Hands grip me and roll me onto my stomach. At least my face is out of sight. They don't know I'm awake yet. Sure fingers probe at my gunshot wound, and a scream tears past my teeth as my chin lurches off the mattress.

"Well, she's awake."

My eyes flare wide to a room full of bright artificial light. For a moment I'm confused. The place has that overworked, stale smell layered with the requisite aroma of antiseptic, but it's no hospital. That much I know.

I can't hold my head up any longer. The innocuous face of a middle-aged man drops eye level with me where my cheek presses flat to the bed. He wears wire-thin glasses that sit on the middle of his nose.

"Hello there, I'm Dr. Phelps. We're going to get you patched up. What's your name?"

"Doctor?" I repeat, like I don't understand the word's meaning. In a way, I don't. Last time I checked, I was in the middle of nowhere, sans civilization. How am I suddenly in the care of a doctor?

"No, *your* name, my dear," he prods with a smile, and I realize he's making a joke. "I'm the doctor."

He's the doctor. This plays over and over in my mind. As in a real doctor. Someone who might help me not die.

"It's okay. Doc's going to take care of you."

I lift my head at the familiar voice, searching for and finding Boots. Only he looks more dangerous than I remember. His hair near black. His features more angular. His jaw rigid in the harsh lighting. The room is mostly white, and he stands out starkly against the sterile surroundings. There's little in his face that matches the voice that sang softly to me as he carried me across the desert. But then he moves closer, placing a palm over my forehead, holding it there with a gentleness that makes something inside me flutter loose.

"You brought me here," I say dumbly.

"I said I'd get you the help you needed." He flashes me a smile, his features easing, losing some of their harshness. "Now do yourself a favor and get better." His gaze holds mine, like he can *will* me to health.

I feel him leaving me, the warmth of his body departing, slipping from me. I grab for him. My fingers meet skin, firm and solid under my fingertips. He has become that familiar thing. Something to hang on to.

His face lowers close to mine.

"Shh." His voice still strikes me as lyrical and deep. Like a low purr. "You're safe here. You're in good hands. Better than whoever was helping you before. We're the best. I won't let anything happen to you." I feel myself soften, relax, but I don't let go. My fingers have a mind of their own, and more strength than I would have thought. Especially when I'm this weak. This hurt and tired.

His hand squeezes mine back while he places his other broad palm to my forehead again. It's how a mother would comfort a child. How mine once comforted me. "You can let go." His voice feathers against my cheek.

I can let go.

I believe this. I believe him, for whatever reason. Maybe because it's just been so long and I need to believe in something. In someone. Or maybe just because I don't have any other choice. My hand unfurls from his.

"There you are," he murmurs approvingly like I've done a great thing—as though he understands the leap of faith I just made.

He bestows a final smile on me and turns away, disappearing from my line of vision. I listen to his steps fade away. My ears strain long after the sound of his tread dies.

With a pained whimper, I drop my head back to the bed— or gurney, rather. I can see now that I'm laid out in the middle of an exam room.

Another person walks around me and squats eye level to me. He's a little older, early twenties, with a serious buzz cut. Only the slightest shadow of hair hugs his scalp. My gaze immediately goes to the imprint on his neck. "I've got some questions for you. For starters, your name." Even if I didn't recognize his nasal voice, I'd know this is the guy who was talking to Boots earlier—the one unhappy with my arrival. The one I don't like. I wish Boots had stayed.

"Davy." I doubt last names matter here.

"Caden said she came from some special camp," Dr. Phelps volunteers. "That's what she told him."

His name is Caden. I turn my head as though I can still see him somewhere in the room even though I know he left.

"There, now." A hand on my good shoulder eases me back down. "Take it easy on her," Dr. Phelps—if I'm to believe he's an actual doctor—says as he bustles around me, wheeling a cart closer that nudges Buzz Cut out of the way. "You can ask her questions later."

"This is important for the security of the compound—"

"And if I don't get this bullet out of her, she'll likely die, Marcus."

Marcus makes a sound in his throat that tells me he doesn't care overly much about that. He wants what he wants from me.

"We need that information now—"

"You can get information out of her later. Caden didn't feel it critical to interrogate her at this very moment, so why should—"

"Anderson is not in charge," Marcus snaps, angry color flooding his face. Apparently his name is Caden Anderson.

"Neither are you," Phelps returns in a decidedly calm voice that Marcus doesn't seem to register. He just keeps talking.

"Just because his old man started this cell doesn't mean he's in charge here. Dumont runs this cell now."

"And he's not here," Phelps reminds him, sounding bored. Like a parent talking a child down from a tantrum. "Now I need to be alone with my patient."

Marcus makes another sound, part grunt, part sputtered protest. Phelps's body steps in front of him, blocking him completely, as if that is the end of the subject. After a moment I hear Marcus's steps fade from the room. A door slams after him.

"You shouldn't make him angry," a soft female voice speaks up. I didn't even realize anyone else was in the room, although there had been a lot of hands touching me earlier.

"He's a bully. I'm here to administer medical care. That's what I'll do."

A tool glints and swings past my vision. I suck in a sharp breath, knowing it's going to be used on me. He doesn't miss the sound of my gasp. Or maybe he simply notices how tense I've become.

"Sorry. This will hurt a bit. I'm afraid we have to ration the use of our sedatives. I'm going to have to dig that bullet out of you. If you ever need surgery here, you'll thank me for my temperance when you really need those meds."

I don't even allow myself to consider that I'm going to stay here—wherever *here* even is. Instead, I just say through my cracked lips, "You mean I'm going to hurt more? That doesn't seem possible."

He chuckles. "She's got a sense of humor, this one."

A girl lowers her face to observe the doctor work on my shoulder. She watches with rapt fascination. Her nose wrinkles at whatever she sees. A nose covered with brown freckles. She's sporting a short boy-cut that complements her round features.

"That bad?" I mumble.

Her moss-green eyes lock on mine. "Oh. Sorry. I'm just squeamish. Trying to overcome that. Working in the infirmary, I really need to."

"Hopefully it won't hurt too much more, Davy," Phelps continues in his easy manner. "Cross your fingers the bullet is easy to dislodge and hasn't shredded too much of the muscle. I don't think it struck bone. You're very lucky."

I'm a carrier. I've lost my family and the only friends I have left. Sean probably thinks I'm dead, and he's gone, headed to a refuge without me. Unless they were captured.

I don't feel lucky.

I brace myself. "Go for it, Doc. I've had worse."

"Tough, huh? That's good. We need more strong ones in here."

Again with the implication I'm going to be here for a while. "Sorry. I'm not staying."

"No? That's a shame. Well, maybe you'll reconsider once you're up on your feet and see our setup. We have a good thing going here. Some resistance cells are little more than campsites. They've got to move every day. Always running. Looking over their shoulders. Never enough food."

A good thing? Are there good things left? For carriers? I don't allow myself that hope.

"Doc," the girl says warningly. "You shouldn't be handing out invitations. You don't know that she can stay."

"You young people," he mutters. "All so serious."

I snort. Now who's the comedian? He's one of the first

adults I've met who doesn't seem to be taking anything seriously. Even the bullet in my shoulder, and that's a troubling thought, since I'm depending on him to get it out.

"Where'd you go to med school?"

He chuckles again at my question. Instead of answering, he says, "All right now, here we go. Hang on. And remember to breathe."

Then I'm dying.

Or I wish I was, because he's digging into my shoulder and searing pain flares through me. I open my mouth wide on a silent scream, my teeth scraping the mattress.

He mumbles something. Assurances or sympathetic words or advice to himself. I'm not sure. I just want him to shut up and finish already. But he's not. He digs a little deeper and I bite down on the mattress, clenching the sheet between my teeth.

"There we are." I hear the sharp ping of a bullet as he drops it in the tray.

I unclench my teeth and sag into the mattress, panting, all tension easing from me. A sharp ache takes the place of the searing pain. The warm sensation of blood trickles down my side, but there's a cloth suddenly there to catch it, wiping at my flesh. Phelps and the girl clean me up. I wince as needle and thread puncture my serrated flesh.

"Now you'll need to remain in the infirmary for a few days," he explains as he sets to stitching me up. "You're going to be in a great deal of pain, and it will be best for you to be in here where I can keep an eye on you. Something tells me you're the type who might not want to stay in bed."

"I need to find my friends." My lips brush the mattress as I speak. "They crossed into Mexico. I mean I hope they did. If they weren't captured—"

"Nah, we would have heard on the wire if any carriers were captured or killed last night in this area. Although they're lucky they made it. Few carriers make it across without our help. There are other groups out there, but none as efficient and organized as us. But you can worry about them later. In your condition, you're not going anywhere for a while."

His words, even as I register their logic, fill me with bitter frustration. Every moment that passes makes the gap between me and the others stretch wider. It's like I can almost touch them, my fingers stretching, reaching, but they keep getting farther and farther away from me.

"What is this place?" I ask.

Phelps pats the back of my head. "Hasn't anyone told you? Welcome to the resistance."

2016 Conversation between Colonel Anderson and General Dumont

COLONEL ANDERSON: You know where this is headed . . . this Wainwright fella. People are actually listening to him. Important people. People with power.

GENERAL DUMONT: I'm guessing you don't see our forced retirement as an opportunity to finally write that memoir?

COLONEL ANDERSON: Let them think we're perfectly satisfied to take an early retirement. I want them to have no suspicions.

GENERAL DUMONT: What do you intend to do?

COLONEL ANDERSON: The same thing we do every time we head into war. Start preparing.

GENERAL DUMONT: Well, you're not doing it alone.

EIGHT

I SPEND THE NEXT TWENTY-FOUR HOURS SLEEPING, waking only occasionally to sip some water. Despite the limits on their medical supplies, they slip me something and it makes me really drowsy. This new world I find myself in, complete with Dr. Phelps and his assistant—who always looks one breath from hurling whenever she checks my shoulder—blurs before my eyes whenever I emerge from unconsciousness.

On the second day, I sleep on and off, and take the broth that Phelps and his assistant—whose name I learn is Rhiannon—force on me. Every movement jars my body and reawakens the pain. If I lie very still and barely breathe, I can *almost* not hurt. I do this a lot. Holding myself close, like if I move I might splinter apart, and taking tiny sips of air.

"So this resistance . . . how many are there of you here?" I still have yet to get a clear answer on where *here* is, exactly. That seems to be confidential. Cue Marcus flipping out when he learned I wasn't blindfolded before being brought in. Despite waking up to that less-than-cheerful welcome, I know I'm lucky to be here. Lucky that Caden found me.

Rhiannon turns swiftly from where she is organizing the contents of a cabinet. "You're awake."

"I think I've slept as much as I'm going to today." Gritting my teeth, I start to roll on my side. I don't normally sleep on my stomach, and despite the discomfort in the back of my shoulder, I can't take it anymore.

Rhiannon hurries forward and helps me turn. "Easy," she cautions. "You don't want to tear your stitches."

On my back, I stare up at the girl, panting and hurting. "Tell me where I am."

"You're in an underground facility—"

"Like literally . . . underground?"

She nods. "It's how we're able to remain undetected. We have about forty permanent residents. A dozen or so carriers pass through en route to Mexico any given week. Sometimes more. Depends how many carriers we're tasked with transporting."

I shake my head. "I don't understand."

"Let me put it like this . . . we're a cell. A single hub on the resistance's underground railroad." She smiles. "You're lucky

Caden found you. Patrols could have picked you up. Or some other lowlife trolling the border."

The heavy steel door clangs open as Dr. Phelps breezes into the room. He wears a faded graphic T-shirt. A washed-out yellow smiley face covers his chest. "Ah, our patient is awake." He drops down on a stool and rolls over to me with a clatter of wheels. "How are you feeling?"

"Like I've been shot."

He chuckles, scratching his scruffy chin. "Yeah, I bet. Good thing Caden found you when he did."

"Yeah, if it had been Marcus, he would have left you out there." Rhiannon grimaces. "He's not the kind of guy to stick his neck out for strangers, even though that's sort of the whole point of what we're doing here." Rhiannon wrinkles her freckled nose as she goes back to organizing her cabinet.

A flicker of something flashes in Phelps's eyes, like maybe he's going to add a comment about Marcus, but then it's gone. "If you're up to it, I'd like you to try standing today. A little exercise will help. Don't overdo it. Just move around a bit."

Unease shoots through me as I realize I'm probably not going to Mexico anytime soon. The doctor must see some of that sentiment reflected in my face, for he continues, his voice softer, almost consoling, "You won't be able to travel for some time. We don't send anyone out without a clean bill of health. The journey is risky enough. The Agency knows there's a bigger, more organized resistance cell in these parts. They're constantly looking, so we have to be careful. You need clearance from me if you want to go out with the next convoy."

I suddenly imagine them as prairie dogs, sticking their noses out of burrows to see if the coast is clear. Mental image aside, finding them, being among them here, saved my life. Yes, I'm grateful for that, but I need to find my friends. I need out of this place. My skin itches just thinking about the last time I was in a place full of carriers.

"When do you think I can leave? When will I be healthy enough?"

Phelps smiles uneasily, his gaze flickering to Rhiannon and back to me. "It's . . . delicate. We'll get this all sorted out and figure out what to do with you. Tomorrow or the next day we'll see about moving you into one of the dorm rooms."

Suddenly it feels like the walls are closing in. I'm back in the Cage again. Someplace to stick me, contain me. An animal. I shake my head, fighting the feeling. I remind myself that we're all on the same side here. These people don't work for the Agency. They're like me. Just trying to survive. They're helping me.

Still, I hear myself asking, "Who's in charge? I need to talk to them."

Dr. Phelps stares at me with such over-the-top patience that I feel like a child making unreasonable demands, and I feel bad. He's been good to me . . . kind. I'd probably be dead if it wasn't for his care. He sighs and slides his glasses higher up the bridge of his nose. "Very well. I'll let them know, but you're only going to hear what I've already tried explaining."

I nod and offer up a smile. "Thank you."

Shaking his head, Dr. Phelps places his hands on his knees

and pushes to his feet with a sigh. He leaves the room with quiet steps, the door clanging heavily after him.

Rhiannon closes a cabinet sharply, deliberately. It echoes in the mostly empty room.

I study the girl's back. "What?" I ask, preferring to get to the point.

She whips around, slamming a bottle of peroxide on the counter. "We saved your life." Color heats her skin beneath her freckles. "You should be thanking us instead of . . ."

"Instead of?"

Her chin firms. "Instead of being a bitch." It's almost funny. Watching her spit that word out like it's something she's never tasted before. She's here. She's a carrier. Swearing can't be the worst of her transgressions.

I hold her stare for a long moment, showing no reaction to her insult. Really, it's hardly the worst thing I've been called since my life spiraled into this.

I finally point to my neck. "See this?"

She crosses skinny arms over her chest. "Half the people in here have those. Is it supposed to impress me? Scare me? What?"

"It should let you know what I am. Am I grateful you people saved my life? Yeah, I am." I incline my head in a small nod of acknowledgment. "But I still need to leave."

Her top lip curls. "Maybe they should just let you go. Waste all our efforts so you can get yourself killed for good this time." Turning, she marches from the infirmary. I resist calling her back. The old impulse to apologize is there. To be a polite, well-behaved girl. I remind myself that I'm not staying here. No need to invest myself, but some habits are hard to kill.

Mom had drilled manners and societal niceties into me since I could walk. It went right along with the voice and instrument lessons. It was important to her that her children be well-bred. I assumed that was simply what a woman like her, raised with everything, did. Now I understand there might have been more to it than that. It might have mattered to her simply because the world was sliding into a place where such things no longer existed. No one asks. They do. They take.

And no one apologizes.

Mom would have better served me and Mitchell by teaching us less about manners and more about how to be ruthless. How to survive. It's a bitter truth.

Alone, I drop my head back on the bed. Tension eases from my muscles as I lower my guard. I can relax here in this place. At least for a little while.

I carefully test my arm, seeing how much I can comfortably move it. I wince when I rotate my shoulder and quickly put a stop to that. I glance at the door, wondering how long I'll have to wait for someone to come and speak to me. It seems like forever ticks by as I lie there. The silence grows oppressive. Or maybe it's just the knowledge eating at me that I'm actually underground. I shove off the notion that I'm buried alive in one giant coffin with a swarm of carriers, ants ready to devour one another.

Exhaling a heavy breath, I lift myself up on the gurney and swing my legs over the side. I stare at my cotton gown for a moment, plucking at the paper-thin fabric, and deliberately don't think about the fact that they undressed me. A flash of amber-brown eyes fills my mind. Heat scores my cheeks, and I can't help hoping he didn't see that much.

The memory of him chases me. His eyes. His voice. The singing. *Caden.* My interaction with him was like something from a dream, fuzzy snapshots, but I recall the deep timbre of his voice as they cut my shirt from my body. He'd been right there. Of course he noticed.

"Perfect," I mutter, easing my bare feet down to cool concrete. *Are we really underground?* A shiver passes through me. It doesn't seem possible, and yet I know it is. People have been making underground bunkers, *dungeons*, for centuries.

I glance up as if I expect to see dark earth, complete with dangling worms and tree roots. Instead a typical ceiling stares back at me, including air vents.

Facing forward again, I take cautious steps, easing toward the door that didn't seem so far before but now feels miles away as I inch toward it with shuffling steps. Maybe I'm still under the influence of whatever they gave me to help me sleep. It's easier to accept that than that I'm really this weak.

Sweat trickles down my spine. All of me is flushed with suffocating heat. I'm panting by the time I reach the door. My hand seizes the latch desperately, clinging to it as if the slim hook of metal can support me and keep me from falling.

I pull down. Then up. Nothing.

I rattle the latch wildly, confirming that it's locked. Grunting in defeat, I glare at the door like it's a living thing standing in my way. An opponent. One in a long line of many.

They locked me in like I'm some sort of prisoner. I slap the door with my hand, ignoring the sting in my palm as I shout. "Open this door! You can't keep me trapped in here!"

Of course that's just what they're doing. *I didn't escape Mount Haven for this.*

I don't know how long I shout, but I'm hoarse and exhausted when the door suddenly flings wide, nearly knocking me down. I stumble, catching myself, my hand flying to my racing heart.

Caden enters the room, closing the door firmly behind him. I blink at his sudden appearance. The bright fluorescent lighting reveals him to be much different from my hazy recollections of him inside a dim cave or against the dark mountainous landscape.

His hair is untamed, like he just finished running his hands through it. The dark strands gleam with moisture and jut in every direction. He looks decidedly cleaner than I remember. I can smell the soap on his tan skin. Probably just stepped out from a shower. He's freshly shaved, too, and the strong cut of his jaw and cheekbones is more pronounced.

"Caden," I murmur, my gaze moving up the familiar boots, past the clean yet well-worn fatigues.

"You've learned my name." He pauses to smile at me. "Davy."

Someone told him my name? Had he asked about me? I

just assumed that he forgot about me after dumping me here. Girl rescued. Chore done.

I nod.

He crosses his arms, pulling the fabric of his shirt tight over his firm-looking chest. I realize he's waiting for me to say something when he adds, "You needed something, Champ?"

I drag a sharp breath into my lungs. "Champ?"

"Yeah. For someone sporting a gunshot wound, you're really . . ." His gaze scans me, and I'm hyperconscious of my thin hospital gown, which could stand to be a few inches longer. "Durable."

"Durable?"

"Yes. Fit. As in strong, athletic." He shakes his head. "Did you just raise hell so I could come in here and you could repeat everything I say?"

"Maybe I just wanted you to return for an encore performance?"

He angles his head, a slow smile curving his lips. "Ah. You remember me singing."

"Maybe. A little bit." I straighten, swiping the short strands of hair back from my face. It's an automatic gesture left over from when my hair was longer. The strands feel awful, grimy under my fingers, and I envy him his shower. "Why did you do that?"

"What? Sing?" He shrugs. "I dunno. It felt like the thing to do right then."

I moisten my lips. A part of me buried away could understand when singing just felt like the right thing to do. "Weren't you worried someone could have heard you?" *Like people who prefer us dead.*

He rubs at the back of his neck like he's a little embarrassed. "Yeah. I was a little worried about that." But he did it anyway. He sang. "Crazy as it sounds, you were in bad shape, and I thought it might help."

"Bob Dylan as medicine," I murmur. Yeah. I get it. Well, not anymore, but I used to. And I can't deny the fact that his voice hauled me back from the brink.

He drops his hand away and looks at me sharply, his eyes bright, interested. "You know Dylan?"

I nod once, uneasy . . . unwilling to continue discussing music with him. How can I without explaining how music is something I've lost? Something I can't hear inside myself anymore?

"I don't think I've met anyone around my age who's ever even heard of him." He looks me up and down, and I turn my face away, scanning the room. My gaze lands on the door. "Are you into music then?"

"Why am I locked in here?" I ask, changing the subject.

He takes his time answering, and it's like I can see the thoughts turning over behind his amber-bright eyes. "You shouldn't leave this room. You shouldn't even be out of bed yet—"

"Dr. Phelps said I needed to get on my feet today," I quickly counter.

"So you were going to take a stroll out of the infirmary in nothing but that?" He flicks a finger up and down.

The heat returns to my face in full force. I tug at the hem of my flimsy gown. It feels like paper between my fingers. "You didn't answer me. Why am I locked in here? Am I a prisoner?"

He considers the word, angling his head to the side and tossing all that dark hair off his forehead. A thick, rebellious chunk of it falls forward again. "More like a guest."

I tear my gaze off his hair. "A guest you lock in?"

"This is a compound full of carriers. Some of us have been here a while now and are known to each other. Trusted. Some not."

"Some meaning me?"

"At any given time we have visiting carriers. Even though we're trying to help and get them relocated to refuges in Mexico, they're strangers to us. We need to take precautions. It's just smart."

"And you keep them *all* locked in? These visiting carriers?" Also known as me.

"They're always watched." Not exactly a direct answer.

"But not locked in? That honor is specific to me?"

He sighs. "You did try to brain me."

"Of course. And you told them that. No wonder they're treating me like a prisoner. I heard that guy. Marcus. He doesn't want me here."

"Let me deal with Marcus. Trust me."

Trust. It's the wrong word to use. Everything inside me seizes up and tightens. The pain in my shoulder actually throbs deeper. Inhaling through my nose, I hug myself, feeling suddenly cold. I take another step back, craving distance.

He watches me, those eyes glinting like fire beneath the slash of his dark brows. He looks at me like I'm some sort of puzzle he's trying to figure out.

"I'm sorry I attacked you, but I woke with a bullet wound. In a strange place with a stranger. Who happened to be a carrier."

"I know that. I don't hold that against you. You were out of it. Which is why I brought you here at all."

As opposed to leaving me out there to die.

I do not mistake his meaning. When he found me, he viewed me as a wounded bird. Broken. He did not blame me for pecking at his hand. *Then.* From the way his jaw locks, I can see he won't forgive me again if I try something like that a second time.

I point to the door. "I want it unlocked." He simply stares at me. Doesn't move. Doesn't talk. Air shudders past my lips. I nod. "I get it. I'm a carrier." Just like when I was stuck in the Cage. Forced in there because of what I was. Not *who*. No one cared about that.

"Yeah. You are. Just like we all are in here."

Studying the planes of his face, I can appreciate his honesty. Nodding, I murmur, "And at the end of the day, no carrier can be trusted."

"I didn't say that."

I snort.

"I don't know you yet," he adds.

Yet. That word hangs between us. It tempts me. The thought that I might find a friend in him is something I hadn't considered. The only friends I have are Sean, Gil, and Sabine. That's why I have to find them.

Turning, I walk back to the gurney. "I won't be here long enough for you to get to know me." My legs tremble as I pull myself back onto the thin mattress. Mostly from exertion. *Mostly.* "I asked Dr. Phelps to get me whoever is in charge." I start arranging the blanket around my legs. "I guess he didn't convey that message. Or your boss doesn't care. Maybe you can let—"

"He did."

I look up. "He did?" He lifts a dark eyebrow, the motion faintly smug. "You?"

"Don't sound so surprised."

"But you're so . . ." *Not who I want to deal with. A guy who looks like you and sings Bob Dylan. Who cares whether I live or die.* "Young."

"I'm nineteen."

"And you run the show here?" I glance around the infirmary, considering all the work and effort that must have gone into creating an underground facility. He couldn't have been solely responsible for that.

"My father built the compound three years ago. He saw this coming. When they fired him from the army because he tested positive for HTS."

He utters this so evenly, his voice devoid of all emotion, but it's there. In the twitch beside his eye. He's affected.

I moisten my lips. "Where is he—"

"He died a year ago." He says this quickly. Like he feels no sentiment over the matter, but I know that's not true. Emotion edges the tightness in his voice. "His second in command, Dumont, is in charge, but he's away . . . on important business right now."

Important business. In other words none of your business.

"And while he's gone, you're in charge of this . . . cell."

"It's not a dictatorship. I'm one of three captains. We operate under careful guidelines. Dumont trusts us to keep things operating smoothly in his absence. Two of the three of us have to agree. Majority rules. This is to keep us from making risky or stupid decisions."

Despite his age, he's a leader. It's in his bearing, the way he stands with his shoulders back, his legs spread apart like he's at the prow of a ship. It's etched into his face, the grooves bracketing his mouth you can almost mistake for dimples. He reveals nothing unless he wishes to. He compels people to obey. Hadn't he commanded me to live when he found me, clinging to life by a thread?

"Decisions like what to do with me?"

He doesn't respond, but he doesn't need to. His silence only serves as confirmation. My fate, at what point I might leave this place, is entirely up to him.

He advances slowly, closing the distance between us with long strides. "You sent for me. I'm here. What did you need?"

"I need to leave."

His lips twitch like I've said something of great amusement. "You're in no condition to go anywhere."

I bite back the instant argument that springs to my lips

and inhale through my nose. "When, then?"

"Do you have someplace to be?" An innocent question, but there's an undercurrent to it. A hint of curiosity and something more. He's fishing. Nosing for information about me. Like I could be something more than what is present.

I hold his gaze. "I was going to Mexico. With my friends. I need to find them."

"Do you know where they're headed?"

"My friend Gil got in contact with someone. Clearly not as organized as your group." I shrug helplessly, wishing I knew more. "We were going to a refuge over there."

"There are half a dozen refuges you could be talking about."

Despair swells in my chest. Why didn't I know more? Why hadn't I asked more questions? Why hadn't Sean or Gil explained our plans more fully to me? Of course we could have gotten separated. I see that now. That should have occurred to us. To me. I drop my head into my open palm. "I'm so stupid."

"Hey. No one plans on getting shot."

Helplessness washes over me. "I'm stuck here, and they probably think I'm dead."

Sean's not coming back for me. Even if he wants to. He's practical. He's always been practical. He was willing to leave me at Mount Haven if I didn't escape with him. He never was one to lose his head over emotion. He'll have calculated the odds of me being alive . . . of him finding me . . .

A lump rises in my throat. By that math, he would never return.

"Why don't you give me the names and descriptions of your friends? I'll send a message through our network."

"You mean that? Their names are Sean and Gil and Sabine."

"If they're at one of the refuges, I'll eventually find out."

I look up at him, hope stirring in my chest. "How long is eventually?"

He shrugs. "A week. Two."

Two weeks here? I swallow past the lump in my throat. As if he can read some of my thoughts, he adds, "You can heal and rest during that time. You'll be comfortable. But while you're in here, this door remains locked. For your protection. Understand?"

The tightness in my chest loosens as I stare into the velvet depths of his eyes. I nod, understanding then that the door is not simply to keep me *in*, but to keep me safe. "Okay." It's been a long time since I've felt comfortable. I'm not sure if I *can* be comfortable, if that's even possible, but at least I'll be safe. "Okay."

The door opens and Phelps steps inside. "Sorry to interrupt, but I need to check on my patient."

Caden nods and moves to the door, holding the edge with his hand while looking back at me. "We'll talk again later, Davy. I want to hear more about this camp you came from." And then he's gone.

I wince slightly at his parting words. The last thing I want to do is talk about Mount Haven, but if it can help Caden and what he's doing here, then I will. For no other reason than that I owe him for saving my life.

"Let's change your gauze and check on your stitches."

Shaking off my thoughts, I nod and permit Phelps to inspect my shoulder. Rhiannon soon joins him, wearing her perpetual look of revulsion at the sight of my wound. It's almost funny, considering she works in the infirmary.

"Looks good. No infection."

"I could really use a shower."

Phelps glances at Rhiannon. "I think with Rhiannon's help you could manage that."

The girl gives one terse nod.

"Thank you," I say.

Phelps beams, and I realize with a cringe that it's probably the first polite thing to come out of my mouth. He pats my arm. "You're going to be fine. Shower today. Maybe tomorrow, if you're feeling better, Rhiannon can give you a tour of the facility."

She snorts. "Why don't you ask Caden to do that? She's his little project."

I look at her sharply. Why would she think that? Because he saved my life and brought me here? Or was there something more to the comment?

The smile leaves Phelps's face. "Caden's a captain. He has responsibilities. I don't think I need to remind you of that. You can do your part."

Rhiannon ducks her head, looking like a child who just got her hand slapped. "Sure. Okay. I can do it."

"Thought so. Fetch her some fresh clothes, too."

She nods.

"Thanks," I say again, looking at her this time, searching her face. If she's going to be doing all this for me, I should try for friendly. Otherwise she might bring me a burlap bag to wear as punishment.

NEWS RELEASE

For immediate release

Contact: Department of Justice—
        Office of the Attorney General

June 3, 2021

News out of Nogales, Arizona, today reports the discovery of a cell of carriers numbering approximately thirty in the Meadow Hills area. Local law enforcement and agents of the Wainwright Agency arrived and evacuated the surrounding area. By 9:50 a.m., members of the DHS used tear gas and stormed the building. Officials on-site declined to comment. It is not known at this time if any carriers survived the siege. . . .

NINE

THE COMPOUND OUTSIDE THE INFIRMARY ISN'T exactly what I expected. Even utilitarian, it's bigger than I imagined it would be. Industrial gray paint. Sparse décor. Mostly metal tables and chairs in a large central room with corridors shooting off it that open to various rooms; living quarters, storage rooms, kitchens, showers, a controls room. This central room serves as a gathering place. Rhiannon waves at the large space as we walk along the upper level, a railing to our right. "Everyone eats there, as well as congregates for all major announcements."

She nods toward an area full of exercise equipment and

mats. "You can work out there when you feel up to it. It helps. Especially when you feel the cabin fever coming on."

"You never go up top?" I ask.

"I'm not a scout. And it's dangerous out there. I prefer it down here. A lot of us do."

Dozens of eyes trail me as I struggle to keep up with Rhiannon. One girl pauses from kicking at a punching bag. She wipes at her brow, carelessly flipping her dark braid over her shoulder as she follows my movements.

"Who's that?" I ask Rhiannon with a nod toward the mats where the girl works out.

"In the black tank? That's Tabatha." A touch of something, awe maybe, hugs Rhiannon's voice. Tabatha arches an eyebrow like she knows we're talking about her and then goes back to pounding the bag. "She's one of our scouts."

"I take it she doesn't prefer it down here?"

"Yeah, she likes to go where the fighting is. Both her parents were carriers. They were shot when they escaped a detention camp. Only she got away. She made it all this way on her own. Now she's our best scout guiding people across the river."

"Then she'll be taking me . . ." My voice fades.

Rhiannon slides a glance at me. "Maybe. We'll see. She's not the only scout."

A pair of amber eyes fills my mind. A small shiver chases down my neck at the thought of him leading me to Mexico. He's a captain. Would that be part of his duties? "Caden?"

"Yeah. He's a scout, too. Along with Marcus and Terrence."

At my confused look, she adds, "They're our three captains. But they have a lot of other things keeping them busy while the General is gone. They've been scouting less since he left. It's enough work just keeping us fed."

Noticing how much I'm laboring to keep up, Rhiannon slows her pace and drops even with me. I smile gratefully, my hand skimming along the railing for support.

"There's probably hot water," she offers. "Not too many people are showering in the middle of the day. If not, you'll just have to settle for cold."

"I'll be happy with anything. I've had worse than a cold shower lately."

She looks me up and down as we continue on our path to the showers. "We all have. We're lucky just to be here and not in some detention camp."

I nod. "Yeah."

My steps slow when I notice a guy—a man—watching me intently. He sits alone, peeling an orange over his tray of half-eaten food with slow movements.

"Who's that?"

Rhiannon glances from me out to the main floor. A flicker of something, distaste maybe, crosses her face before vanishing. "That's Hoyt. He got here a few weeks ago. He's Marcus's cousin. Traveled all the way from Oregon, I hear."

"He's a carrier, too?"

"We're all carriers here. That goes without saying."

Yes, it does. We're all in the same boat here. Whether any

of us are true killers is beside the point. We are all the same in the eyes of the world.

She keeps walking, not looking his way again. "He's not like Marcus, though."

Considering Marcus doesn't possess such a winning personality, I'm not sure what that means.

She elaborates with, "He's a creeper."

"A creeper?"

"Yeah. You know. Always creeping up on you. Quiet as a mouse, but when you turn around, he's there. Watching you." She looks at me and repeats, "Creeper."

Like it's the most obvious and natural thing. Like this place is full of them. I shrug off my sense of disquiet and remind myself this place can't be worse than Mount Haven. The carriers here want to be here. They're helping one another. And others on the outside, too.

I nod and move on, still feeling his stare. *Creeper.*

We enter the women's showers. Basically a locker room. Poor lighting. Concrete on every side. There are hooks and cubbies.

Rhiannon puts the fresh clothes she carries for me inside a cubby and picks up a towel from a folded stack. "Here."

I take the towel. The fabric is rough and scratchy, but clean at least. I follow her to where the floor slopes into showers that are sectioned off with curtains. I'm almost surprised at the nod to modesty. Everything else feels so utilitarian . . . like such a thing would be beyond concern.

She helps me ease the gown off my shoulders. With careful fingers she peels back the gauze. "Try not to get it too wet. I know you want to wash your hair, but do the best you can to keep this dry. There should be some bottles of shampoo on the ledge in there."

"Thanks." Letting the gown pool to my feet, I step behind the nearest curtain. Even lukewarm, the water is heaven. I let it gently beat down on my battered body. I shampoo my hair twice, rubbing my scalp clean with my fingertips, noticing that the water darkens for a moment with some of the residual dye. Remembering Rhiannon's advice to keep my shoulder as dry as possible, I finish the rest of my shower quickly and shut the water off. The towel appears through the curtain as if by magic, and I realize she must have been waiting on the other side the entire time. Like some kind of bodyguard. I shove off the uneasy sensation.

"Thanks." I accept it and pat myself dry. Satisfied, I pull back the curtain with a noisy screech of the iron rings—and freeze. A girl stands there, but it's not Rhiannon. It's Tabatha. With her hands propped on her hips, her toned arms are highlighted to perfection. My gaze skips over her and skims the room.

"Where's Rhiannon?"

"Doc needed her. I volunteered to stay."

Because I can't be left unsupervised?

Wrapped in the towel, I step from the shower, my modesty suddenly returning in the presence of a girl who looks like she works out every spare moment.

"I wanted to meet you anyway." She studies me as I move toward my clothes. I feel her gaze on my neck, lingering on the band and the encircled H. This sleek—yes, sexy—dangerous-looking girl evaluates me. I'm almost surprised she doesn't bear an imprint, too. There's an aura of power about her. She definitely seems very capable of dispensing violence. They would have loved her at Mount Haven.

Even though a voice tells me I shouldn't respond to her comment, I hear myself asking, "Why would you want to meet me?"

"I heard about you. The girl who Caden found. Who survived the wilderness alone . . . complete with a bullet wound." The words are right, but there's something to them. A lack of respect that crystallizes the point that she really isn't impressed with me.

"Well, I wasn't exactly alone, was I? Like you said, Caden found me."

"Hm." She lowers herself to a bench and watches me clinically as I dress. "But you got away from the patrols shooting you. So you have some skills." She looks me over as if searching for evidence of this and not seeing it.

"None to speak of," I hedge, hoping to appear nonthreatening. Let her think I'm a carrier passing through like all the rest.

"So what's the deal with this camp you came from?" She brings her braid around her shoulder and toys with the end of it, running the dark strands between her long fingers.

At my sharp look, she shrugs. "I heard them talking

about it." I wince internally at the thought of anyone sitting around . . . discussing me. "They were training you to be some kind of specialized killer, huh?"

"Not really."

"Did they train you in techniques and stuff?"

Finished dressing, I stand. "Ready?"

She hesitates, clearly wanting me to answer her. Shrugging, she drops her braid and rises from the bench. "Sure." Even as lukewarm as the water had been, the air outside the room is decidedly less humid, and my breath flows easier out of my lungs.

We don't make it very far before the iron-grate floor beneath us rattles with the weight of someone coming toward us. I look up and my gaze collides with the dark eyes of a guy who must have played football in his past life—or wrestled. His neck sits thickly on his shoulders. The great width of it only draws more attention to his imprint.

"Enjoyed your shower?" Reproach laces his voice. Like I'm somehow not entitled to such a thing. But it's a voice I recognize. The nasal quality impossible to forget.

I stare at him, managing a nod.

"We met when you first arrived. I'm Marcus. Captain here." As though he's the only captain. He nods to the guy standing close behind him. He's big, too, with close-set eyes. "This is Ruben."

I hold silent. Standing between Tabatha, with watchful eyes, and Marcus, I don't exactly feel like I'm among friends, even though these people and this place are the only things standing between me and certain death.

"Glad to see you're on your feet. Maybe we can talk now, but not here." He glances around, his dark eyebrows drawing together. His hair is shaved close to his head in a military-style crew cut. He's in his midtwenties and holds himself rigidly, his muscled chest pushing against his tight camo T-shirt. "Let's head to the interrogation room."

Interrogation room? What is he—a police detective?

I moisten my lips and glance around, searching for Rhiannon. There's no sign of her, and I turn back to Marcus.

He cocks his head, considering me. Waiting. And I know it's not a suggestion.

I look at Tabatha, but there's no help there. The expression on her face tells me she thinks this is a great idea. She would probably sit next to him and add her own questions to the inquiry.

Suddenly I feel very alone.

Marcus's gaze lifts right and settles over my shoulder.

"That's enough time on your feet for one day, Davy. Let's get you back to the infirmary."

I shouldn't have been surprised to hear the low rumble of Caden's voice behind me. I blame my injuries. I thought my situational awareness—at least ever since finding out I have HTS—was better than that. Seems I still have things to work on.

I'm not sure if it's Caden's voice or his hand settling on my arm, but I shiver.

"Hey, Caden." Tabatha straightens, gifting him with a

bright smile. He nods hello.

"We were going to put a few questions to her, Anderson." Marcus's eyes take on a new gleam as he directs his attention to Caden. "We haven't had an opportunity to do that yet given her unorthodox arrival. I'm sure you can see the wisdom in that. Your old man, the Colonel, was the one to set up such protocols, after all." Ruben nods beside him.

Caden grins then, his teeth a flash of white against his tan face. He chuckles softly, and I think I catch him murmur the word "unorthodox."

Marcus must have heard him, too—or he just doesn't care for Caden's amusement. He snaps, "That's right. We have protocol in place. Protocol established by your father when he first started this cell. Protocol we're trusted to maintain while Dumont is gone. *Protocol* that you broke when you failed to blindfold her." He stabs a finger directly in Caden's chest, and just like that all levity leaves Caden's face.

The air thickens, and I'm convinced one of them—or both—is about to launch at the other one. By now I know carriers. Whatever else they are, they're aggressive.

"I don't need you to lecture me about my father."

"I think I knew the man better than you." Ruben makes a grumbling sound of assent. Marcus nods and claps him on the shoulder as he continues, "I served under him for five years and Ruben here served under him for three . . . while you were some snot-nosed kid hanging out on a skateboard back home with your mommy. The General only made you a captain when you came here out of some screwed-up sense of loyalty to your dad."

"Shut up." Caden's jaw tenses, and I know he wants to say more than that.

Marcus ignores him. "Following protocol keeps people alive. Your old man never got around to teaching you that lesson, I guess. For all we know she's an Agency spy."

"I don't work for the Agency," I can't stop myself from protesting. I grab at my throat, stretching my neck for all eyes although it's not necessary. My imprint is clear as day. "Does this mean nothing?"

"For all we know they put that on you so you could fit in better." This from Ruben. I glare at him, standing so confidently beside Marcus.

"Really?" I feel my eyes go wide. "Are there many volunteers out there who would take an assignment where they have to get themselves imprinted?"

No one would want that stigma. I know that much . . . have lived through the ostracism firsthand. Family. Friends. The life that you thought yours all of a sudden vanishing. As fluid as water slipping through your fingers.

"Who said it was your choice?" Marcus shrugs. "Or maybe the Agency promised to remove your imprint after you completed your job."

I pull back, feeling myself shrink a little inside, because it's close to what Mount Haven dangled before me—that if I successfully completed their training, I could have a future without this imprint around my neck. But that ship sailed the day I escaped.

I'm not a spy.

Caden's fingers adjust on my arm, just a light flexing. I could easily shrug him off, but that would leave me facing others who look ready to drag me away into some interrogation room. I envision it like in one of those old police dramas—with them beating me with a rubber hose to get whatever answers they want out of me.

"Back. Off." Caden punctuates each word with a meaningful pause.

"Caden," Tabatha says, and there's a cajoling tone, a lilt to her voice that irks me, driving home the fact that while Caden and Marcus might not get along, Caden and Tabatha are a whole other story. She plays with the end of her braid again, curling the dark strands around her fingers with an elegance that belies her hard-as-nails-camo-wearing persona.

He shakes his head once at her. "We're not doing this now, Tab."

I glance at the hard set to his jaw. Not now. But later? This time I tug my arm free. The action liberates me, but I sway a little on my feet.

"See? She can hardly stand." Caden wraps an arm around my waist.

Tabatha's eyes narrow on that arm and her gaze feels heavy on me, heavier than Caden's arm. Like a shackle. Caden walks us past them, still holding me like I might drop. Marcus stands aside at the last moment, letting us pass. My hip brushes with Caden's and I try to lean away, but he yanks me back, tucking me to his side.

I glare at his profile. "I can walk."

"Keep moving unless you're in the mood to be interrogated," he says near my ear.

"I thought you were in charge here," I toss back.

"I told you . . . there's not just one leader here." He jerks his head back to the group. "If Marcus wants you badly enough . . . and convinces everyone else that you're some spy, well then, there's not much Terrence or I can do for you."

My throat tightens as his voice fades. I swallow against the thickness rising up my windpipe. "Why not let them take me? Aren't they your friends?"

"Marcus is not my friend, nor is his sidekick, Ruben," he growls, his hand exerting the slightest pressure at my waist. "He's power hungry. All this is a pissing match between him and me."

"And I'm in the middle of it? Great. Maybe you should care a little less for my welfare then. Maybe I'd be better off."

His mouth curves in a half smile, and that sends a warm little flutter through me—to know I made him smile. *Perfect.* I give myself a mental punch to the face. That's what feeling so alone and starved for friends and companionship does to you. It's made me weak and overly affected at the first smile a cute guy throws my way.

That's not all it does. It makes me care. Again. Like before.

I nod as the knowledge twists sickly through me, curling around my heart. Yeah. Right. *And caring makes you do things like kill.*

I suck in a breath at the reminder of Sean. I don't regret saving his life, but taking the life of another? I can never shake that.

"Hey, Cade!"

I look up as another fatigues-clad guy advances. This one doesn't look nearly as intimidating as Marcus and Ruben, however, even if he's big, too.

"Been looking for you!" He holds a notepad, his face animated at whatever he's got written there. He's probably in his late twenties, but at the moment he looks like a kid who just discovered a forgotten lollipop in his pocket.

"Terrence." Caden stops and nods at me beside him. "This is Davy."

"Oh." He blinks down like he's noticing me for the first time. "Heard Caden found you out there . . . there was a lot of static on the wire about your group. They were going nuts trying to get you guys. Glad the others you were with made it across. Pretty lucky. More are captured than succeed. Except us. We rarely fail."

"Yeah, it's a real relief." Whatever happens to me, at least there's the comfort of knowing they reached the other side.

"Last night I was actually worried with Caden out there and the patrols so thick."

"Yeah. I guess I'm lucky he was out there, though, to find me."

"No doubt." He takes my hand in a firm handshake. "Nice to meet you."

"You too."

Terrence drops my hand and waves his pad at Caden again. "I've got some exciting intel about activity east of—"

"I'll meet you in controls in a minute, T," Caden says calmly.

Terrence looks ready to argue, but then he glances from Caden to me and seems to compose himself. He squares his shoulders, and his expression loses some of its animation. "All right." He nods. "See you in a few."

Caden holds the door to the infirmary open for me. I feel instantly more at ease once I step inside the familiar room. Phelps is there with Rhiannon. They're peering over a microscope on the far counter. They lift their heads to give us the barest glance before returning their attention to their work.

Caden helps me toward the bed. "Kind of hard to stop now."

I pause, looking at him in confusion, both my hands flat on the bed, ready to lift myself up.

"Caring," he clarifies. "About you."

The words send hot prickles throughout me. I quickly drag myself all the way onto the bed, hardening everything inside me. I don't know why he's saying such things or being kind. It's tempting to trust him. To let myself lean on someone else. "It's *not* hard," I insist, staring at him intently, begging with my gaze. "You just stop." I say this like that's the easiest thing to do. I want to add that if you don't stop now, it only hurts more later. I know this. Later, when the world crashes all around you, it will be too late.

He pulls the blanket over my legs like I'm an invalid. "Rest. Get better. We'll talk tomorrow." He glances to where the doctor and Rhiannon work. His voice lowers as he considers them. "Try to avoid Marcus. It doesn't take much for him to stir up trouble. I'm sure you can understand how tense everyone is."

Tense? With the world wanting you dead or under lock and key in a detention camp? With patrols swarming above us hunting for carriers? Yeah. I guess I understand why tempers might be quick to flare.

He continues to study me, adding, "I know it feels like you're trapped here, but this place is freedom. The closest we can get, anyway, these days. This compound exists for the sole purpose of helping carriers find freedom. You'll get your chance. Just hang in there. I'll help you. You just have to trust me."

I shake my head at him, all my nerves squeezing tight. Resisting him and that impossible thing he suggests.

He sighs, a faint smile on his lips. "I know what you're thinking. You don't do trust."

The corners of my lips tentatively lift. It's a humorless smile that feels all wrong on my face. "It's not in me." To trust. To wait for life to happen to me. That's not possible. Not anymore.

"You can't go out until I say it's safe. Do you understand?

You can't act without considering the whole group. None of us can. That's how we've made it this far, and I'm not going to let everything my father built crumble to hell." A hardness enters his voice. "If one of us is captured, or a group that goes out is taken, this entire cell is threatened. That won't happen. I won't let it."

Staring into his earnest face, I know he's for real. This place is his priority. As kind as he's being to me, ultimately it's the group he's looking out for.

A whisper of respect weaves through me for this guy who would take on so much, who would fight for a cause ... for an entire population of people he doesn't even know.

I shove down the surge of emotion. I'd prefer not to feel this way . . . not to feel anything for him at all. If there's respect, then before I know it, I'll be liking him. I'll *care*. My stomach twists.

"You don't know me." As much a reminder for me as him.

"Just because we're carriers doesn't mean we have to live without a conscience. The minute we forget that, the minute it's every man for himself ... then all is lost. We've become the monsters they say we are."

There's a chord of something in his voice—a plea? I roll over onto my side, away from him, almost hating him in that moment for reminding me of the person I used to be—the person I assumed I would always be before everything was taken away from me. My eyes burn, and I blink them hard once. He makes me remember and yearn for that girl again. He makes me think that maybe ... just maybe, I can be her a little bit.

His sigh gusts above my head. I don't acknowledge him there even as I can visualize him looking down at me. I wait for him to go. He does, his steps a soft tread on the tile. It's not until the door to the infirmary opens and shuts that I finally let go of the breath I've been holding.

SAN DIEGO TIMES

April 17, 2018

A killer is still at large in the greater San Diego area. The latest victim is student Shannon Gomez. She is the third young woman to fall prey to a murderer police are no closer to apprehending. A source close to the case claims they are seeking Hoyt Mackenzie, a registered carrier and Ms. Gomez's neighbor, for questioning and are unable to locate him. . . .

TEN

DARK EYES SHOWS UP AGAIN. I'VE DECIDED TO refer to him in this way until I can come up with an actual name for him that doesn't seem snarky or disrespectful. Ghost just seems somehow belittling and brings to mind old *Scooby-Doo* cartoons. And Guy-I-Killed doesn't fully capture my guilt. It's a hard thing.

He sits across the room on one of the stools beside Phelps's lab table. He watches me with those eyes that glitter like flaming coal, hands braced on his knees, his posture as quiet as he is, his mouth a deep slash of lips, unspeaking. Brown eyes. Bullet hole. Black-red blood.

I wish he would speak. If he just broke out in speech like a normal person, not a dead-come-back-to-haunt-me person, then I could talk to him. Reason with him. Explain why I had to do what I did. Then maybe he would be at peace. And so would I.

"You're back," I say, and then realize just because I don't remember him being around in the last couple of days doesn't mean he hasn't been with me all this time. That's a sobering thought. Maybe he's been here every time I close my eyes. I was just too sedated to notice.

He'll never really leave me. I know that.

I glance around the room. There's a small glow of light coming off some equipment in the corner. Dr. Phelps sleeps behind a curtained-off area. His gentle breathing scratches the air.

When my gaze swings forward again, Dark Eyes moves from his seat. In a fraction of a second, he's before me, bending at the waist in an eerie, unnatural way, crouching in front of me so I can see the shine of his eyes.

Gasping, I lurch back, but his hoarse voice fills my ears. A single word. It travels through me like a deep vibration, settling in my head and spreading outward through the rest of me.

It's urgent and desperate, the syllables stretching long, sinking deep and biting into me. "Waaaaaaaaaaaaaaake."

Wake. Because I'm asleep.

The sound reverberates in my ears as though someone had truly just shouted for me to wake up, and my eyes fly wide open.

Relief rushes over me. I was dreaming. I drag in a lungful of air. My chest swells, holding the breath in before expelling it in a silent rush.

I can practically feel my pupils dilate to take in more light. It's in this eerie little moment, flashes of something . . . innate hit a chord, a buried memory of when humans were more animal than man, both prey and predator, and I feel my instincts take over.

The same faint blue glow suffuses the room as in my dream. Peering into the shadows, I see that Phelps is gone, however. The curtain to his sleeping area is pulled back, revealing his unmade bed. Maybe someone got sick and he had to go to them. Whatever the case, it's just me in the infirmary. That's my thought as I roll onto my side, hoping to get back to sleep and that this time no visitors wait for me in the dark of my mind. Especially ones sporting a bullet hole to the head and who appear to be growing more vocal. *Wake?* Why would he have wanted me to wake up?

I rub at the center of my forehead and release a shuddering sigh. Closing my eyes, I settle back onto the mattress. With a small snort, I remember that he was just a fabrication of my subconscious. He didn't command me to wake up. I did.

I did. . . .

My eyes flare wide open. The room is pitch-black now. The low blue light is out, and I know that someone plunged the room into darkness. Someone. Someone who is in the room with me.

My scalp pulls and tightens under my hair. I know, with

the same instinct that tells me I'm not alone, that it's not Phelps or Rhiannon. It's not even Caden. Whoever's here is not friendly.

I can feel his intent, rolling in dark, malevolent waves toward me. It's almost a tangible odor. Like burnt leaves in my nose.

A switch flips inside me as instinct takes over. Everything drags to a slow crawl. My heartbeat stutters to a deep thud in my ears. I sit up on one elbow and pivot my neck, scanning for any shapes, a flicker of movement against the blanket of dark.

Muscles tense, I push the covers off my legs and drop to the cold concrete. I step slowly in the direction of Phelps's lab table, going after a weapon. I can see the medical instruments in my mind, where Phelps left them on the stainless-steel rolling tray.

I move blindly, listening, seeing with my memory, feeling with my skin.

I jump as wheels roll across the floor with a whir. A gurney hits a wall with a violent crash. I spin around, staring, my breath a loud saw of air.

Then I hear it. Someone else breathing, too.

Too late, I realize my mistake. I should have kept going for that weapon. I let myself be distracted. My training from Mount Haven kicks in, and all at once I hear my instructors' advice drilling into me.

Be faster. Outrun your opponent.

I take off for Phelps's tray table of instruments as those voices play out in my head.

Get your hands on a weapon.

My bare feet smack hard over the concrete.

Embrace the fact that they will always underestimate you.

I feel him behind me before I actually *feel* him. The rush of air as a hand swipes near my head. Fingertips graze strands of my hair and then latch on, knuckles curling hard into my scalp and then yanking.

Crying out, I drop, counting on the weight of my body to break his hold. Tears spring to my eyes as hair rips free from my scalp. I let gravity do its job; my feet dive first like a baseball player sliding into home. I crash into the stand holding the tray of instruments. Everything rains to the floor in a deafening clatter.

Hopping up in a crouch, I pat the ground until I find something. Fumbling, I wrap my hands around cold steel. The sharp tip of it scores my palm, and I quickly reposition it sharp end out. It's slick in my bloody palm, so I clench tightly and stand. I swing blind, again and again, in every direction, hoping to make contact. My weapon whistles on the air, but nothing. No contact.

Wild, animal-like sounds escape my lips, but over the sounds I can hear the ragged breathing of another person.

Something crashes into my cheek. I go down hard, fall on my shoulder, and it's double the fun. I still manage to keep my weapon, but I'm stunned, the pain in my shoulder worse than the throbbing in my face. Something wet trickles down my back and I know I'm bleeding again—the stitches ripped free.

Panting, I shake my head, trying to force myself to move, to *think*. A body pins me, the weight heavy, punishing. Thighs straddle me and I know I'm screwed. He's bigger and I've lost the upper hand, if I ever had it.

He scoots up until his knees find my shoulders, anchoring me there, fixing me to the floor, incapacitating me. It's agony. White-hot agony. The pain is so intense I can't even struggle. A scream starts at the back of my throat but is swiftly killed as two hands grab and squeeze, crushing my windpipe. My lips work, choking, gargling for speech as those hands clench tighter.

Do something! Fight! Move!

I swing, embed the slim blade into flesh. A deep shout tells me I hurt him. I'm not sure where I've struck. His arm or his side. The hands on me loosen for a brief moment before tightening again with renewed determination. Clearly I didn't hurt him badly enough. Or he's just so unhinged that pain takes a backseat to his thirst for killing.

He shakes me as he's choking me, and the back of my head cracks against the floor. Bright spots flash over the darkness. I flex my hand around the weapon and yank it out, then plunge it in again. This time there's no shout. He stiffens above me. Wetness spills over my fingers like a geyser, and I know I hit something vital. His hands release me, fingers slipping from around my throat, and he slumps over me.

I struggle to push my face free so that I can breathe. My fingers claw an opening for myself, and I suck in air.

I can't move for the longest time. Even as my body grows wet under him, soaked in his blood, I just lie there in the dark, spent.

My muscles spasm and quiver. I'm a useless lump. If someone wanted to finish me off right now, they'd find no resistance. Every breath hurts passing through my ravaged throat. I try to inhale through my nose, but I'm too starved for oxygen. I can't stop my lungs from pulling air in and out of my mouth, even though it feels like nails clawing the inside of my throat.

The door to the infirmary suddenly opens, and I hear the click of a switch the second before fluorescent lighting hums to life.

Dear Davy,

I haven't heard from you and I know I shouldn't expect to, but I can't not write to you. The house is so quiet without you. Mom and Dad try to act like everything is okay, but they hardly talk to each other—or me. Our family just isn't a family without you. It's like you were our captain, steering us through life, and we didn't even know it.

I watch the news every day. I've joined a group. We protest the Agency . . . make posters and circulate petitions. Next week a huge group of us are rallying at the state capital. I tell myself I'm doing something, but it doesn't seem enough. I don't know how long I can stay here. Not with everything that's going on. Not with you out there.

I hear the rumblings about the resistance cells. Word is they're popping up all over the country, smuggling carriers from checkpoint to checkpoint, working toward undermining the Agency and camps. The media insists it's all exaggeration, but I think the Resistance is real. They're out there and making a difference. There are more people questioning the validity of HTS. Things have got to change soon, Davy. Just hold on.

—Letter sent from Mitchell Hamilton
Destroyed upon receipt at Mount Haven

ELEVEN

BY THE TIME PHELPS ROLLS MY WOULD-BE-ASSASSIN off me, he's made enough noise, shouting and calling for help, that a mob quickly crowds the infirmary. I wheeze, speech impossible.

Caden isn't the first one to the room, but there's a shift in the air once he arrives. He may claim not to be in charge, but everyone looks to him when he bursts through the door, shoving past bodies. Even Marcus looks at him. Or glares really. But Marcus has been glaring since he got here and crouched beside me and the dead guy, looking back and forth between the two of us with the oddest expression in his eyes.

Caden searches the room, takes it in with one sweep. His eyes light on the body of the man I killed. He's still right there beside me, the copper-rich scent of him indistinguishable from my own smell. I reek of death. The entire room does.

Since the light flipped on, I've studied him, too. My would-be-killer. Another face for my nightmares. Although I won't suffer guilt this time around. Not for this one. He didn't have to creep into my room in the middle of the night and try to choke the life out of me. No one forced his hands around my throat. That was his choice. Killing him was mine, and I don't regret it. Not when it came down to him or me.

I recognized him at once. The creeper.

Caden's gaze locks on me. He moves to stand beside Phelps, who still inspects me, prodding at my neck, and it takes everything in me not to shrink away from the contact. Right now I really don't feel like being touched. "Choked you, huh?" Phelps murmurs.

Caden's hands lift, slightly flex on the air as though he's not sure where he can touch me. If it's okay. If I'm not spinning toward death even now. Whether the copious amount of blood covering me and the floor isn't mine.

I stare at Caden's hovering hands, hoping he doesn't touch me. I don't want the comfort. I need to remember hard, crushing hands strangling the life out of me. That will keep things in perspective. Keep me sharp. Alert to danger, to threats. I can't let someone lull me with a tender touch. I'd dropped my guard here, and it nearly cost me.

"You're bleeding?" It's more question than statement as his

eyes do a quick dance over me.

"No." The word is a hoarse croak. His eyes narrow in on my face, that fiery brown warm and alive in the unkind light. "Well. Maybe." I wince and shift my shoulder as much as I can bear. "Most of it is his." I nod toward the dead guy.

"Your voice—" Caden starts to say, but Phelps cuts him off.

"She's alive. She's fine." Phelps lifts a hand and pats Caden on the shoulder.

As though being not dead is all it takes to be fine. I bristle, wondering how he knows that. I want to shout at him, *I don't feel fine. I'm not fine.* But I pull myself together with a rough breath.

"Get that out of here." Phelps motions for a few of the guys crowding the room to grab the corpse and then he's behind me, arms hooking under my shoulders. There's fresh pain, but I barely register it as he drags me off to the side, away from the wide puddle of blood. I glide easily enough over the floor, the blood slick under me. My entire body feels like it went toe-to-toe with a semi. It could be worse. I guess Dr. Phelps is right, because I could be dead and not feeling anything at all anymore.

Rhiannon helps him get me up on an exam table. At least I'm not on the floor now—I felt too vulnerable with everyone towering over me—but all the movement has made me dizzy.

Caden stands off to the side, listening to something Marcus is saying, but his gaze flits back and forth between me and the body with a scalpel sticking out of its neck. That's where I stabbed the winning blow.

Marcus's hands slice the air and his voice lifts. I can't focus on the words, but Caden doesn't look happy with whatever he's hearing. He shakes his head and tries to step around him, but Marcus stops him with a hand on his arm. Caden knocks it away. Marcus's face turns several shades of red, and I know they're about to get physical. And then Terrence is there, stepping between both of them, speaking in a low voice impossible for anyone but the two of them to hear.

My gaze slides away, drawn to my attacker. His body is gathered up into a sheet and hauled out the door. There's so much blood left behind on the floor.

Rhiannon touches the back of my hand lightly, and I flinch.

She pulls away, her expression sliding into something cautious and distant. "Let's get you showered."

I shake my head, still staring at the dark puddle of blood like so much tar on the floor.

"You can't stay like this. You're covered in blood, Davy—"

"I can't walk." This last word catches, vanishing in my destroyed throat. My eyes swing to her, resenting that she's making me say it. At Mount Haven they taught us, *Never show weakness.* But here I am. So weak. A broken bird. I have no fight left.

Rhiannon looks toward Phelps, and her gaze must communicate something because he places cool, gentle fingers at my neck, peering closely. I'm not sure what he can determine. Most of the skin there is covered with ink, but he frowns. "Is it too uncomfortable to speak? Can you say something more for me?"

I moisten my lips, my gaze slipping to the pool of blood and back to him again. "Y'all really need to work on your welcome here."

His mouth lifts in a half smile. "Your voice should recover." His gaze flicks to my shoulder. "Anything else wrong?" He peels back my collar. "How are your stitches?"

I shake my head.

He nods. "Okay. I'll stitch you back up, but shower first." His lip curls as his eyes skim me. "You're a mess."

I glance down. Every inch of me is covered in blood.

"C'mon. You treat carriers." I swallow against my ravaged throat. "You must see this all the time."

"We rarely have violence here," Rhiannon defends, a touch of accusation in her voice, a sharpness to her eyes. Like I somehow brought this with me.

I grunt. "It's just me then. I incite violence by . . . taking up space."

Her lips compress.

Just then Caden approaches, the lines of his face set grimly as his amber eyes assess me.

I look up at him and swallow before speaking, trying to work moisture into my mouth and ease the words out. "Rhiannon was just telling me about what a peace-loving operation you run here."

The corners of his mouth pull downward, and he suddenly appears older than his nineteen years. "This isn't usual."

This only aggravates me further—and the fact that I had started to believe myself safe. That I was beginning to relax here.

He continues, "Hoyt has been with us for a while and never showed any signs. . . ." His voice fades. A muscle ticks in his jaw. He glances to Terrence, who stands silently beside him, taking in our little play.

"Never showed any signs of violence," I finish for him. "Right? That's what you were going to say?" My last few words are just a rasp, a scratch of whispery sound, but he hears them.

"That's right," he agrees, his eyes like molten earth as they peer down at me, his expression unnerving in its intensity.

Am I the only one here who hasn't forgotten what we are? No one is trustworthy. Deep down they know that, or they wouldn't be concerned about blindfolding people.

Marcus materializes beside Caden and Terrence. "Why should he have wanted to kill you?"

"I don't know," I growl. "I didn't know him. Did he need a reason?"

Marcus snarls. It's the only word for it, and I go from strongly disliking him to hating him right then. I was the one nearly strangled.

"Maybe you invited him in here and then turned on him?" Marcus arches an eyebrow like he's landed on some genius possibility.

"When would I have done that? I've been escorted anytime I've ever left this room." I snort. "And why? Just for the pleasure of killing him?"

Marcus shook his head. "There must have been some reason my cousin came in here."

That's right. Hoyt was his cousin. *Great.* Now this guy will never get off my case.

"I don't know why he wanted to kill me." I ignore the way every word I utter feels like a razor slashing into my windpipe. "Maybe he just wanted to kill me because, oh, I don't know"—I angle my head to the side and look from Marcus to Caden—"he's a carrier and that's what carriers do?"

This shuts them up. They look to each other and back to me again.

"That's not what we believe here," Caden says, and he actually looks slightly disappointed in me. "We don't prejudge."

I blink. "So this is some perfect utopia you have here then, is that it? Really? How's that working out?" I motion to myself as evidence. "And that's why you locked me in? Why you guard new carriers? Right."

Marcus's expression shifts from angry into something mild, but there's a sly cunning there, just beneath the surface. It reminds me of so many other carriers to cross my path lately. I suppose there is uniformity, a sameness to be found within people whose moral compass isn't quite set right. Not a comfort, though. I would actually prefer open hostility.

"Maybe it's you," Marcus suggests in a silky voice. "Maybe Hoyt recognized a bad seed. Maybe he saw something in you that needed eliminating."

"Marcus," Caden warns.

"She's not all she seems, Anderson. You might be blinded

by a pretty face, but I'm not. Why don't you let me handle her? I think you've lost objectivity."

I suck in a tight breath, waiting, watching. Tension feathers Caden's jaw before he speaks. "And you just lost your cousin. You're lacking objectivity, too."

Terrence nods in agreement beside them, but I am stuck on one word. *Too.* As in Caden agrees with him that he has no objectivity when it comes to me?

"Give her to me," Marcus insists. The hands curling at his sides tell me he's not that unlike his cousin. The apple doesn't fall far from the tree.

A growl escapes me. Builds up inside my chest. For some reason my primitive side surfaces around him. Or maybe that's just an excuse. Maybe it's just a result of coming out on top of a death match not even a half hour ago. Maybe this is my norm from here on out. A bracing thought, but nothing that really shakes the foundations of my world. This is what I've become. I kill when I need to.

Like before.

And yet not like before. Yes, I just killed someone, but this time is different.

Still. My body count is at two. I wince. Is this going to become a thing? Where I need to start keeping count? Is everyone right and I have a knack for it? My stomach knots and I compress my lips, afraid I'm going to be sick.

Caden moves in front of me, blocking me from Marcus's gaze, and it's a relief. "Not happening, Marcus."

"All right. Why don't you all leave us now?" Phelps

announces in a voice that declares he's finished with the little drama unfolding in his infirmary. "We've got to get her cleaned up and check on that shoulder." Phelps closes in on me, Rhiannon with him. Together, they help me to my feet. I whimper when she lifts my arm to drape it over her shoulder. I used to think I had a pretty good pain tolerance, but now I realize I was giving myself too much credit.

I gaze toward the door, and my heart sinks at the distance. It seems so far away. I want to weep when I think of the walk stretching from here to the showers.

Then suddenly I'm not thinking about it at all, because I'm swept off my feet into a pair of arms that are becoming far too familiar. Too strong. Too comforting.

"What are you doing?" My fingers clutch Caden's shirt like I need to hang on in case he drops me. The warmth and breadth of his chest singes my fingers, and I snatch my hand away.

Faces blur as he carries me from the room, Phelps and Rhiannon following. The air is cooler outside the infirmary, less sour.

"What are you doing" I demand a second time, glaring at his profile.

"Getting you to the shower sometime this decade." His gaze dips to mine, and suddenly the heat washing through me has nothing to do with adrenaline or outrage. Especially when his lips lift in a half smile. "You're welcome."

I jerk my gaze away. He's always doing that. Saying something that makes me feel like I should be grateful to him. As if we should be friendly with each other—if not actual friends. Looking at me with eyes that make me feel . . . well. They make me feel.

"I'm sorry I'm such a burden," I grumble.

His hands flex where they hold me. My skin shrinks at the sensation, and I pull inside myself. "It's not a problem."

I tuck my hands under my sides, squeezing myself tighter, trying to hold myself apart from him as we head down the hallway.

I feel his eyes on me. "I'm not going to hurt you."

I know that. Even though he's a carrier and someone in his flock just tried to kill me, I know that. Guys who rescue girls from certain death don't then hurt them. But for some reason he makes me uncomfortable anyway. "I don't like being touched."

"I noticed. Is that a chronic condition?"

"Meaning have I always been this way?" I think about the girl I used to be before her life ended. She loved people. Touching didn't scare her. If anything, she was a hugger. "It might surprise you to know that I was homecoming queen." I don't know why I throw this out there. Maybe for shock value.

His eyes glow like the sunset, all amber and red tones buried in the brown, and I know he's amused. I shake my head and squeeze myself a little tighter. How can he find amusement in anything? He lives in an underground bunker because the world up top rejected him. *Us.* "Actually, that doesn't surprise me at all."

"Liar."

"No. I can see you in a dress like some sort of beautiful princess. With some lame guy—let me guess, quarterback?"

"Rugby captain," I supply.

He shrugs. "Close." His gaze fastens on my face in a way that makes my skin flush. His voice drops low. Husky. "I see past this tough armor you wear. Homecoming princess. Admired by friends. Sweet. Confident. Boys couldn't help but stare. And in secret, you jammed out to Bob Dylan and enjoyed a juicy cheeseburger. Let me guess. Bacon?"

I nod. "With onion rings."

"I knew it." His smile widens, showing off his straight white teeth.

I swallow and wince at the pain in my throat, regretting ever letting him know that I heard him singing. "Yeah. Not much of a princess anymore, though, am I?" I motion to my blood-caked self and arch my throat where the imprint circles me like a collar. My dark, hacked-off hair no doubt completes my ensemble. "This is me now, okay? And I don't like to be touched or handled, so stop it with everything." *Stop the smiles. Stop making me like you.*

His eyes darken, the sunlight there dimming. "You're overdoing it. Quit talking."

I clamp my lips shut. He's right. I shouldn't try to talk. Tabatha watches us with a bemused look on her face as we pass. Several others are awake, emerging from their rooms, standing in the open space of the main floor, gawking at the sight of me, covered in blood.

Once we're in the showers, he deposits me on one of the

long benches. He glances at Rhiannon and Phelps. "Got this?"

"Sure." The doctor waves him off. "The tribe is restless. They need you out there herding them back to bed. God knows you can't leave them to Marcus, and Terrence isn't exactly one for many words. He's probably already back in the controls room."

Caden nods like he understands and moves to go. Suddenly he stops and turns back to me. My neck falls back to look up at him, and I wince. Even that simple movement stretches my bruised flesh uncomfortably.

His expression is serious, intent. "I'm sorry this happened to you. It shouldn't have happened here. It won't again." His deep voice is like a physical touch, and I shiver.

I moisten my cracked lips and try not to let his words weave a spell around me. I can't drop my guard again. Hoyt attacking me proves that. "Don't make promises you can't keep."

The skin near his eye jumps. "I don't."

And then he's gone. Rhiannon turns on the shower, and soon steam fills the space. I stare at the door where Caden disappeared as she helps me from my clothes. They hit the floor with a heavy smack, ruined. From the corner of my eye I see Phelps open his kit and start taking out what he'll need to re-stitch my wound. I sigh and brace myself.

More pain ahead.

Gentlemen, ladies, I know it took a great deal of risk to get here. A risk that will not diminish as we come together for these talks. The reason you're here is because you've sacrificed so much already. You are true patriots. Now let us get to the heart of the matter. How do we take down Wainwright?

—Private meeting between General Dumont and
fellow Resistance leaders
Undisclosed location in the United States

TWELVE

THEY DON'T TAKE ME BACK TO THE INFIRMARY. After Phelps finishes with me, I'm assigned a cell. With a roommate. Apparently they sleep two to a room. Except for the General and captains. They have their own rooms, Rhiannon explains as she escorts me to my new quarters.

Each room contains bunk beds. Like at a summer camp. Or prison. My roommate is Junie. She's a scout like Tabatha. Only she's really friendly and talkative. She's like a normal teenager. Well, except I learn she's twenty-three. She doesn't look it, though. She's small and fine-boned and looks like she could be fifteen. She hops around the room like some kind of quick-moving ninja, making space for me. Not that she has a lot of stuff to begin with.

She immediately offers me the bottom bed. I'm in no condition to climb to the top one.

"Thanks. I just need a bed," I tell her, sighing as I sink onto the bottom bunk. The shower really wore me out. Oh, and nearly getting choked out. "And sleep."

"Of course," she replies.

"Phelps will check on her in the morning," Rhiannon informs her before leaving.

Pulling the cool sheet over myself, I lie there for a moment, considering how completely unbothered I am to find myself in a strange new room with another stranger. I guess I'm too tired to care. And my body aches. Plus, Phelps took pity and gave me something for the pain. I feel that starting to work its magic and relaxing me. I know I should have resisted. I need my wits, but I figure the odds are on my side. Two attempts on my life in one night? Could I be that unlucky?

Junie turns out the light and bounds with ease to the top bunk. I guess I see why she's a scout. I jerk a little when she hangs upside down, dangling her head near mine, twin braids flopping like dark ropes. "Get some rest. I can't believe Hoyt attacked you . . . well, I kind of can. He was a little off. Rhiannon dubbed him a creeper the day he first arrived here."

"Yeah." I squeeze the bridge of my nose between my fingers, trying to assuage the ache starting to form there.

"You look beat. We'll talk tomorrow."

"Thanks," I murmur, relieved.

"Good night," she chirps.

"Night." My eyes shut, and instantly I'm asleep.

I wake to a hand on my brow. My vision clears to see Phelps leaning over me. I yank away, unable to help myself.

"Now there," he chides. "Just making sure your fever hasn't returned. You haven't been very kind to that shoulder. Hopefully you won't get an infection."

I resist the urge to bite out that it wasn't *me* being unkind to my shoulder but the world in general, but then I catch sight of Caden hovering near the door to the room, his arms crossed over his chest as he observes the exchange. I forget about everything else in the face of his watchful gaze.

"Hey," Caden greets me, unfolding his arms. His army-green T-shirt nicely molds to his firm chest. "You slept through breakfast. Want me to call for takeout? I know this great Thai place."

Phelps chuckles. I resist smiling. Holding silent, I let the doctor poke and prod me as he examines my shoulder. He changes the bandages and makes a happy humming sound, apparently satisfied that it didn't bleed too much overnight.

I glance around the room, confirming what I already suspected. Junie isn't here.

"What time is it?" I ask.

"Almost noon."

I shake my head. "I don't usually sleep so late." It shouldn't matter, but it's one more thought in the chaos of my mind. I blow out a breath, wishing I could silence all of it.

"You had a rough night. It's allowed."

Phelps stands. "That should do it. I would stay in bed and rest today. Let me or Rhiannon know if it starts bleeding through the bandage. I'll check on you later."

I nod.

Phelps looks at Caden. "Will she be staying in here?"

"I don't want to go back to the infirmary," I interrupt, realizing that my move here might have been temporary. I'm sure they've cleaned everything up. Still, I don't want to set foot in that place again. The blood flashes in my mind. Thick, dark as tar.

"Would you prefer to stay here? With Junie?" Caden trains his gaze on me. Surprising, really, that he's giving me a say. I haven't had a say in anything since we met.

"Yes. Thank you."

Silence stretches as we stare at each other, assessing.

Phelps looks between us, and there's speculation in his gaze. With a shrug, he grabs his bag and leaves the room.

It's just the two of us now. I glance around so I don't have to look at him, but I can feel his attention focused squarely on me. Too bad my roommate isn't around. "Where's Junie?"

"Scouting."

My gaze snaps back to him. "You mean outside the compound?" Impatience snakes through me. I want to be outside. I want to be *gone* from here. After last night, I want this more than anything else. That sensation of being trapped down here is stronger than ever. "I thought you weren't sending out any people—"

"Across the river?" he finishes for me. "No, we're not right now."

"But Junie—"

"She scouts. That's what she does. She's good at it. Sending convoys to Mexico isn't the only thing we do here. We gather supplies, monitor patrols. I'm leading a group out tomorrow to—"

Hope swells in my chest. "But you just said—"

"I'm staying stateside." And just like that, my hope deflates. "There's a station east of here that Marcus wants to check out," he adds.

At my questioning look, he explains, "It's a checkpoint— went up after the Agency partnered with Border Patrol. If I let Marcus go on his own, he'll probably blow the place up and the Feds will rain down on us afterward. The goal is to make an impact that doesn't beg for them to use every bit of manpower at their disposal to track us and wipe us out. At least that's my goal. Not always so with Marcus."

"So you're going along to keep him on a leash?"

"Something like that."

I scan him. Hands half-buried in his pockets, even with his forearms tense, he looks . . . relaxed. Not at all like someone about to go on a dangerous mission. "Why not just let him blow it up? They can search for you all they want. You're underground. They want us dead. Or in cages." I sweep a hand around us. "They've forced us to hide like fugitives."

He studies me for a moment. "You think I should do that? Let dozens of people die? They can't all be bad, can they?"

I snort, hating that he's making me feel small and . . . wrong. "They think we're all bad. Evil."

He pushes off the doorjamb and approaches me where I recline on the bed. "You're not as merciless as you act."

This annoys me. I angle my head sharply. "All you need to know about me is this." I point to my neck. It's funny how I actually believe that now. I didn't at first. I fought so hard to deny that HTS determined anything about me at all. In so short a time, I've become a realist. But then I had to. Optimism can get you killed. "Isn't that enough?"

He smiles again, his lips curling like some kind of sexy lead singer in a boy band, and I really dislike him right then. That he can look so normal. Like a boy I would have liked in another place, another time.

"I think there's more to you than that, Homecoming Queen."

My hands clench at my side. I've already shared too much.

His gaze flicks to my hands, then back to my face. "Not gonna let me in anymore, huh?" With a sigh, he turns and opens the door to my room—my cell. "Maybe when I get back we can talk some more."

"About leaving and finding my friends?"

He hesitates, one hand on the doorknob. "All right."

"All right?" This is the last thing I expect him to say.

He nods. "I'm not the bad guy. Maybe you'll believe that someday."

I do already. "All I know is that I need to sleep with one eye open here."

"And that I saved your life," he reminds me, his gaze so open, guileless. "You know that, too. I can be your friend."

"I don't need a friend. I already have friends. I just need to get back to them."

He does that smiling thing with his mouth again. What does he have to be happy about? "Why are you so . . ." I grope for the word. *Happy. Pleasant.* Instead, I just go with, "Don't you ever get mad?"

He shrugs. "Sure. Everyone does. You don't have to be a carrier to feel that emotion."

"But you are," I remind him. "A carrier." So how come I haven't seen a whiff of true anger from him? Not a raised voice, not the flash of fury in his eyes. Nothing.

Something passes over his face. For a moment, he looks uneasy, but then he blinks and it's gone. "We all handle anger . . . stress . . . differently."

"I would think being here . . . doing this, would bring that out in a person."

"What about you?"

"Me? I tried to kill you the first moment we met."

"You were reacting to the situation. Out of your head with sickness and pain. You were afraid. Not angry."

"You're splitting hairs. It's the same result."

"No," he says evenly. "Fear and killing—anger and killing, for that matter—don't necessarily go hand in hand."

"Have you ever killed someone?"

It's like a shutter falls over his face. The light in his eyes dims until he stares at me with flat brown eyes. A fire banked. No longer amber. Just brown.

"I take that as a yes," I murmur, not wanting to feel kinship with him, but I suddenly do. Because clearly he's not proud or happy that he ended a life. Maybe we're a little alike in that way. I suck in a breath, crushing that thought before it takes root. I don't need thoughts like that. Especially about him. Especially as my days here are numbered.

"We all do things to survive. I've accepted that."

And in that moment I realize I have, too. I had to kill Hoyt.

"The things we've done to survive don't make us undeserving of happiness. It's a hard lesson," he adds. "But one you need to learn if you'll ever—"

"I've learned plenty already, thank you very much." I smile then. I can't help myself. "Guess I'm not such an ideal recruit, am I?"

He looks me over thoughtfully. "So you have a few rough edges. Who doesn't in here?"

"Don't get any ideas. I'm not staying."

Grinning that infernal smile again, he shakes his head. "We'll see." He exits the room, the door clicking softly after him.

We'll see. What's *that* supposed to mean?

My chest feels tight and uncomfortable as I stare at the closed door, thinking over his words. *I can be your friend.* His eyes fill my mind, that melting brown tugging at some hidden part of me, the part that used to believe I had a right to happiness. With a jolt I realize I haven't felt this way since Sean. Since before everything that happened at Mount Haven.

Rolling to my side, I pull the covers up to my chin as if that will somehow shield me. My mind drifts, eyes scanning the bare wall before me. I think about Caden leaving on his mission. Heading into danger. He might not even come back. People drop like flies around me these days. Another reason I shouldn't let anyone in. Still. My lips whisper a plea.

God, please keep him safe . . . bring him back.

I spend the rest of the day alone with my thoughts. A dangerous pastime. Rhiannon brings me breakfast, lunch, and dinner. Phelps drops in to check on me twice. They're the only break I get from wondering about Caden's mission. About Sean and the others. Are they at the refuge already? They think I'm dead, lost forever. I'm convinced of this. Are they broken up about it? I know Gil has to care. I haven't known Sabine very long, but she's a survivor. She'll move on. No pieces to pick up. Sean, I'm not so sure. Yes, things had been tense between us. I shut him out. But he cared about me, and he had convinced me to escape Mount Haven. He's probably blaming himself. That much I know about him.

I sleep restlessly that night, waking frequently. Junie returns late. I can tell from her stealthy movements that she's trying not to disturb me. There's no clock, but all the small sounds that alert me to life and activity in the compound have fallen silent. It's like someone flipped the off switch.

I crack open an eye to observe her. She's turned on the lamp, so I can study her in the dim light. She looks bedraggled as she grabs a few things and heads out again. When she returns half an hour later, her hair is wet and her face scrubbed pink from a shower. She looks so young. Nothing like a tough soldier girl.

"Sorry," she mutters as I stir when she pulls herself up to the top bunk. "Didn't mean to wake you."

"I was awake. How'd it go?"

"I'm wiped out. Covered a lot of ground." The mattress springs squeak above me as she settles into bed. She chatters about her mission and I listen closely, absorbing every word in case she lets something useful slip. "Patrols are thicker out there. Must be because of you and your friends. How many were in your group again?"

"Three. And me," I reply into the dark, looking up at the bed above me as if I can see her there, through the mattress.

There is a pause, and the mattress squeaks as she shifts her weight. "If your friends made it across, we'll track them down. Caden sent a message."

"What?" I demand sharply, forgetting my shoulder and sitting up on my elbows, then dropping back down with a cry of pain.

Her head pops over the side, wet hair dangling. "You okay?"

"Yes. Fine. What did you just say?"

"Caden had me get a message over to one of our contacts.

It will make the rounds to the refuges. We should know soon which one they made it to."

My heart thuds faster in my chest. He meant it when he said he'd help me. I flatten my hands over my stomach, excitement rushing through me. Caden's going to get me across. I see his face then, the eyes, that smile I want to distrust. But I can't. I wait to see if she's going to volunteer anything more, but soon her breathing drifts down to me in slow, measured pulls, and I know she's asleep.

No longer alone in the room, I feel my muscles loosen. I test my shoulder, rotating it slowly, wincing at the soreness. I finally feel the tug of sleep. Her presence actually makes me feel better, and that's when I realize just how uneasy I've been all day. I'm not sure what to think about that. I'm not looking for friends. I know better than that.

This is probably the reason Caden assigned me to her room. It's not simply that she has an extra bed. He knew she would put me at ease. I don't know why I'm so sure of this about him, but I am. Shaking my head, I chase off the idea that he's someone I might *want* to know better. That's a dangerous thought.

The following morning Junie coaxes me out of bed to breakfast by singing an old Celine Dion song. Apparently she was raised in foster care, and one of the women who watched over her was a big fan. She makes me grin . . . even if her voice is reminiscent of a dying cat.

"She might have had terrible taste in music," Junie says, talking about her "warden," as she calls her, "but she would pop us popcorn before bed." She shrugs. "She wasn't so bad. I've had worse. A lot worse." Hearing this, I can't help but think of Sean. He was brought up in foster care, too. Those children were tested earlier for HTS, almost as soon as the science became available.

"Did you ever get placed anywhere? In a real home?" Sean was placed in one with a few other boys, and from all that he shared with me, it was a true home to him. The other boys were like brothers to him, and his foster mother genuinely cared about them all.

"Nope. No one wanted to let a kid with HTS into their house." She utters this matter-of-factly, but there's a brief flash of emotion in her eyes. She wasn't as unaffected as she would like me to think.

I instantly sense a difference when I step into the main room. There's a tension that hadn't been there before. Everyone seems on edge. Maybe it's because Caden and Marcus are gone. Terrence stayed behind, and he's a captain, but his silent watchfulness doesn't seem to lend much comfort. Several eyes stray to the metal stairs as if waiting for Caden and Marcus to appear. I can understand their anxiousness. At least regarding Caden. I'd feel better if he were here, too.

"Coming, Davy?" Junie asks, picking up a tray at the end of the food line. There are only a few people ahead of us.

Nodding, I accept the tray she offers me.

She leans close and whispers conspiratorially, "Avoid the

eggs. They're that fake crap. Now, the French toast is good. Fried in butter and sprinkled with sugar, you can't tell the bread is stale."

I smile again, glad Caden placed me with this girl.

Janie drops a plate of French toast on my tray with a wink. "There. You'll almost feel like you're back home and not in some underground bunker."

Yeah. Almost.

Please advise if you have recently taken in three carriers. Two males, one female going by the names Sean, Gil, and Sabine. Awaiting reply.

Message sent to Refuges 1, 2, 3, 4

THIRTEEN

THE FOLLOWING DAY, I VISIT PHELPS IN THE INFIR-
mary, and I let him look me over. Junie accompanies me. I
can't help enjoying her company. I sit beside her during meals,
and she's introduced me to a few of the other permanent residents of the compound. Without Caden, her presence makes
me feel safe even though part of me wants to keep my distance.

The other refugees who are waiting for the next convoy to
Mexico sit grouped together and mingle very little with the
rest of the general population. I should join them. I have more
in common with them, after all. I'm just passing through. And
one of the permanent residents did try to kill me. Surely Hoyt

has made some friends in the ranks. Someone who might desire a little payback. His cousin can't be the only one upset over his death. But I somehow can't make myself cross to the convoy group.

To my relief, I'm not quite the spectacle anymore. Hardly anyone stares at me as I walk around the compound with Junie. I join her as she trains. I do some leg weights, careful not to jostle my arm in its new sling. When she meets with other scouts and they pore over a map, sharing information about where they last spotted border patrols, she lets me observe. I stand back, absorbing everything in silence as they point to areas on the map . . . although no one reveals precisely where we're located. Still. It feels good to be accepted . . . to maybe have found a friend in Junie.

That should lull me to sleep at night and make the air flow easier in and out of my lips. And yet it doesn't. Not entirely. Nothing does until two days later, when shouts ring out through the compound. They're back. *Caden* is back.

I didn't realize how tense I had been all this time. How tight the breath had been in my chest, trapped there. I toss down the English-to-Spanish dictionary Junie loaned me—I figured I better brush up—and slide off my bed, joining everyone else who crowds into the main room, looking up at the dozen figures clambering down the iron ladder, heavy boots clanging on the grated steps.

Junie appears at my side, breathless like she has just run from somewhere. "They made it."

I don't even glance at her face. I know she's smiling. I can hear it in her voice. Everyone cheers. My eyes find Caden, skimming over him, searching for injuries. It's a purely calculated move on my part. I trust him the most here. He's promised to get me to Mexico. Of course I want nothing to happen to him. That would be bad for me. I tell myself these things and almost believe them.

He drops down onto the main floor, light on his feet, and he's rushed like a returning hero. Marcus joins him and receives similar treatment. Claps on the back. Words of praise. Questions about how it went.

They carry several packs, which Terrence starts looking through. He pulls out a box, glances at it, and tosses it to Phelps, who turns it around in his hands. "Antibiotics?"

"Courtesy of the Wainwright Agency." Satisfaction rings in Caden's voice.

"You raided their supplies?"

"Couple of us snuck in and might have borrowed a few things."

Phelps whoops and moves to investigate the rest of the bags' contents. A faint glimmer of respect fills me. It really is remarkable what they've done here. They're trying to build something civilized here while helping other carriers at the same time. My gaze returns to Caden. He could just run. Look out for his own neck and flee into Mexico. Especially since his father died. Nothing holds him here. And yet here he is. It's an admirable thing.

The group starts to disperse. Caden's gaze scans the crowd like he's looking for someone. I force myself to breathe. My chest loosens a bit as air passes out of my expanding lungs.

Suddenly someone steps directly in front of him, blocking him partly from my line of vision. Tabatha. I recognize the long rope of her dark braid. She stands up on her tiptoes and plants her mouth on his. Several whistles ring out. My face grows hot. I don't want to watch, but I can't look away.

Junie snorts beside me. "Not subtle, huh?"

I glance at her. "They're a thing?"

"Used to be, but Tabatha has a hard time letting go."

"I see that." I watch as they pull apart. Her hands roam over his chest. "He doesn't seem to mind, though." His hands move to her shoulders, but he hardly shoves her away.

"He's just trying not to embarrass her. Caden is respectful that way."

I study Junie thoughtfully, noting the way her eyes follow Caden. I release a small puff of breath. Part sigh. Part laugh. She's infatuated with him, too. Shaking my head, I glance heavenward. I guess most girls with a pulse would be. Especially here with such slim pickings. He's good-looking. Confident. That goes a long way.

"C'mon. Let's get you back to our room." Junie takes my elbow.

"I can make it on my own."

Nodding, she lets go of my arm, but she's quieter than normal, and I know she's still thinking about Tabatha laying that kiss on Caden. I'm also thinking about it a little too much, wondering if he really doesn't reciprocate Tabatha's feelings. It's hard to imagine. Especially when she looks the way she does. Didn't I just note that good looks and confidence go a long way? The girl is hot, and she doesn't even have to try.

Once in the room, I sink onto the edge of the bed, watching Junie drag a small laundry basket out and start folding the clothes. She works in silence.

"Need some help?" Because really, what else do I have to do?

She arches a dark eyebrow. "You ever fold laundry?"

"What? Do I look like someone who never folded laundry before?" Forget the fact that I rarely did. My family had a housekeeper. I didn't have time for laundry amid all my activities. I was busy with voice lessons, orchestra rehearsals, school. And Zac. So much of my time had been devoted to Zac and my friends. Mom never made chores a priority for me, because all those other things that were so important to me were equally important to her. I wince. Caden was right. I was a bit of a princess. I know that now. I'm not sorry to see that part of me gone. The pampered, deluded, naive girl needed a reality check. Maybe that was the one good thing to come out of this.

"Knock yourself out." She grins at me as I start to fold and do a less-than-spectacular job.

"It's my shoulder," I say defensively. "I'm not at full function."

"Then I'd love to see you at full function."

"Why?"

"'Cause you're kind of a badass." And I realize she's not talking about laundry anymore. A lump rises in my throat, because it's not something I want to think about. Killing never is. I'd avoided the subject of Hoyt with her this long. "You killed Hoyt when you were still laid up from a gunshot wound."

I inhale through my nose, her words confirming my fear. Here, that's all I'll ever be known for—killing Hoyt. Staying here—not that I'm contemplating it—seems like even less of an option now. "Are people mad at me for that?"

She shrugs. "No one particularly cared for him. He was really quiet, you know. Always watching the girls." She shivers a little. "Everyone tolerated him because of Marcus."

I nod.

"But people are definitely talking about it. About you. He wasn't some weak-ass guy, and you took him out." She waggles her eyebrows. "You're a regular mystery."

"Not really."

"Hey, roll with it. I wish I had an aura of mystery. Might get certain guys to notice me."

And by certain guys I'm guessing she means Caden. Clearing my throat, I set a poorly folded pair of pants on top of the pile. "Where could I find Caden right now? I'd like to discuss when he thinks I might be ready to leave."

She considers me, her gaze skimming my shoulder as if she can see through my shirt and the bandage to the wound underneath. "That shoulder needs to heal up more, don't you think?"

"I'll be fine."

Shaking her head, she takes my pile of clothing from me and starts refolding. "He's three doors down on the right."

"Thanks." I stand, readjusting my sling.

I do a quick scan when I enter the hall, and I'm relieved it's empty. Especially knowing that everyone is talking about me. At the third door, I knock.

A muffled "Come in" drifts through the panel. I turn the latch and push the door open. As I step inside, my face instantly flames. I spin away from the sight of Caden, shirtless, finishing doing up the snap on his pants. It's the first glimpse of the firm chest I'd felt more than once beneath his shirt, and the image burns an imprint on my corneas. He isn't heavily muscled. But there isn't an ounce of fat on him, either. He is lean, his tanned skin tight over a well-defined abdomen and smooth, flat pecs.

"Oh, sorry—"

"It's okay. I'm decent."

Decent. I almost laugh at the double meaning there. It's funny in a sad kind of way, because he's a carrier. And ironic, too, because, so far, he might truly be just that. *Decent.* As much as I struggle to refute it, he presents a strong case for the possibility of being both a carrier and a decent human being.

"You can turn around."

His voice hums deeply on the air and makes me tremble. Hero fixation. I tell myself it's just that. He saved my life. I've lost Sean. I'm needy. Vulnerable. And he *is* easy on the eyes.

Slowly, I turn, and my breath catches. "You're not dressed."

His lips lift in that half smile of his. "You've never seen a guy without his shirt on?"

I've never seen *him* without his shirt on. And the sight

makes my chest tight. He's showered. His hair is wet and looks black as ink. He runs his fingers through it, sending the longer strands at the top of his head flying in every direction. I inhale the clean, soapy scent of him.

"No boyfriends? What about the rugby captain?" His gaze skims over me, and my face stings even hotter.

"Of course. I have—*had* a boyfriend." I wonder at the slip and whether I'm talking about Zac or Sean. I'm not even sure.

"Ah, so you're experienced then?"

"I didn't say that, either," I snap, not liking the implication that I'm a girl with a lot of mileage. That's the last thing I want him to think. With that idea in his head, he might start to think I'm an easy conquest for him. That I'm just another girl ready to rush at him with kisses when he returns home from a mission. Yeah. Not happening. Save that for Tabatha.

"You said *had*. You don't have a boyfriend now, Davy?"

I pause, not sure what Sean is to me. Things weren't right between us when we parted, and with this time away from him I'm starting to see that whatever romantic future we had was lost when I pulled the trigger on a man to save his life. Right or wrong, things were never the same after that. They never can be. But that doesn't mean I don't care about Sean. That he's not special to me and my friend. That I don't want to get back to him and Gil and Sabine.

And that doesn't mean I'm somehow available or interested in a new guy. Decent or not. Romance is the last thing I need in my life. Merely existing is complicated enough. Hard enough.

"Davy?" he presses in that deep, lyrical voice of his that makes my skin contract . . . like his voice is something I can actually feel. A feather brushing my skin. "You do, don't you?" he continues. "You have a boyfriend. There's someone." His brown eyes stare at me flatly, the bright amber there dormant, like he's burying a part of himself away as he announces this.

"I didn't say that."

He moves to the door behind me, his bare arm brushing me as he passes. "You didn't have to say it. That's why you're really in such a hurry to leave here. He's who you want to get back to, right?" He closes the door with a soft click, sealing us in. My nostrils flare. Instantly, I feel caged, penned in.

I turn in a half circle, following him with my eyes.

"What's his name, Davy?" He angles his head, looking at me intently, waiting like he has all the time in the world. The sound of my name on his lips wakes my skin with a shiver. It feels so intimate. Like we have some connection to each other.

I shake my head, pressing my lips into a hard line, refusing to go there with him . . . to get this personal, this close.

And there's also the niggling little voice in me, warning that if I say Sean's name out loud, then it's an acknowledgment of what Caden is asking me. That Caden is then somehow right. That Sean *is* my boyfriend. He's many things to me— all complicated, but he's not that.

"It's not a trick question." He arches one eyebrow. "His name?" The question hangs in the space of his room. I glance around, scanning the surroundings. Bed. Desk. A single chest. A large map covers one wall. Very utilitarian. For some reason

I have a flash of my girlified bedroom back home. That room that belongs to some other girl. That girl would never be here. This place looks like a soldier's cell. And Caden the consummate warrior. Even if he does smile too much and come off as *decent*, his body hums with a tension, an energy, that puts me on edge. Like he could snap into motion at any time. I saw a glimpse of it when I woke in that cave with him. I'm sure if I stay here much longer, I will see evidence of it again.

Maybe being alone with him isn't such a good idea. I curve my hand over my arm resting in the sling. Like hugging myself can somehow protect me.

He pulls back slightly, cocking his head again as he crosses his arms over his chest. I remember how solid that chest felt when he carried me. My eyes flick over him for a moment, skimming his lean torso, the golden-brown skin, before locking on his eyes again. *Don't go there.*

He continues, "So which one is it? Sean or Gil?"

I compress my lips.

His eyes glint. Clearly he's enjoying himself. "Not going to admit it then? What's wrong? Have I gotten in your head? You can't resist me and don't want me to worry about this MIA boyfriend...."

Outrage burns through me. I inhale sharply and for some crazy reason I feel the need to run. "No!"

He chuckles that damn laugh of his and I know he's teasing me, but I'm not amused.

"You talk too much," I accuse, pushing back down that swell of panic.

He laughs harder at that.

"And laugh too much," I add.

His smile deepens, if that's even possible. "Now, what's wrong with laughing?"

"What's wrong is that there isn't anything to laugh about, is there? Certainly nothing to be happy about."

"You don't believe that. Now more than ever, it's important to find reasons to smile and laugh. To have friends. To love."

For some reason, heat swarms my face. I blink at him. Suddenly his gaze feels too much. Too probing. I struggle to sound normal and unaffected as I demand, "Are you kidding me? How do you manage to be so unflinchingly optimistic?" I wave my good arm wide. "We're in an underground bunker in the middle of nowhere." I start counting off, trying to pretend that I don't notice him inching closer, wearing an expression of mockery. "The United States government has herded our kind into detention camps that we've barely escaped. They'll shoot us on sight. Isn't that the current protocol? And we're fleeing into a country that doesn't want us, either. They haven't declared outright war on us yet like here, but I'm sure it's only a matter of time before they decide to put more effort into stopping us. Then what? How will these refuges"—I air-quote with my free hand—"hold up? There's nowhere in the world for us to go."

Still smiling, he says, "You worry too much."

I stare at him in horror . . . and he chuckles again. "Isn't this the time when we should seize every bit of happiness we can? Enjoy ourselves?" His gaze flicks over me, and my horror mounts. I'm immediately hyperconscious of what I must look like. Not a stitch of makeup on my face. My dark hair is a hacked-up mess, and I'm wearing a brown T-shirt and camo cargo pants, courtesy of who knows. Not Junie. She's too small. My quick glance in the mirror today revealed that my face is still pink from my fading sunburn. Freckles that had never been there before generously dotted my cheeks and my nose.

I must be wrong. He's not looking at me in that way at all. Not when he has girls like Tabatha flinging themselves at him.

"Isn't it okay to take what pleasure we can find? Especially now?" His voice is softer, and goose bumps break out across my flesh.

"I don't know," I whisper. "It's not that easy. It hurts when you lose . . . when it all goes away." God, does it hurt. To have everything you know and love ripped away.

His eyes crawl over my face, focused and intent, and it's like I feel him peering into my very soul, reaching deep inside me.

"So you'll keep yourself hidden away, because that's safest." He's not smiling anymore. "That's sad."

Anger sparks inside my chest, spreading outward, suffusing me with warmth. "You don't know anything about me." An angry tirade continues in my head: *Not where I've been, what I've been through.*

"And you're not going to let me know anything." It's not a question but a statement of fact. He looks a little disappointed.

Or maybe just thoughtful as he frowns and studies me. Shaking his head, his troubled expression clears. "Did you have a reason for coming here, Davy? To see me?"

I blink and square my shoulders, gathering my thoughts, wondering if just like that he can switch from prying into my feelings to being all business. The guy is bewildering. "Junie told me you had her send a message to see which refuge my friends are at."

He nods. "Yes."

"When will we hear back?"

"I don't know. Our system of communication isn't the most reliable." He studies me a moment longer. "You doubted that I would send the message. I told you I would help you."

At this reminder, I lift my good shoulder in a partial shrug. "And you think I should just believe everything I'm told?"

"You can believe me. You gotta trust sometimes. Someone . . . eventually. Right?"

Like trust is such an easy thing for a carrier to do. He should understand that. He doesn't trust me. He can't. I rub at my temple with my good hand. "You make my head hurt."

He sighs. "Don't worry about it. Junie sent the message. Now we wait to hear something. If your friends reached one of the refuges, we'll know soon."

I drop my hand and look up at him. I don't need a mirror to know that my face reveals all the hope swelling inside me. "Really?" It can be that easy?

"You'll be on your way before you know it." His voice sounds harder, clipped.

He reaches for a shirt draped over the back of his chair. His desk is littered with papers and maps and a few books.

There's just one bed. My gaze strays to it. Full-size, it looks cozier than the one I've been sleeping in. The thick blue comforter is inviting. I guess being the quasi leader has its perks.

He pulls the gray cotton T-shirt over his head. It does nothing to hide the strong body on display moments before. "You should stay off your feet and rest up for the trip. It's not the easiest journey. You'll need stamina."

"All I've been doing is resting." Well, when I haven't been working out with Junie or sitting in on her meetings with other scouts. I've also spent a fair amount of time people watching (trying to predict who might be another Hoyt). Eyeing his desk, I inch closer. I know I should leave. I got the information I wanted, but it's not like my hours are full of stuff to do.

Dipping my head, I touch a book and turn it so that I can read the spine. *Guerrilla Tactics and Principles of War.*

So he's not the pacifist he appears. He had made it sound like Marcus was the one given to violence, but apparently he's not totally opposed to it. Of course. As a carrier he wouldn't be. I feel somehow validated at this.

His hand comes down on the book. His long fingers brush mine, and I jerk away at the contact.

His lips curl in amusement, and I mutter a mental oath at myself. If I want to show how unaffected I am, I shouldn't be so jumpy.

He sets the book aside, sliding it to the far corner as if

trying to distance me from it. I glance at him warily. Is he trying to hide what he is because it smacks down his Boy Scout image? I never bought into that anyway. My gaze travels over the imprint circling his throat. He's got the propensity for violence in him just like the rest of us.

"Don't see too many books around these days," I murmur.

"Books might be old-fashioned but they're reliable. Terrence is our tech specialist and hacker extraordinaire. He's rather possessive of all our equipment. He claims it's too precious for me." His mouth twists into a wry smile. "Claims I'll break it. He's not giving up any of our technology so I can read a downloaded book. And these belonged to my father. Some kids got *Goodnight Moon* at bedtime, I got books on hand-to-hand combat. But I wouldn't have changed it. It prepared me for where I am today."

Of course. Even as a child, he probably reveled in it. Some kids got bikes for their fifth birthdays. He probably got an automatic rifle.

I wonder if I would have reveled in it, too. If my father hadn't been a banker. If my mother hadn't been an interior designer.

"Interesting childhood," I murmur. "Mine mostly consisted of voice and violin lessons—"

"You sing?" he cuts me off, the amber of his eyes glinting with interest.

"Not anymore."

His expression turns to disappointment. "Too bad."

Did he actually think I would sing for him? Here? What?

Did he want me to put on a concert out in the main room after dinner?

I move around his desk. Not caring if I look nosy, I pick up a packet of papers and skim them. My eyes widen, and I raise my gaze to him. "This is how to construct some kind of . . . bomb?"

He plucks the papers from my hands. "You shouldn't look at that."

"Why? I'm not to be trusted?" I fling this out at him, angling my head, daring him to say he can't trust me after he's stated more than once that I should trust him.

"There are security protocols—"

"Right. *I* need to trust you implicitly, and be happy and laugh while you're building a bomb to do God knows what?"

He drags a hand through his hair, compressing his lips before expelling a heavy breath. "If I knew you were staying . . . joining us, then I could let you into the fold, Davy."

Everything inside me freezes at what he's saying. "W-what?"

"I'm asking you to stay and be a part of this." He splays his hands wide like he's offering me something, handing it to me. "It's better than hiding in some camp in Mexico, crossing your fingers, hoping that you're never discovered, that the Mexican authorities never decide to get serious about hunting you down."

"My friends—"

"We can send word you're alive and well. And you can stay here and do some good. Have a purpose beyond surviving."

I open my mouth to argue, but this last bit resonates,

tempting me. A purpose beyond surviving. That's the only thing that separates us from animals. Purpose.

"You obviously have some skills. That much you've proven. We could use you, Davy."

Because I killed a man. Someone bigger, stronger. While I was weak from injuries, no less. Like it or not, the cred I wanted so badly for myself when I was at Mount Haven? I've earned that here.

He's moved closer, I realize. The clean smell of his skin swirls around me, and I feel a stab of loneliness. Yearning. That's maybe the worst part of this new life. The always being apart . . . alone even when you're surrounded by others.

The gold flecks that make his brown eyes look so fiery are easy to detect standing this close to him. Stupid lashes. They're longer than any girl could hope for even with the best mascara.

"I—I have to go." Because being here with him makes me feel like a traitor. Even though those feelings I had for Sean died, I still shouldn't feel myself leaning toward him like he's something I need. Food for the starving.

"Always running. From this place to Mexico." His lips curve, but he doesn't look amused anymore. Not this time. "From me."

I shake my head, refusing to believe he's talking about him and me like there might be something there. An *us*. It's so wrong I could laugh at the idea of it. If it didn't terrify me so much.

"I'm not staying here." I turn for the door and hesitate to

add, "As soon as you get word—"

"I'll let you know," he finishes, his voice flat, emotionless.

I stare at him for a moment, not liking the feeling sweeping over me. That I'm somehow a disappointment to him because my purpose isn't his. That I'm failing to do the right thing here. That used to be my MO. To do the right thing, perform the way everyone expected. My parents. My teachers. I even did that at Mount Haven.

Not anymore. From now on I'm going to be smart and live for me.

Text Message

8:19 a.m.
Tori:
Hey, hot stuff. Big anti-carrier rally at the capital. You coming?

8:52 a.m.
Zac:
What about a normal date for once? You know. Movies? Dinner?

9:09 a.m.
Tori:
Where's your commitment to the cause?

9:10 a.m.
Zac:
Your cause. Not mine. I'm not into it. You know that

9:11 a.m.
Tori:
Fine. I'll go with someone else. Let you sit around and sulk, thinking about her

9:14 a.m.
Zac:
I'm not thinking about her

9:14 a.m.
Tori:
Liar

FOURTEEN

THE DAYS ROLL INTO A WEEK, AND I BEGIN TO FEAR
that we'll never get that message. We'll never learn which refuge shelters Sean, Gil, and Sabine.

Maybe they didn't make it.

I ignore that negative inner voice, squashing it like a bug,
hoping that it won't get back up and come at me again.

I see little of Caden. I gather from Junie and Phelps that
he leaves almost every day. Goes above to do whatever it is he
does. I don't get to know that kind of information. That much
is clear.

I busy myself working out, determined to regain my

strength, increasing from a walk to a light run on the tread-mill.

I ignore Rhiannon when she suggests—repeatedly—this might not be a good idea with my arm in a sling. I need to get back in shape. It helps. Makes me feel like I have some control over my life again. When the message comes through, I need to be ready to go.

I jog lightly on the treadmill after lunch one day. My eyes scan the room. I have several faces and names memorized by now. Few talk to me, but I remain vigilant. That happens when someone tries to kill you on one of your first nights some place.

Caden steps from one of the rooms where they often hold meetings. By *they* I mean the "inner circle."

My pulse jumps at my throat. It's one of few glimpses I've had of him since we last talked. There's been no sight of him at meals and the thought crosses my mind that perhaps he's avoiding me, but then I dismissed it. That's giving me too much credit. I have no hold over him.

He's dressed in his usual fatigues. Tabatha walks beside him, her strides long to match his. She talks with her hands. He nods, his expression intent as he listens. Terrence, follow-ing one step behind them, catches me looking and glances between me and Caden with a lifted eyebrow. My face heats, but I don't look away.

Marcus and Ruben bring up the rear. In addition to hating me for killing his cousin, Marcus craves power and sees me as a threat. I've learned that much from what Junie has said as well as what I've inferred. Caden broke procedures to bring me here. Letting that slide undermines Marcus.

Caden spots me over Tabatha's shoulder and stops. He frowns, his gaze skimming me as I jog in place. His disapproval reaches me, palpable as smoke in the stale, recycled air. I stumble and catch myself. My face burns hot as I recover and continue running. I try to look straight ahead, but my attention strays back to him, trying to see if he's amused over my clumsiness.

He's not. He only looks more disapproving.

Tabatha follows his gaze and frowns, too. He makes a move toward me, but she stops him with a hand on his arm. I almost wish she would let him approach. It would ease my boredom at least. Talking to him might give me a headache and drive me crazy and make me feel things in general when I'm trying my best not to feel anything, but I can't stop the flicker of longing.

Tabatha says something, motioning to me. Caden shakes his head no, but she keeps talking. Finally, he gives a single nod and stalks off, leaving her smiling. She comes toward me, her every movement satisfied, confident. I can't help myself. My gaze drifts to Caden, watching his back as he walks away, wondering what he wanted to say to me and why he changed his mind—what *she* said to change it.

At least now I know. He's avoiding me. My chest tightens. I shouldn't care one way or another. I've given him every indication in word and action that I'm not interested in a friendship . . . in anything with him.

Tabatha stops in front of me. "Hey, there. You're looking better."

"I am," I reply, determined to appear strong. I punch off the machine and slow to a halt. "Sling can come off in a couple days." Phelps said a week, but I see it otherwise. The sling will come off tomorrow. Day after at the latest.

"Great. You should be ready for travel then."

"What?" Surely I didn't hear her correctly. "Really? I'm leaving?"

"Junie just got word. Your friends are at refuge number four."

Everything inside me slumps and tightens all at once. It's a combination of relief and a jolt of adrenaline for the trip to come . . . the reunion ahead. *I'm actually going to see Sean again. Gil and Sabine.* It's really going to happen. Until this moment, I didn't recognize that a part of me doubted that it would.

"When?" I demand.

"Day after tomorrow."

I frown, disappointed it's not sooner.

"Hey," she adds, smiling, but there's nothing nice about it. It's judgy, tinged with contempt. "We have to get the group ready that's been waiting to go out. This isn't all about you."

I clench my teeth, resisting the impulse to defend myself. She doesn't care about me, so what I say doesn't matter.

Marcus appears then, moving to her side. "So this one is finally leaving."

"Yep. Heading out Wednesday." Tabatha nods.

Marcus steps closer and looks up at me where I stand on the treadmill. "Watch yourself out there. The world isn't as gentle where you're going as it is in here."

"You think it's a gentle world in here?" I snort. "Your cousin trying to choke me out wasn't bad?"

"You don't know bad," Ruben voices from behind Marcus.

I feel my lip curl over my teeth. I know I shouldn't rise to his bait, but I just can't seem to help myself. Maybe it's what's in my blood, coursing along with my DNA, that sets me apart from the average person and marks me as someone capable of killing. "I've had to deal with my share of thugs who lurk behind someone bigger and stronger because they're really nothing but cowards."

He snarls, attempting to step around Marcus. "You think you're so tough."

Tabatha laughs, her body lifting with the motion. Clearly she's ready to watch some action.

Marcus holds Ruben back with a hand on his chest. "Easy there, Ruben."

Ruben stops in his tracks, looking from Marcus back to me.

Marcus stares at me grimly. "You don't belong here. You know that." My skin prickles as his words sink in. It's like he knows that Caden asked me to stay. "Why don't you just keep your mouth shut and stay in your room until you leave. If you want to get out of here in one piece . . ."

It's no empty threat. I see that in his steady gaze. And I can't imagine this is just because he doesn't trust me. It's more than that. More than that Caden smuggled me in here minus a blindfold. I killed one of his men. His cousin. Never mind that the guy attacked me, I killed him. He won't forget the fact. The sooner I leave here the better.

"I'll do that," I whisper, holding Marcus's gaze because I know that he's the one who matters. Not his goon.

I step down between him and Tabatha, careful not to let any part of us brush. Almost like if we were to touch, we would ignite in an electrical reaction. We're two properties that should never meet. And yet here we are, thrown into a fishbowl together.

Just two more days.

I suck in a breath as I head to the room I share with Junie. I find her there, removing stuff from her pack.

She smiles when she looks up. "Hey, did you hear the good news? Your friends are okay, and they're at refuge number four."

I smile. "That is good news."

"I bet they're going to be relieved when they hear that you're all right and coming to join them."

"Yeah." I sink down on the bottom mattress.

Her smile slips. "You don't look too happy."

"Of course I am."

She stares at me, disbelieving. Sighing, I admit, "Just had a little run-in with Marcus and Ruben."

She rolls her eyes. "Those two. Don't worry about them. They're just in a perpetual bad mood because everyone looks to Caden first. You would think Caden is older. That makes it even more of a sore point for Marcus, I think."

"Why does everyone trust Caden so much?" I ask, even though I already suspect. Caden has a way about him. He's the kind of guy who makes you believe in silver linings. The kind you trust your life to. That is, if you were the kind of person given to trust anyone.

She looks at me blankly. "Wouldn't you trust Caden first? I mean, between the two of them?"

I smile and nod grudgingly. Without a doubt. "Yeah, but then I might be biased." Caden did save my life, but I don't remind her of that. "Marcus hasn't exactly been warm and fuzzy with me."

She gives me a look that says, *Yeah, well, you did kill his cousin.* Instead of going there, though, she says, "Marcus wants to rush out guns blazing." She shakes her head. "Some of the schemes he has suggested . . . I mean, they're suicide missions. He might be a badass soldier, but he's no military strategist. The only reason we've made it at all these last couple of months without General Dumont is because of Caden's good sense."

The hero worship is evident in her tone, and I can't help but smile. I remember feeling that way when I met Sean. Well, not at first, but eventually. He'd been marked as a carrier for most of his life. He knew how to handle living with the circumstances that had suddenly been thrust upon me. All the misery and injustice . . . he endured it all and seemed stronger for it. Honorable. Proud. If I had to be a carrier, I wanted to be one like him. He gave me hope.

And now there's Caden. He's all that and maybe even more. Because he refuses to run. He's staying and fighting.

With his faith in carriers, in mankind. In me.

Now he's the one. The one whose smiles pull at something inside me and make me want to smile, too. The one I wish I could be more like.

Victoria (Tori) Samantha Chesterfield died Saturday afternoon while attending a peaceful protest outside the state capital, one of four victims senselessly shot by a lone carrier sympathizer. A life cut down much too early, she died standing up for her beliefs, a true patriot for her country who will be greatly missed. She is survived by her parents, Eric and Hannah Chesterfield, a younger brother, Brandon, and countless friends. The service will be held at Sleepy Hills Memorial Home Wednesday afternoon at four p.m. In lieu of flowers, her family requests donations be made to any anti-carrier group of your choice.

FIFTEEN

I'M IN THE INFIRMARY WITH RHIANNON THE NEXT day, helping her catalog the new supplies, when Caden finds me.

Even though the infirmary was the location of my attempted murder, I gravitate toward it now. For the most part, I've been cared for here. It's been safe, quiet. Fewer prying stares. Usually it's just Phelps and Rhiannon. Only an occasional patient.

Rhiannon has come around, treating me almost warmly as I read off the names of the medicines for her to enter into the computer and then stacking them neatly beside me.

"There you are," Caden murmurs, the door clanging behind him. His gaze shifts from me to Rhiannon. "Mind if I borrow your helper?"

Rhiannon shakes her head.

Caden offers me a hand and pulls me to my feet. He holds on to my hand for longer than necessary. We're almost to the door before I slip my hand from his. I tuck a short strand of hair behind my ear as if I needed my hand free to do that. Which is a little lame. It's not as though I need an excuse *not* to hold his hand. Why would we be holding hands? We're not a couple. The very idea makes me drag a deep, shuddery breath into my lungs.

I keep pace beside him. He leads me down the narrow hall into the controls room.

Terrence looks up from where he's sitting at a table full of several high-tech-looking computers and equipment.

"Hey, T." Caden nods at him. "Can you give us a minute in here?"

Terrence almost looks like he'll refuse, but then he sighs and removes a pair of headphones from his ears. He exits the room, and I feel a little uneasy as he shuts the door behind us. We've been alone together before, but not since I turned him down when he asked me to stay.

I uncross my arms and force a smile. "Did you need something?"

"Actually, yes." He moves past the computers to stand before a large map on the wall and waves a broad hand at it.

"Before you leave, you could help me."

"Help you? How?"

"Well, help us. You're not the usual carrier passing through here." His amber eyes roam my face, and something warm blossoms in my chest and spreads through me. For a moment I think that maybe he really sees something in me that sets me apart from everyone else here. That he might think I'm special. That I'm not my worst nightmare but still a normal girl. Crazy, I know. I might believe my carrier status doesn't define me, but it definitely makes me anything but normal. Although he's a carrier, too, and it doesn't appear to stop him from . . . well, from *anything*. He's here, living, fighting. He's not full of shame. He's determined to carve a future not just for himself but for others.

"Your special camp . . . can you show me where it is?" he asks, and I deflate. Just because I was in a special camp does not mean *I'm* special to *him*. "It could be useful to know."

I step up to the map and study it. Several flags of different colors riddle the country, most concentrated in the Southwest, but some flags reach as far north as New England. "What are all these?"

He points to the red flags, which are the scarcest. "The red flags are known Agency checkpoints and headquarters." He moves to the green flags scattered throughout the country. "These are detention camps."

I point at the concentration of yellow flags along the border. "Those?"

"Border checkpoints. And these." He motions to the little black tacks. "These are the locations of known resistance cells."

I look at him sharply. He stares back at me, so open and forthcoming. He trusts me enough to show me this.

Nodding, I turn back to the map and point to New Mexico and wave west of Albuquerque. "We were about an hour west of here. I don't know more than that." I didn't exactly take note when we were brought there, and I especially was in no frame of mind to pay attention when we left. Plus, it was the middle of the night then.

"Were there other camps? Like the one you were at?"

I shake my head. "I don't think so. At least they made it sound like we were the only one. There was always the threat that if we didn't cooperate or perform up to level, they'd send us to a detention camp."

"What were your supplies like there? Food? Weapons?"

"Plenty of both. They trained us with all kinds of weapons, and we were always well fed."

Frowning, he stares at the map, and I take advantage of his distraction and study him freely. The dark fall of his hair against his forehead. The straight bridge of his nose over well-carved lips. He doesn't have dimples exactly, but twin brackets dent his cheeks, right beside his mouth. My chest tightens.

Shaking my head, I follow his gaze. "I'd leave it alone."

He looks at me again.

"The camp," I add. "I don't know what you're thinking, but I wouldn't mess with it. There's a reason we ran from there."

"And what was that?"

"It was changing me. And that was the point. Their goal. They wanted to shape us. You're thinking you might find carriers there with training . . . special skills. Right?"

He nods.

"Well, you'll find that, but you'll also find something else."

"What's that?"

"They're taking away their hearts. Training them to be machines. Some of those carriers there . . . they were only too happy to become mindless assassins."

He assesses me for a moment before saying with conviction, "They could never have done that to you."

I snort. "You don't know anything about me."

"I'm a good judge of character. My father always said I could size a person up. It's a particular talent of mine." He grins almost smugly, and I have to fight down a smile of my own. He's even better-looking with that cocky grin.

"Yeah? You've sized me up then?"

"Yep."

A frisson of discomfort rushes through me, but still I hear myself ask, "And what do you see?" I have to know.

"Someone way too hard on herself, who needs to stop believing what others say about her . . . especially what some stupid lab report says. She needs to stop believing that a test can define who she is."

I laugh hoarsely and hug myself, my fingers flexing on my arms. "You see all that, huh?"

He looks back at the map. "You chose to escape that place.

That says it all. You didn't stay to let them warp you into some heartless machine. You escaped. And now you're here."

I'm here. With him.

Something loosens inside me as I realize he's right. I didn't stay. Leaving Mount Haven . . . yeah, that means I'm different.

My skin shivers as the idea takes hold and settles deep . . . as his gaze drills into me, seeing beneath the surface to the real me. The me I'm not even sure I know anymore. It's disconcerting to think he sees more than I can of myself—but a relief, too. Because listening to him, the girl he sees when he looks at me isn't lost. My stomach flutters beneath his amber-eyed examination.

"You have an amazing voice," I blurt, both deliberately and not. He does have an amazing voice. I haven't been able to get it out of my head. But I also feel desperate to break free from his scrutiny.

He blinks at the sudden change in topic. "Thanks." He shrugs like it's not a thing. His voice. My compliment. "I played around with the guitar a bit in junior high. Couple friends and I actually thought we could put together a band. We'd just started to get serious and practice when my father got reassigned again. . . . And eventually—" He stops and waves a hand, motioning at the bunker around us. Enough said. I try to picture him in his life before but have trouble grasping it beyond who he is now. Here. In this world.

"Where are you from?" I ask.

"South Carolina."

I thought I detected the barest southern lilt to his voice.

"Let me guess. Football?" Bred in the South. It seems a certainty. I cross my arms and assess him with an air of drama.

A plan that backfires, because once I start checking him out, it's hard to stop. My cheeks grow warm, heat creeping all the way up to my ears as I skim his broad shoulders. The cotton T-shirt looks so soft. It rests across his chest, hugging the flat lines of his torso. I remember the sensation of me curled against that chest. The power of his arms, flexing biceps as he carried me. Aware that I'm ogling him, I jerk my attention back to his face. I'm worse than a boy who can't keep his eyes off a girl's chest.

He smiles that grin that makes my stomach flutter again. "No. No football."

I angle my head. "Not the golden boy, huh?" It fit. At least I thought so. He's so strong and in command here. He seems like the kind of guy who would lead his team to a state championship or something. Then it dawns on me. "Oh, I get it. You were the army brat. Bet you rebelled."

The idea of this is kind of hot. I picture him luring some Goody Two-shoes (who resembles me a lot) onto the back of a Harley and speeding out of the school parking lot. I glance away, afraid my burning face is bright red now at the totally ridiculous fantasy.

"Am I that predictable?"

I feel my eyes widen. "Oh my God, am I right?"

"Hey. It wasn't cool moving around every couple years.

One year I changed schools twice. So. Yeah. I might have acted out a bit. First day of school I might have made a beeline for the kids who looked most likely to skip school and get high in their parents' basement. I had a nose for them." He taps the side of his nose.

"And wild girls," I say before I can catch the words.

He stares at me for a while. "Well, I was wild. They were the only ones I could get."

This I doubt. All he needed to do was flash that grin, and any girl would have followed him.

"The good girls knew better," he adds.

Maybe he's right about that. I would have known better. The Davy Hamilton of before would have given him a wide berth, watching from the window of her chemistry class as some other girl hopped on the back of his bike and took off to make out in some basement.

This Davy Hamilton? She could be tempted.

My cheeks sting as this thought slides through me to settle into the mass of butterflies kicking to life in my belly.

"Guess we're all bad here," I say, unable to look away from him. I can hardly breathe. My chest feels tight as he watches me intently, like he's waiting for me to say or *do* something. Like he can read my mind.

"Well, we're all rebels. This is true."

I nod, waving at the map with flags dotted across it. "Literally."

"You were the good girl," he declares abruptly.

I snort and tuck a strand behind my ear self-consciously. "What?"

"It's stamped all over you." He moves closer. "You were the girl. The one."

I hold my breath, watching as he stops just inches from me. The notion of personal space is lost.

"The perfect princess." His words are a warm breath on my face.

I open my mouth to deny the image, but can't grab the words. They're not untrue exactly.

His lips twist into a crooked smile. "You wouldn't have even looked at me."

Not true. I would have seen him. I know this deep in my gut where muscle meets bone and wraps tight. I wouldn't have been able to *not* look at him. And if I'd ever heard his voice . . . if he ever sang? I don't know if I could have stayed away. Good girl or not.

He continues, still standing too close. I can smell the clean, soapy scent of his skin. "I would have been one of dozens looking at you. Just another guy who can't help himself when he sees this amazing girl out of his reach."

I avert my eyes, stunned by his words. I've been complimented before. But not often since I became known as a carrier. And not since I hacked off my hair, dyed it, and exposed my face to so much sun it resembles leather. "I doubt—"

"Yes," he's quick to say. "I think you're the most beautiful girl I've ever seen."

I moisten my lips and shake my head. I'm not beautiful. I know this. Not because I suffer from low self-esteem or anything. I know my assets. I have good hair (well, had). My legs are pretty decent. And yet there were far prettier girls at Everton than me—and even here. Tabatha's face floats across my mind. I'm too thin. As far as my chest goes, there isn't much to it, and my nose has a slight bump. So I can't fathom where he's coming from when he calls me beautiful.

As though he's reading my mind, he says, "And I'm not just talking about your face. You're strong. Brave. And even though you try not to show it, you care about people. You're beyond loyal. All you've wanted to do is get back to your friends. I can't tell you how jealous that has made me."

Jealous? My gaze snaps back to his. His eyes are like amber lit from the sun, blazing down on me. I flinch—but not in fear—as he brushes the hair back off my forehead.

"You can stay here, Davy. Join us. Join me."

My nerves snap then, bloom into full-scale panic at the mere suggestion. His eyes are too warm, too compelling. I have to look away, but even then I can still see them. They still pull me to look back at him. When I do, he's somehow moved closer. Our lips are a hairbreadth away.

Him. His words. The temptation hits me strong. My throat constricts, making the air impossible to flow.

"I—I have to go." Squeezing past him, I stumble from the room.

Breathing heavily, I hurry down the hall, one hand pressing to my thundering heart. It's not right. The way he makes my heart beat. I feel wrong, panicky. *Guilty.*

I'm leaving this place. I'm going to find Sean and Gil and Sabine. I don't need to be falling for this guy who's committed to an impossible cause. Who will likely end up getting killed on his next mission. Who makes me wonder if there isn't a little bit of something special . . . something other than tainted blood . . . still inside me.

Dear Mom and Ashlee,

I know you expect me to come home. Nothing is keeping me here. Dad's gone. It's still such a shock. We all thought it would be something else. That nothing short of a bullet would take him from this world. Who knew he even had a heart problem? Maybe if he hadn't been forced into early retirement, they would have caught it in time. Maybe. I think that word a lot lately. *Maybe*. And *if*.

I thought I could come home. I planned to. I told myself there's no need for me to be here anymore. Except there is.

They do need me here. More than ever now. I have to stay. For Dad. For everyone. Even for you and Ashlee. I can't stand by and do nothing while this happens. I hope you understand. I hope you can forgive me.

Love,
Caden

—Email sent from Caden Anderson following the death of Colonel Anderson

SIXTEEN

THERE ARE TEN OF US DEPARTING FOR MEXICO, including myself and Tabatha, and five men, one woman, and two children. I'm not sure if the children are carriers or just there because of their parents. I don't know. I don't ask questions. No names. No life stories. If I don't ask theirs, they won't ask mine. Maybe I can still have some distance.

Still, I find myself staring at the little girl. She's maybe ten with carrot-red hair. Her nose and cheeks are heavily freckled, her skin mottled shades of white, brown, and pink from a past sunburn. She stays close to her mother. Does the mother have HTS? Or the girl?

Whatever the case, I think of my own mother. Try to imagine her here, running across the border with me. It's impossible. I can only see her with her manicured nails and silk blouses.

Tabatha is our appointed scout. I had hoped Junie would be leading us, but apparently not. Junie joins me in the main room, near the stairs leading up to the exit. My stomach churns and twists the way it used to right before a roller-coaster drop.

"Don't get killed out there." She jerks her head to where Tabatha talks to Caden. I've been avoiding looking at him. It makes me think about his offer for me to stay. An offer I can't take. And for some reason that makes my stomach churn even tighter.

Junie shakes her head, and the action tosses twin pigtails over her shoulders. "And don't expect that one to look after you. Keep up or she'll leave you behind. Or worse." *Worse?* It doesn't take much imagination to figure out what's worse than that.

I scan Tabatha. Dressed head to toe in fatigues, dark hair pulled back beneath a hat worn low on her head, she's practically sexless. For some reason I see her in my mind, plastered against Caden. *Far from sexless.*

"Don't worry. I don't expect her to stick her neck out for me." I don't expect that of anyone.

Junie flings her arms around me and hugs me then. I pat her arm awkwardly, the most I can bring myself to do. "Take care of yourself," she says.

"You too," I murmur, wondering if she'll even be alive a year from now. A carrier scout, she'll probably be shot or captured. Suddenly I'm hugging her harder, forgetting my issues about getting close to another person. For a brief moment, I let myself feel. A swift squeeze and then I'm stepping back, arms falling at my sides.

She grins at me brightly like we're not two people stuck in the middle of a war. Like we might run into each other at the mall. "Maybe we'll see each other again someday."

"Maybe," I allow, but I doubt it. Not unless she intends to leave her work here for a refuge in Mexico.

"Let's go," Tabatha announces. Taking the lead, she starts up the stairs. I fall in last. At least I think I'm last, but then I hear a deep voice behind me.

"Can you manage the steps?"

I turn. Caden stands with one boot on the bottom step, his hands gripping the railing on either side of us. The others move ahead. I can hear the *thunk* of their shoes on the grate steps, but I don't look up. I train my gaze on him.

"I think I can handle a set of stairs. I hurt my shoulder, not my legs." My tone escapes more biting than I intended. My stomach is all knotted up, and it's impossible to talk in a way that makes me sound . . . *better*. Nice.

His eyes move to my arm, and I know he's measuring me. I took the sling off last night. It hurts when I move my arm too much. I can't rotate my shoulder at all. Even without the sling, I hold my arm close to my side, the elbow partially bent. With his eyes focused there, I force it straight down, fixing my expression so it reveals none of the discomfort the simple action causes me.

His eyes fasten on my face, and despite my attempt to disguise my pain, he looks at me knowingly. "Well, I hope so, considering you're leaving. You don't want to get out there and realize you've made a mistake and shouldn't have left."

"I haven't made a mistake." I swallow and correct myself. "I'm not."

Something flickers in the amber depths of his eyes, but then it's gone. He waves ahead. "Then by all means. Let's go."

My heart lurches against my chest. "You're coming, too?" I look him up and down. He carries no gear.

His mouth lifts in a half smile. "I don't know if that's hope or horror I hear in your voice."

Hope. It's hope, and that disappoints me. I know better. Hoping for more than I need, more than I can have, only leads to pain. "I—I just didn't know. . . ."

He shakes his head. "I'm just seeing you off at the top. Making sure you're all properly blindfolded before you step outside."

Right.

"Oh. I see." My heart settles back in my chest. A chest that feels a little hollow knowing this is it. He's not coming with us.

Turning, I continue up the stairs, his boots falling heavy on the steel steps behind me.

At the top we reach a platform with a tunnel that stretches both left and right. I don't see the others. They've already moved on. Shadows loom in both directions.

"This way." Caden steps past me and leads me to the right, his boots clanging over the grate. As we move the shadows deepen, enveloping us like we're sinking into night.

His strides fall swiftly. Clearly he doesn't need to see where he's going.

I follow, studying the vague outline of his lean frame, the slope of his shoulders, careful not to walk too closely and run into him if he should stop. Ahead, I can hear the voices of the others, a soft rumble on the air.

"Almost there," he says over his shoulder, as if he senses that I need the reassurance.

The narrow tunnel opens to a small space with three steps that lead up to a circular steel door reminiscent of the kind you would see on a submarine. Muted blue-tinged light glows from a fixture positioned near the door.

Tabatha is securing blindfolds to everyone as she issues instructions. I try to step closer and listen, but Caden's presence is a distraction. Especially when he makes no attempt to hide the fact that he's watching me, his dark eyebrows pulling tight. My skin prickles. His gaze is like a physical touch to my face, invisible fingertips moving, sliding over my jaw, my cheek, the bridge of my nose.

"At no time are you to remove the blindfold unless I tell you. It's dark out there. You're not going to be able to see where you're going anyway, with or without the blindfold, but the blindfold must stay on. We'll hold hands and make a chain. We just need to make it a few yards, and then we'll be in the van that will take us to the halfway point."

The ten-year-old is bouncing up and down with excitement, so much that Tabatha has a hard time fastening the blindfold around her.

Caden's stare grows heavier on me. I swing around and glare at him. "Would you stop it?" I hiss, my voice low enough that no one notices.

"Stop what?"

My stomach feels like it's bubbling with a thousand butterflies. "Staring at me." This is it. Good-bye. He knows that. We both do.

His eyes glint darkly in the muted light. "You're really going through with it?"

"Leaving? Yes. And why wouldn't I?"

"Because the right thing to do is to stay here, where you can help and serve a purpose." His voice has a hard, desperate edge to it. He's convincing. I'll give him that. He almost makes me feel necessary.

"Stay here?" I laugh.

"Yes."

Stay here. Where no one wants me except him? And honestly, he scares me the most. I know Marcus's kind. Caden I don't understand.

I shake my head and press a hand to my rioting stomach. What's wrong with me? Maybe I'm getting honest-to-God sick? "You're wasting your time."

"Evidently. I guess I just misjudged you."

I should just let that remark go, but I can't. "Oh? How so?"

"I thought there was something special in you. I thought you were someone who gave a damn. . . ."

His words find their mark. Sting as they shouldn't. As someone that everyone once thought was special, remarkable even . . . I still hunger for that. My stupid longing for more, for my life to be something extraordinary—in a positive way—it's still there, buried beneath the scrapes and bruises.

"You thought wrong," I whisper thickly.

Tabatha steps between us, her gaze curious and faintly suspicious. "Here." She dangles the thick black strip of fabric out. "Turn around."

My gaze flicks to Caden, locking on him, memorizing. Once that blindfold is on, I'll never see him again. For some reason, I crave a picture of him in my mind with a suddenness that rocks me.

"I got it." He takes the blindfold from her.

Shrugging, she turns away. "I'll go check and make sure everything is clear." The well-oiled door doesn't make a sound as she unlocks it and pulls it open.

"Go ahead," I say, lifting my chin and trying not to care that this is my last glimpse of him. That it's for the best. A good thing. He pushes too much. Makes demands.

He steps closer and lifts the fabric to my face. I watch his eyes, holding them, fixing on those tiny flecks of gold that give them an amber tint. I feel his breath on my cheek as he brings the cloth over my eyes and works on knotting it behind my head. The knot catches on a few strands, and I wince.

"Sorry," he murmurs near my ear.

He's so close, his chest brushing my own. I tremble even as everything inside me tenses, eager for him to step back and go away.

"There." He lowers his arms. My pulse skips as his skin grazes my cheek. I blink, my lashes brushing the fabric blinding me. Drowning in darkness, I move my head to the side, listening. Feeling. All my senses thrum in hyperalert.

Are you still there, Caden? Say something.

The words knock around inside my head, threatening to spill loose like pebbles chipped off a boulder. Sheer willpower dams them up inside me.

The others speak in low tones around me. I sense their hovering presence, their soft movements. The tension is thick, swirling like smoke as we wait for Tabatha to return.

Suddenly I hear the click and grind of a door opening. Tabatha's voice rings out, "Okay, we're clear. Let's go."

Shoes shuffle as Tabatha starts lining everyone up, instructing them to hold hands. I turn in the direction of her voice. I know Caden's still here but have no idea where he stands. I sense him. *Feel* him.

Then he touches my shoulder. I know it's him and not Tabatha. There's just something in the heat and pressure of his hand on me . . . in the sparks that flare from the simple contact.

He turns me around. "I should have handled you differently."

I bristle. "Handled me?" No one handles me.

He sighs. "Okay. Poor word choice. It's just that I—I

listened to you. I let you push me away." Again, I can feel his breath on my cheek.

My chin goes up. "That's what I wanted."

"Yeah, you wanted that, but it's not what I wanted. And it's not what you needed."

I snort even though his words are finding their way beneath my skin, arrowing straight for my heart. My hands shake a little, and I press them against my sides. "And you know what I need?" We just met, but he thinks he knows me as well as that?

"I think you're scared and running."

I nod once, swift and certain. It's hard to admit, but what's the point in arguing? I am scared. What carrier isn't? I should be scared. It's logical. "Of course I am." I step back, feeling the heat of him radiate, close to me, following.

"I'm sorry I couldn't change your mind."

There's a slight shift in the air. For a fraction of a second, I understand his intent, that he's moving in. His hands slide along my cheeks, holding my face for him, the calloused pads of his fingers exerting the barest pressure. And then his mouth is on mine.

I startle, jump a little as our lips meet. They're cooler than I expect. Soft and dry. Not that I have given kissing him great thought. It's been one thing I deliberately avoided considering, but an awareness has always been there. Maybe this was inevitable. Two forces destined to collide.

His lips move over mine, slanting one way, then the other, kissing me like some sort of snake charmer working to coax a response. I finally give in and lean into him, my mouth softening under his, moving, kissing him back like it's the last kiss of my life.

And maybe it is. At least it's our last kiss. The first and the last.

That familiar heat sweeps over my face. *How does he do this to me?* So quickly? So easily? And was breathing ever this hard before? I feel like I'm stuck in a windowless room without any air-conditioning in the middle of summer. It's something that only happens to me around him. I breathe just fine any other time.

"Caden!" The sharp sound of his name is like a sudden douse of ice water. His mouth lifts off mine. I turn in the direction of Tabatha's voice, tempted to wrench the blindfold from my face.

Instead, I hold myself still, waiting to hear if he says anything more. That deep, velvet voice one more time before I go.

"I'll take her from here, Caden," Tabatha says tightly, and I feel her cool, slim fingers wrap around my wrist, her hold tight, unyielding. Like she's ready to drag me bodily from the compound and Caden if she has to. I almost smile at the image. It's unnecessary. One kiss changes nothing. If anything, it just confirms how fast I have to get away from this place. From him.

"Good luck, Davy." His voice rolls over me. It sounds deeper, a little husky, and makes my lips tingle with the memory of his taste.

"Good-bye," I say.

Tabatha tugs me and I move, slide one step and hope she's

not about to lead me into a wall. Or off a cliff.

I strain, listening for his voice, convinced that his eyes are still on me.

"Here," she instructs. "Take his hand." She shoves my hand at one of the other carriers. My fingers get lost in the larger, sweaty grip of a man. I'm the last one in the chain. "Don't let go," she whispers near my ear. "I'm happy to leave you behind out there."

I just bet. In moments the man in front of me is moving, pulling me after him. It's start and stop. I collide into his back several times. No one slows, though, as I ease my way over the door. There's momentum in the chain by then, and I nearly fall and lose my grip on the carrier's hand in front of me.

He yanks hard as he pulls me up. Free of the underground compound, the air feels crisper, laced with a lingering heat left over from the day. I sniff the aroma of mesquite and cedar. In the distance, I think I hear the door clicking shut, sealing us out. Sealing Caden in.

He kissed me. I curse under my breath. What did he go and do that for? That kiss is the last thing I needed.

And no matter where I'm going, I know I will always remember him. The dead already haunt me. Now I'll be haunted by the living, too.

PART TWO

CROSSINGS

911 Transcript

911 DISPATCHER 02910: What's your emergency?

BETTINA MORGAN: Oh my God! Help! Help us! We're dying!

911 DISPATCHER 02910: Ma'am, calm down. Can I have your name?

BETTINA MORGAN: Bettina. Bettina Morgan.

911 DISPATCHER 02910: (typing) Bettina, where are you?

BETTINA MORGAN: I'm at the Wainwright Headquarters on Fourteenth Street. Th-there's been an explosion. Bodies are everywhere. I'm hurt. My leg . . . oh my God. My leg . . . (sobbing) I—I can't walk. I'm just twenty! God, oh God! I don't want to die!

911 DISPATCHER 02910: (typing) Stay where you are, Bettina. Can you do that? Help is on the way.

BETTINA MORGAN: (whispering) Please, p-please. I can't feel my leg.

911 DISPATCHER 02910: Can you look around and describe your surroundings? Are you on the first floor? Bettina? Where are you in the building?

BETTINA MORGAN: I was on the third floor, b-but the explosion . . . there's debris everywhere. I don't recognize anything. Everything's been leveled.

There's light to my left. Maybe an opening that way.

911 DISPATCHER 02910: (typing) Good. Can you call out? Shout for help?

BETTINA MORGAN: I never wanted to work here. My dad said the internship would look good on my résumé. You know my driver's ed teacher turned out to be a carrier. He was a nice old guy, but they sent him to a camp. (sobbing) He was a grandpa. He kept pictures of his grandkids on the visor. I shouldn't be here. I should never have—

911 DISPATCHER 02910: Bettina, I need you to calm down so that you can help me help you. Understand?

BETTINA MORGAN: This is my punishment. Don't you see? We're all being punished. . . .

SEVENTEEN

TABATHA IS RIGHT ABOUT THE VAN AT LEAST. WE don't have to go very far. Thankfully. We all make it, even me, the caboose, holding my free hand out in case I fall, stumbling blindly over broken and uneven ground.

Once we're inside the back of the van, Tabatha is good to her word and announces we can remove our blindfolds. The windows are blacked out, so we won't be seeing much of anything besides one another's faces, but still. I look around, almost as if I expect to see Caden somewhere in the van with us. As if that final glimpse, that taste, of him wasn't the last.

I note the outline of a man behind the driver's wheel, his

shape shadowy and indistinct in the gloom of the van.

I turn back to the windows and strain my eyes as I stare at the painted glass, wondering about the direction of the compound. Then I wonder why it matters. I've left that place. Never to return. My future lies ahead.

We drive maybe an hour before the van stops. We don't have to put the blindfolds on again before we're urged from the van and herded through the brush into a small clearing. There's a small fire pit, so I know they've used this spot as a camp before. In the not-so-far distance, I think I hear the gurgle of running water. I stand off to the side, listening as the van drives away, leaving us, feeling very alone even though I'm not.

The others mingle together, familiar with one another. I hadn't spent any time at the compound with them. It didn't seem important. Or necessarily wise. We'll part ways soon enough after we cross. Maybe some of them are going to the same refuge as me. Maybe not. I don't care either way. Can't afford to. Caden's face flashes across my mind like a blinding bright snapshot and I kill it, shove it back into the dark. My lips hum, and I resist the urge to brush my fingers there.

My chest feels hollow as I look out at the horizon. Morning tints the sky, edging the landscape in orange as several of the carriers find a place to sit. I stand. I sat long enough inside the van. A restlessness buzzes through my muscles. I can hear the river, just a faint murmur in the distance, and know we're close. We'll cross today. I'll leave the country of my birth behind. My family. Regret pinches my heart. But then I left them behind months ago. The moment I tested positive for HTS. Even Mitchell. As much as I love him and he loves me, my brother is virtually as far from me as the moon.

My nerves stretch and thrum with tension. I glance around, feeling exposed and vulnerable out in the open like this. Despite the attack on my life, there was a measure of security within the compound. Out here, in the open, anyone could find us. Border Patrol. The Agency. Vigilante civilians. Or rogue carriers—which yes, seems to be a bit of an oxymoron in itself. Or even people from Mount Haven. If they're still looking. The list of threats seems endless. And my life feels dark and hopeless with the possibilities swirling around in my head.

"You thought you were going to stay, didn't you?" There's a definite smirk to her voice.

I hadn't even heard Tabatha approach. I turn and stare at her blankly. "What are you talking about?"

"Caden. You thought he wanted you to stay."

I don't bother letting her know that he asked me to more than once. She obviously has a thing for him, and me getting on her bad side—even more than I am—when I already have to rely on her to get me across the border is just all kinds of dumb.

So I play ignorant and kick at the dirt with the toe of my shoe. "I don't know what you mean."

"What was that kiss? You trying to tempt him to let you stay?"

I stare at her. Is that what it looked like to her? That I

kissed him? Shaking my head, I turn and look out across the camp. "You got it all wrong."

"Oh, I had you pegged from the moment you showed up. I saw the way you looked at him like a bitch in heat."

I inhale through my nose sharply. "I did no—"

"Hey, I get it." She shrugs her slight shoulders. "He's hot. He's powerful and in charge and can get you nice things when there's just not a lot of nice things to be had for carriers these days. What's not to want?"

I snort. "So you think I want to be the first lady of your resistance cell? No, thanks."

"Yeah, you say that now 'cause he threw your ass out with the rest of them." Her gaze skims the group, and I see how little she thinks of us all.

Unable to stand another word from her, I start to walk away.

"Hey, where are you going?"

"I need to go to the bathroom."

"All right," she responds, as though I asked her for permission. "Don't go far. We'll be leaving here soon, and we're not going to wait on you. Once the guide is in position on the other side and gives the signal, we're moving out. Any minute now."

I give a slight wave of acknowledgment and keep walking, leaving the campsite behind. I rotate my shoulder gingerly, working the dull ache there as I walk. The ground is rocky, full of rises and dips and short scrub and brush that grab at me like greedy hands. I don't really need to relieve myself but figure I might as well. I don't know when I'll get the next chance.

The ground breaks suddenly, dipping into a small gully. I jump down, the soles of my boots skidding for a moment before I catch my balance. With a quick glance around to make sure I'm alone, I do my business.

Buttoning up my pants, I rise and slap a hand on the ground at eye level above me, prepared to haul myself up. That's when I hear the first shot. Screams and shouts follow.

Everything inside me seizes as I'm flooded with the memories of the last time gunfire riddled the air. When I was shot. The wound stings and pulses and my right hand drifts there instinctively, curving over my shoulder. Trembling, adrenaline pumping hotly through me, I haul myself out of the gully. I inch forward in a crouch in the direction of camp.

Pop! Pop!

Staccato gunfire cracks the air, rapid-fire, and then the shooting stops. The screams and shouts fade away, and that silence chills me even more than the noise. My mouth dries and I swallow.

Everything in me tells me to run, get away. But I have to see. I have to know.

The closer I get, the lower I drop to the ground, practically belly-crawling. Cacti and all manner of plants tear at my flesh, but I keep going, ignoring the pain. The camp comes into view, and I stop, holding myself still, peering through the knee-high scrub and weeds. I convulse at what I see and press a hand to my mouth, stifling a cry. I bite down on my finger, my throat contracting against the surge of bile.

Bodies are everywhere. The ripe, coppery scent of blood stings my nostrils. Tabatha is there, facedown, her cheek turned to the side on the ground, facing me. She's as still as stone, her eyes wide and glassy. The surprise is caught there, etched in her frozen expression, captured forever in the moment of death.

A dozen men walk amid the bodies, prodding at them with the barrels of their guns. My chest pushes against the ground, my breath laboring as I will myself to disappear. To be anywhere but here.

I look away from Tabatha. My gaze moves on, fastening on one small body with carrot-red hair tangled in the dirt, the light strands stained with blood so dark it looks almost black in places. I didn't know her name, and this seems so wrong. I should know her name. I wish I knew her name. I bite my hand harder, muffling the cry that swells up in my throat, the stifled sound mingling with the salt of tears.

"Looks like your tip paid off, Allister," one of the men congratulates, slapping another man on the back. "Good work. Bet you get a promotion for this."

"Yeah." I can hear the grin in Allister's voice. "I was a little skeptical, too, but turns out the informant was legit."

I register this dully. I'm still grappling with the fact that everyone who sat in the back of that van with me only minutes before is now dead.

One of the bodies moans, and Allister turns to the offending carrier and squeezes off another round. I jerk at the sharp crack, feel its vibration rattle through me and bleed into my bones. I must have gasped or made some small sound. One of the men swings around, lifting his weapon level with his waist.

I sink down, pressing myself as flat as possible while peering through the tall grass. Tense, I don't breathe. He inches in my direction, setting his boots down carefully, one after the other. He stops just a few yards from me, scanning the far outskirts of the campsite, his gaze fixed directly above me as he searches the horizon.

After several moments, he lowers his gun, lets it point back down at the ground. One of the other men calls out for him, and he turns. My body sags, some of the tension ebbing away.

"All clear," a guy calls out. A radio crackles, and he speaks into a small handheld device, his voice too low to hear. My eyes fly over them, noting their attire. Not uniforms exactly, but they're all dressed in browns and khaki. Like Caden and his bunch, but their clothes look a little better. Less rumpled, less worn. Better quality.

They're not carriers and they're not Border Patrol, either. They would have some kind of uniform with markings to symbolize their law enforcement branch. They must be Agency.

My gaze moves on, and this is confirmed. Two tan SUVs with Agency insignias and one pickup truck sit parked near the campsite. They're systematic, calculating as they look over the dead bodies. One man walks to each one and snaps a photo of their faces. Done with that, the rest of them then lift and deposit the corpses in the back of the truck, tossing them like sacks of corn. I flinch at the thud of each body. Soon they're all gone, collected like garbage to be discarded.

That could have been me.

If I hadn't walked away when I did. Sweat beads my face, and I shake. I squeeze my eyes in a tight, pained blink. Lucky doesn't begin to describe it. Maybe it's fate. Or maybe there is a God . . . some entity greater than everything and everyone, looking out for me. The instant I think this, I feel sick. Selfish and stupid. Why would I think myself any more important than all those people in the back of that truck? No. Not people anymore. Bodies. Corpses.

The men survey the campsite again, tossing a few bags and other miscellaneous items into the back of the truck, leaving nothing behind.

Doors slam shut as they clamber inside the vehicles. Engines rev and dust billows in the air as they drive off, their taillights fading away in the morning light. Except for the still ripe scent of blood in the air and stained earth, it's like nothing ever happened here. I wait several moments, half-afraid they'll come back. Maybe it's a trick. Maybe they left someone here and he's crouched out in the brush, waiting for me to surface. Maybe that guy who stared in my direction knows I'm hiding out here somewhere.

Or maybe I'm all alone. Stranded.

I drop my forehead against the ground. The grit grinds into my skin, but I don't care. My shoulders shake with silent sobs. I'm alive. But for how much longer?

The bombing of Agency headquarters in Los Angeles only further confirms the necessity of our role in a country ever closer to chaos. This is not a time to weaken our resolve. Greater measures need to be taken to fight carriers. We need to find the head of the snake and cut it off. . . .

—Dr. Wainwright
in a private hearing before Congress

EIGHTEEN

I'M NOT SURE HOW LONG I STAY PUT. AT LEAST LONG enough to convince myself that they are well and truly gone. Long enough to stop shaking so very badly. Long enough to decide that I have to try and get to Caden. Tell him what happened. Warn him.

By the time I lift my face and sit up, it's well into morning. The sun is high in the sky. My scalp feels burning hot beneath my hair, and I wish I had brought a hat with me.

I think of Caden and how when he found me out here we only traveled at night, seeking shelter during the day. There's a reason for that beyond avoiding patrols. I understand that now. The heat is misery, and it's only going to get worse as the day advances.

Rising to my feet, I look around, rubbing my sweating palms on my thighs.

The cicadas' song congests the air, loud as an angry army. I survey the empty camp. Caden will come looking for Tabatha when she fails to return, but I can't stay here. What if the men with guns return? They could, suspecting just the thing that I do—that a search party will venture out.

Glancing up at the sun, I try to determine which way is west. Whoever knew that I'd be navigating a desert on my own?

I'm pretty sure it's not noon yet, so with the river at my back, I face west, surmising from my cursory glance at the map that the compound is that way. I set off in that direction. I know it would be best to travel at night and rest during the day, but I don't see any semblance of shelter nearby, and I'm not going to just sit down where I stand and let the sun roast me. Hopefully I'll run into someone from the resistance. And soon. Before I pass out from sunstroke.

And hopefully it will be before I meet more people okay with killing little redheaded girls.

The heat ripples on the air. I almost laugh when I think that I grew up in Texas and once thought I was immune to heat like this. It's easy to consider yourself tough when you can dive into air-conditioning at a moment's notice. My feet move, one after another, a slow and steady rhythm that I'm convinced will get me somewhere. Eventually. As long as I don't stop. If I stop, if I slow for even a moment, I'll drop and never get back up.

My head aches, the sun beating down on me. I applied sunscreen this morning, and for that I'm thankful. However, I didn't apply it to the back of my neck. When it starts to sting, I lift my collar to try to offer some protection to the exposed skin there.

The day slips away. I work my mouth, parched and desperate for a drink as I stumble along. I study the horizon as I move, holding a hand over my eyes as I gaze into the rippling waves of heat, looking for signs of life. Nothing.

I push ahead through the night, finding a little more energy as the temperature dips to a bearable degree. There's enough moonlight to keep going. At this point, I'm not sure which way is west, but I guess it doesn't really matter. It's not like I know where the compound is anyway. Funny, considering that was Marcus's first gripe with me. That I wasn't blindfolded when Caden took me to the compound. That I might lead the wrong people back there.

I laugh brokenly, the sound brittle to my ears, filling the empty space all around me and echoing out into the night. I can't even lead myself there. Forget about anyone else.

I step into a hole and lose my balance, fall face-first on the hard ground, my reflexes too slow to catch myself. I roll to my side, my chest shuddering. My nose smarts and I reach up to gingerly touch it, pulling my hand back. A hissing breath escapes me at the dark splash of blood on my fingertips, visible even in the night.

Panting, I sit up, resting my elbows on my knees for a long moment. My tongue feels thick, the inside of my mouth like sandpaper. I drop my head into my hands, gathering my strength, preparing myself to get up and keep moving. Keep going. It's all I can do. Either that or I stay here in this spot and die.

Exhaling a heavy breath, I lift my head, bracing myself for the next push.

And that's when I see it. Arcs of light in the distance, jerking wildly through the air. Flashlights.

My heart kicks faster as adrenaline shoots through me. I struggle to my feet, hope surging. It could be anyone, but wouldn't the patrols be in a vehicle? As well as goons from the Agency? Who but carriers would be on foot out here in the middle of the night? I want to believe it's someone from the Resistance. Every fiber of me strains, yearning for it to be them.

Take cover, hide, and die. Eventually. That's my likely fate. Or I can get closer and see who's out there. That's what Caden would do. He'd take a risk. He'd trust.

I push myself to my feet and start walking.

It seems to take forever, but once I'm close enough that I can count them, I stop. Before they can see me, I crouch low and squint at the three shadowy shapes limned in moonlight. Men. They're too big to be females. The one in the middle holds the flashlight. They're not especially quiet. They tromp around, their steps heavy, their voices jarring on the otherwise silent night.

Squatting, I inch closer even though my gut already tells me it's not Caden or any of his crew. They would never be this loud ... lumbering around like elephants in the semidarkness. They might as well announce their presence with a bullhorn. Stupid. I balance my weight on my heels, preparing to wait until they pass.

Suddenly a rattle sings nearby, shaking its feverish warning. I know the sound for what it is. Crying out, I stumble away, landing on my back. I hear the snake strike, hitting the ground near my boot. I yelp. My hands claw at the dirt, trying to get away. I keep moving until the snake doesn't sound close anymore, its rattle fading as it slithers off.

But then there are other sounds. Light swings wildly in the hands of someone running. Feet pound toward me.

"This way! Over there!"

I scramble to my feet and start running, not caring how loud I am. Fear chokes me. Feet shake the ground after me. I push on, wheezing, my lungs burning. Until now, I didn't realize how much the day had drained me.

A body slams into me, and I eat dirt. The immense force pushes the air out of me. A hard hand slams down on my shoulder and flips me over. Terror blocks the pain. It's all I feel rushing through my blood as I stare up at three men. A beam of light hits me in the face. I immediately size them up, not missing the imprints on their necks. One looks young, around my age, but the other two are older. One of the older men is on top of me. He's huge, thick with muscle and fat.

"Look what we have here."

The young guy peers down at me and points at my neck. "Look. She's a carrier, too."

"On the run like us, sweetheart?" The guy pinning me leers. There's no other word for it. His nose is so sunburned it glistens, blistered and peeling at the same time. He pants from exertion, staring down at me like he's caught a prize catfish.

I gulp for breath, trying to get words out. "Get off. You're crushing me."

The other older guy has an infected eye. It's swollen and oozing with pus and turns my stomach. He doesn't look too bothered over it, though. He laughs and slaps the big guy on the shoulder, motioning with his flashlight that he should move. "Get off before you break her, Nate."

Nate clambers off me, but still hangs on to my wrist as if I might somehow make a run for it.

Gross Eye Guy assesses me, looking me up and down. "Kind of a mess, aren't you, girl?"

"She's still a nice piece, Leo." Nate scratches his bristly jaw, and his eyes gleam with a light that makes my skin crawl.

"She is. She is." Leo nods in agreement.

Nate and Leo exchange glances. The younger guy watches me dumbly, unaware of the meaningful look passing between the two older men. But I don't miss it. I know exactly what that look means.

"We've been traveling for a long time," Nate drawls, his

thick, sausage-like fingers flexing on my wrist.

"Weeks," the boy inserts.

"Haven't been this close to a woman in all that time." Leo flicks the flashlight's beam up and down my body. A pause follows. Nate's breath crashes near my ear. I give the slightest tug on my wrist just to check—the motion sends arcing pain straight to my sore shoulder—but he's holding fast.

Leo cuts his gaze to the boy. "Hold her other arm, Andy."

I react to this command like someone just fired a gun at the starting line. I struggle, thrashing my body as Andy makes a grab for my other arm. I catch a glimpse of his bewildered gaze. He doesn't quite know what he's doing, I realize. He's simply accustomed to following these two blindly. He was probably just a high school kid like me when he was told he had HTS. One moment working on geometry, the next hitting the road with these Neanderthals.

Nate's grip tightens and twists, pulling at my skin—a vise I can't escape. I kick him, aiming directly for the shin. I put everything I have into it, and the hard toe of my boot connects with a crack.

He howls an obscenity. His hold loosens enough for me to pull free. Andy offers no resistance, staring slack-jawed at his giant friend.

I tear off, adrenaline shooting through me, and that helps. Wind rushes me. My legs pump faster, my breath escaping in loud puffs. Pants. Sobs.

I hear them in pursuit. Feet thundering. Calling out ugly things in loud, brutal voices. They don't care about keeping quiet. One of them laughs. A demented, crazy sound. I know it's not Nate. His curses burn my ears, still going strong.

I imagine their hands right behind me, reaching, swiping so close. Maybe it's that thought that makes it a reality. The boy brings me down, catching me midstride. Slams me chest-first into the ground. I'm not surprised. He's the youngest, the most fit.

He flips me over with a triumphant smile on his face. It's a hard thing to see, especially as I slide a blade into his ribs.

A knife I hardly recall removing from my pocket. Instinctively, I went for it. And just as instinctively, I buried it inside him. Warm wetness rushes over my fingers. His smile slips into a loose-lipped O of shock. I scurry backward, taking my knife with me. His hand goes to the wound. Dark liquid gushes between his fingers, but I don't stick around to watch.

I'm on my feet. Running again. I don't look back. Not even when I hear the angry bellow from one of the other two carriers. Evidently seeing my handiwork pissed them off. I only wish I had managed to stab Goliath. Suddenly the expression "no quarter given" has all-new clarity for me. They were going to hurt me before, but now they will make me wish for death.

I keep running. I can't stop.

But how long can you keep this up?

The instant the thought enters my head, I kill it. I can do this as long as they can. Longer. I have to. I can outrun Nate surely. And I'm younger than Leo. I have to be faster, even as exhausted as I am.

Fingers catch the jagged ends of my hair and grab hold,

knuckles grinding into my scalp. I scream, enraged, terrified, bewildered. I'm supposed to get away. How did I let him catch me?

We go down in a tangle of limbs. I swipe wildly with my arm, trying to cut him. Feral sounds rise from deep in my chest.

"Davy! Davy! Stop! It's me!"

My eyes focus on the face above me. "Caden?" I choke, shaking with the sudden shock of seeing him. Crying out, I drop my knife and fling my arms around him, squeezing so hard I probably cut off his oxygen. I don't even care about my protesting shoulder. Elation swells inside me, chasing away the terror.

He hugs me back, making shushing sounds, his mouth on my ear. Only then do I realize I'm sobbing. Fear and pain lift from me with each tear. His hand rubs smooth circles on my back. The easy, rhythmic stroking lulls me and quiets my blubbering.

I jerk violently and pull back in his arms, talking fast and feverishly, "Carriers!" My gaze darts around. "They're coming—"

He seizes my arms, holding me steady in front of him. I resist, looking over his shoulder.

"Shhh, it's okay. Junie and Terrence got one of them, and the other guy took off. He's running for the hills. Probably shit himself."

I peer into the night, marking Junie and two other shadows

approaching. I moisten my dry lips and start to speak, but my voice escapes in a croak.

Caden snaps his fingers. "Water," he calls out.

Terrence steps forward and offers me a bottle. My fingers fumble in my eagerness. Uncapping the lid, I drink noisily, water running down my chin and throat. I drink deep and long. They let me have my fill.

Lowering the bottle, I ask, hiccuping, "How did you find me?"

"Well, your little meet-and-greet with those guys wasn't exactly quiet. Everyone within twenty miles probably heard, which means we need to get going and fast." At the mention of this, he looks left and right, scanning the dark horizon.

I stare into the distance, at the boy I killed, his body nothing more than a bump in the landscape. "I killed one of them." Just a kid. Probably younger than me.

"You had to," Caden says instantly, automatically.

Junie steps up, looking so small between Terrence and the other guy I vaguely recognize. "That big one didn't go down easy." Squatting, she wipes her blade off in the dirt. "He was one angry mofo. Didn't run. Not even when Terrence jumped on his back and started in on him. But we got him." She makes a swiping motion to her neck.

Bile rises in the back of my throat. She's so dispassionate as she utters this. And I guess I shouldn't feel sick, especially knowing what he had planned for me. I push a hand against my stomach like that can help settle it.

She jerks a thumb behind her. "The other one ran off, Cade. You want us to go after—"

"No." Caden wraps an arm around me and stares off into the horizon as if he can see the fleeing carrier. "Let the desert have him."

Junie nods, her face softening as her gaze rests on me. "You've looked better. You okay?"

"I'm in one piece." My voice trembles and I swallow. Was I supposed to lie and say I'm okay? I just killed my third person. I guess I do have a knack for it. A third life taken by my hands. Yes, justified, but did that really matter? Dead is dead. How many more will I kill? "Thanks to you."

"Let's get moving." Still with one hand on my arm, Caden starts walking, his head rotating left and right, turning constantly, scanning the horizon. We move in the semidarkness, no flashlight to guide us, Caden leading us, the others close on our heels. Their tread falls silently on the night, a direct contrast with the other carriers—two of whom lie dead behind us. I close my eyes in a pained blink. The ugly thoughts won't go away. Won't stop digging claws into me.

So much killing. It's forever there. Always. I can't ever outrun it.

"Davy," Caden says softly, not looking at me, staring out at the horizon. "What happened to the others? We went to the campsite when Tabatha didn't return, but couldn't find much in the dark."

I swallow past the lump rising in my throat. His hand slides down my arm, his fingers catching and tangling with mine. My chest squeezes, pleasure there, humming beneath my skin, and I stop myself from pulling my hand free like his touch is too intimate for me to bear.

"What happened to the others?" His thumb strokes the back of my palm, just the softest graze, but it sends goose bumps up my arm.

He wants to know what happened. Of course he does. He's the self-appointed savior of this group. And there was more to his relationship with Tabatha. An image of her in Caden's arms bombards me. Whether he initiated that kiss or not doesn't matter. He'll be hurt when he learns that she's gone, and I shrivel a little inside at this, knowing I'll be the one to tell him. To hurt him with the news.

And then I remember *him* kissing *me*. My lips pulse and tingle for an instant. I suck in a lungful of air and shove that away. I can't do that. Not right now. This isn't about Caden and me. *There is no Caden and me.*

He slides me a look, waiting for my response. I squeeze his hand a little tighter, our palms flush. "Executed. All of them." I force the words out. "About a dozen men surprised us. I was going to the . . . bathroom when it happened. I crept closer to see all I could, but it was too late." My gaze swings to Caden. He keeps pace, not breaking stride, but his jaw locks tight. "There's more," I whisper.

"More than that they butchered us? Killed my . . . ?" His voice fades here. His mouth draws tight, and something pinches inside my chest.

He scrubs a hand over his face.

"You don't have to explain your relationship to me," I say softly. She's gone. And he doesn't owe me any explanation.

"No?" He cuts me a glance. "Of course not. You don't care. You left."

There's no heat to his words, but I flinch and resist arguing that I do care. That a huge part of me was driven to get back here not just for my sake but to warn him. To tell him there's a mole in his organization. This could happen again if he doesn't find out who. More carriers just trying to get across the border could die. The compound could be raided.

Caden could die. . . .

I stumble and his arm goes around my waist, steadying me. "Easy. It's not too far from here. You covered a lot of ground today."

I manage a wobbly smile and lean into that arm, reveling in its strength. Because I need the support, but maybe also because he feels so good and solid and I crave that desperately. "I didn't know where I was going."

"Well, you were headed in the general direction."

"Luck," I murmur, because my prayers couldn't have been answered. No one is listening.

They've been answered before.

I sift through memories of me begging, pleading for someone to help me when I was shot. And then Caden found me. A lucky coincidence?

"You said there was more?"

"Someone betrayed you."

He shakes his head but keeps moving, his hand warm in mine. "Impossible."

"Is it?" I glance behind me and lower my voice. Not that I don't trust Junie or Terrence or the other guy specifically. I just don't think it's a good idea for it to get around the compound that there's a spy among them before Caden is ready for it to be known. "Isn't that what you are all so hyperconscious about? I heard the attackers talking. They got a tip from someone in the resistance cell."

Caden glances back at Junie and the other two scouts, apparently understanding my hushed tone. "Not a word of this to anyone. I'll decide what to do when we get back. I don't want to panic everyone. I'll figure this out. I'll figure out what to do." His voice lowers to a mutter here, like he's telling himself this. A mantra that will somehow come true.

Something inside me clenches tight. I want to say that I'll help. That he doesn't need to figure this out alone. That I'm in this with him. It's a crazy impulse . . . the kind I would have had before, when I was a girl who believed in happy endings. I manage to hold these words inside.

He looks down at me like he senses my struggle. He gives my hand a slight squeeze. "Right now let's just get back."

I hesitate, not so sure that me going back to the compound is such a good idea. Do I really want back into that viper's nest?

Do you really have a choice?

Like he can read my mind, he adds, "It's safer than staying out here. Besides, if this spy wanted to expose the compound, he would have already informed on us."

Good point. And one I can't argue with. I'm too exhausted. So I breathe and let Caden lead me. Let the warmth of his hand seep into me and steady the skip of my heart. Viper's nest or not, he'll be there. I try to pretend this doesn't mean so much. Everything, really.

Your experiment has failed. We've been over-run. The carriers raided our arsenal, stole several of the vehicles. Killed three of our staff, injured over a dozen. They were long gone before we could even get up and functional again. . . .

The camp is lost.

—Correspondence to Dr. Louis Wainwright from Commander Harris, Director of Operations at Mount Haven

NINETEEN

THEY'RE WAITING FOR US WHEN WE RETURN. WELL, Marcus and his crew anyway. It's late and most of the compound is asleep. At first glance, I don't notice anyone on the main floor below us. It's quiet as a tomb as we descend the stairs. Until Marcus's voice rings out. "What's she doing here? Where is Tabatha?"

I'm not a face anyone in the compound expected to see again. I realize this as Marcus and his thugs crowd around the base of the stairs, backing away only to give us room when we reach the bottom.

"We found her out there," Caden begins explaining.

"You didn't blindfold her again?" Marcus's gaze flits over us, presumably searching for the scrap of fabric that served as a blindfold.

Junie sighs. "Not this again."

"Yes, *that*!" Ruben takes a menacing step in her direction. She holds her ground, not even flinching. She trains wide eyes on him as she lifts her chin. Like she's more than ready to take him on.

"That's it!" Marcus stabs a finger in my direction. "I want her—"

"They're dead, Marcus. Tabatha. All of them." Caden's voice falls hard. I glance at him. A vein throbs in his temple. I notice his eyes are bloodshot. He's tired . . . and blaming himself.

"How?" Marcus demands, his nasal voice especially sharp. Some of the color bleeds from his cheeks. He's not unaffected.

"They were attacked—"

"And she was spared?" Marcus waves a hand at me, the color flooding back into his face in an angry rush of blood. "Isn't that convenient?"

Caden grasps my arm and skirts me around Marcus and Ruben. "We'll talk about this tomorrow."

Feet pound after us. "No, Anderson. Not tomorrow—"

Caden jerks to a stop and whirls around. "Not now, Marcus. It's late. We've been through enough for a day," he growls, his voice tight and shaking with emotion.

Marcus glares, pressing his mouth into a hard line. He doesn't try to stop us, and I guess he understands that to push any further would be crossing a line. Caden resumes walking, taking us straight to Junie's room.

"Home sweet home," Junie declares, striding into the space after us.

Caden's eyes scan me, and I wish I knew what he was thinking. Those bloodshot eyes stare so intently. I know there's a lot going on inside him. "I'll have Phelps come check you over."

"Thank you."

"We'll talk more tomorrow." His gaze slides to Junie sitting on the bottom mattress, working her boots free. Of course he doesn't want anyone to know that there is a traitor in our midst.

"Yes. Tomorrow." I nod, my fingers reaching up to rub softly at my aching shoulder.

"Get some rest." He turns to go and stops at the door, stands there for a moment looking at me. It's the first quiet moment since everything happened. Since the shooting. Since he found me running for my life from those carriers out there. For a second, I forget that Junie's even in the room. It's like it's just the two of us, communing privately with each other, our awareness of each other sharp on the air.

Finally, he says, "I'm glad you're okay." And then he's gone.

Junie drops one boot to the floor, then the next. "What was *that*?"

"What do you mean?"

"Haven't seen him look at a girl that way before. I would have noticed."

"Don't be ridiculous. We're just . . . friends." It's safe to say that. He's not nothing to me. I can't pretend that any-more.

"Truly. Not even Tabatha." At the mention of Tabatha, she clucks her tongue and shakes her head. "Poor Tabatha. I mean, dying sucks . . . but dying while pining away for some-one who wants nothing to do with you. Blows." She lifts off the bottom bunk and starts undressing.

Caden wanted nothing to do with her? For a moment I debate my reply before deciding it's one of those things that doesn't require a response.

Junie's fingers deftly unravel her braids. Pulling a fresh shirt over her head, she vaults up to the top bunk. "Looks like you'll be staying awhile now."

"I'm still leaving," I insist.

She responds with an indifferent grunt.

I stare at her on the top bunk for a moment. She laces her hands behind her head, gazing up at the ceiling. Only another day for her. When the lights go out, I wonder if she'll think about Tabatha and the others who died today. Will she think about the man she killed? Will she dream of their ghosts?

Her words sink in. *I'm going to be here for a while.* I drop down on the edge of the bed and stare blindly at my dusty boots. I know I disagreed with her, but I'm not sure how I even feel about it anymore. I had wanted to leave so badly, but when I saw Caden tonight—

Phelps knocks once and breezes into the room. "Hey there, Davy, welcome back. Let's look you over again. Heard you had a rough night. Shame about Tabatha."

I manage a small snort at this monster of all understatements.

He stops in front of me, chafing his palms together to warm them. "You just can't stay away, can you?"

Rhiannon follows, looking less exuberant. Her lips press into a grim line as she surveys me. The people who died—Tabatha and the rest—I see them reflected in her gaze. A gaze that settles on me. "Can't say I'm happy to see you again. I figured you'd be in Mexico by now . . . along with the others."

My chest pulls at her words. The others. The others, who are all dead. Of course she isn't happy to see me. Me gone would mean everything is all right. Tabatha, one of their own, would be all right. No one would be dead.

Junie and I are the first to the showers the following morning. Only a few of the scouts are up, working out in the training area. Fists pound punching bags and shoes rain down on treadmills. Junie slides me a look as we enter the women's locker room. "I should be working out with them, but after yesterday I'm not in the mood, you know?"

"Yeah." I nod, understanding. It feels strange to simply continue on like nothing happened. Like all those lives weren't lost.

Beneath the showerhead, I bend my neck and let the spray beat into my tired muscles. I'm not sure how long I stand there, letting the water relax me as thoughts burn through my mind. Maybe I should just ask for a map and supplies and head out on my own. It couldn't be worse than the last two times I set out to get across the border.

By the time I emerge from the comforting spray, Junie's gone. A couple of other women enter, hesitating when they see me. I nod hello, and they nod back warily. Grabbing my fresh clothes, I move into one of the bathroom stalls to dress and escape their stares. The instant I'm behind the flimsy door, they erupt in whispers.

Rolling my eyes, I leave the bathroom. A few more people are up and eating breakfast now. I lock my jaw as I walk past the training area. Ruben is there. He presses weights, his face flushed with exertion, a vein popping in his forehead. He starts lifting faster and harder when he sees me. I look straight ahead. *Sociopath.* I wonder if he's ever acted on those impulses or if he is just a socially inept jerk.

Turning down the hall to Junie's room, I spot Caden there in front of the door. He turns when he sees me, one hand lifted midair to knock. "Hey. You're up."

His hair is damp from a recent shower himself. The dark locks gleam black.

"Yeah." I tuck a strand of wet hair behind my ear. It's a self-conscious gesture—the kind of thing I would have done before when Zac first started paying attention to me—and I'm not sure where it comes from now, since that girl doesn't exist anymore. Caden's eyes follow the gesture, and I can't help it. My gaze drops to his mouth, marveling that those lips kissed me not so very long ago. I never thought I would see him again after that kiss, but here we are.

I snap my eyes back to his as I stop before him. "Did you need something?"

He gives a brief nod that's a little curt for him. His usual smiling optimism has fled him. I guess what happened to Tabatha and the others and the knowledge that a spy hides among us has finally chipped away the last of that. Understandably, but for some reason, this depresses me a little. "Have you eaten?" he asks.

"No."

He gestures back the way I came. We walk side by side down the narrow hall. "How's your shoulder?"

"Good." I rotate it in a small circle, testing it for myself.

As we enter the main room, his hand drops to the small of my back, guiding me toward the breakfast line. I pick up an apple and fill a bowl with cereal, trying to pretend that I don't feel dozens of people watching us.

We sit at a table, just the two of us. We don't say anything for several moments, eating in silence. My spoon clinks against my bowl. "Why do they always stare at me?" Dozens of carriers have passed through here. It can't be that. Is it because of Hoyt?

"Do you really need me to answer that?"

I shrug.

"Why should it bother you? We've always been watched." He taps his neck and then motions to mine. "Nothing new, right?"

I frown. "Before this my biggest worry was how to spend

more time with my boyfriend without offending my best friend."

"Maybe you didn't realize it, but they were watching you . . . or they would have never found out you have HTS. Right? Everyone has always been watched."

I shrug again and look over those scattered among the tables, eating their breakfasts. "They blame me. For what happened with Tabatha and the others," I murmur. "That's why they're staring at me. They all died, but I'm alive. They don't trust me and they blame me."

"Davy, that's not logical—"

"Fear never is, is it?" My fingers tighten around my apple. "Wainwright, HTS testing . . . it was all made possible because of fear. Fear doesn't have to be logical. It's still one great motivator, though."

He inhales and exhales, holding my gaze for a long moment. "You're right. They're scared," he returns. "That's why they stare at you."

"They're scared of *me*?" I hadn't meant that they were scared of *me*. I was being more general. I meant they were afraid of everything going on out there. They were afraid of being caught. Of dying. It still strikes me as crazy that anyone could fear me. Even if I have taken lives. I'm Davy. Former music prodigy who frequently complained of cramps to get out of gym class.

He nods once.

"And you're not afraid of me? Why not? Everyone else is,

but you're sitting here with me. You want me to stay here." At least he did before.

He lifts his gaze from his food. He smiles like he used to before I left this place. Like I amuse him. "No. I'm not scared of you." The warmth in his amber eyes makes my stomach feel fluttery, and I look back out at the room again. "They're just not used to living with fear yet."

I would think anyone marked a carrier would be well acquainted with the sour taste of fear by now.

Silence stretches. He's waiting, his gaze fastened on mine. "Are you used to it yet?"

I shrug. "I've learned to control what it is that I feel."

He chuckles and takes a bite of toast. "You're so full of it. You'd like to believe that. Or better yet, you'd like me to believe it."

I square my shoulders. "Believe whatever you like about me. What are you going to do about your spy?"

His gaze sweeps the room, and he looks tired again. Like he did last night. I resist the urge to touch him. Squeeze his shoulder or something. It's what I would have done for a friend. And he's that to me. At least. No point denying it. When someone saves your life once—make that twice—he can only be called a friend. "I could tell everyone now. But they'll assume the spy is you, of course," he continues, rubbing at the back of his neck. "I don't know if I could even stop them from pouncing on you."

So he's trying to protect me? My chest tightens. "How are *you* so sure it's not me?"

He looks at me, his eyes clear and deep and full of faith. Faith in me. It's humbling and not something that I feel I deserve.

"Because you would have had no way to get a message out to anyone. And you didn't even know where you were going to be. I realize that." He nods out at the room. "But they'll be too emotional to see it that way. And in Marcus's case, too stupid."

"So you're going to keep this to yourself?"

"Telling them will lead to hysteria. And your lynching."

I pull back my shoulders. "Don't worry about me."

His lips lift in a half smile, and his gaze skims me leisurely. My skin shivers, turning to gooseflesh. As though he's actually touching me. "Funny. Little late for that."

The tightness in my chest intensifies. "So what are you going to do then? You can't pretend he isn't here . . . watching us." Waiting for the next time he can betray us. Kill us.

"I'm going to set a trap." He takes a long swig of orange juice from his carton, his throat muscles working. It's a mesmerizing sight.

"What kind of trap?"

"Not sure. Need to figure that out. Our advantage is that this spy doesn't know we know he exists."

Our. That single word fills me with equal amounts elation and trepidation. I don't want to belong here. I don't want to be a part of something again.

I shake my head, wondering if it's not too late for that and feeling a little panicked. "I don't have any ideas—"

"C'mon, you're smart. You have to have an opinion. I gotta

keep things together until the General gets back. If Marcus had his way, we'd be charging off daily, shooting anyone not sporting one of these." He motions to his neck.

My hand goes to my throat, fingers closing around it. It's strange that in this scenario, an imprint is the great unifier.

He leans forward across the table. "And do me a favor— stop pretending you don't care. I see you under your tough-girl act."

I don't say anything, simply suffer his hard, all-seeing stare until he moves, pushing back from the table. "Think about it. I'll stop by later." He gathers up his trash and leaves me at the table.

I follow his progress across the room. He joins Terrence and together they disappear into the hall leading to the controls room. Not a glance back for me. No opportunity to insist that it's not an act. And maybe that would just be pointless anyway, because I suddenly recall my use of the word *us* when talking about the spy.

I already see myself as one of them. As a part of this cell. A part of Caden's life.

Conversation between the United States chief of staff and Dr. Louis Wainwright

SWITZER: It's been brought to my attention that your camps aren't living up to your predictions. They're overrun. The last report showed a remarkably high death rate within the camps, and the number of escapes and escape attempts is alarming. The president is quite concerned. . . .

WAINWRIGHT: What reports are you referring to? I haven't released any—

SWITZER: Do you think I'm not privy to such information?

WAINWRIGHT: Of course, I'm only concerned at the accuracy of the information you're receiving.

SWITZER: Oh, rest assured, my information is accurate.

WAINWRIGHT: Results take time. You need to be patient.

SWITZER: Given the current climate, time and patience are two things the president possesses very little of. Nor you, for that matter. . . .

TWENTY

I KNOW THE MOMENT CADEN STANDS UP IN THE
middle of dinner that he's going to make some kind of
announcement. It's a crowded room, almost every chair occu-
pied. Even my table is full. Junie's friends, Boyce and Roland,
two other scouts, sit with us.

My fork stalls mid-stir in my spaghetti. A hush falls over
the room.

"I knew this was coming." Junie leans back, crossing her
arms over her chest. The guys at the table nod in agreement.

"Maybe we'll finally get some answers." Boyce fingers the
long ridge of scar tissue that drags down his cheek. He touches

it a lot, drawing even more attention to it, which I think is the opposite of his desire. He's always looking down at the ground—or in this case, his plate—and letting his hair fall low on his face. He's not one of those carriers who enjoys looking menacing.

Roland, on the other hand, looks as pretty as a homecoming king. Not a hair out of place. Even in his fatigues, he looks put-together. "Yeah. Let's at least address the fact that we lost Tabatha and an entire group of carriers." Roland looks at me then as he says this, his dark eyes direct and cutting. "Well, except for this one."

"She has a name, Roland," Junie reminds him with an apologetic look at me, tossing her twin braids over her slim shoulders.

He shrugs. "She's not staying. What's the point of learning the names of those just passing through?"

Caden's deep voice floats over the room. "You all know we lost one of our own yesterday."

Heads nod, and a slow murmur breaks out across the room.

"Tabatha believed in what we've built here. She knew the risks." Caden hesitates, either to let this sink in or pausing for composure. "She was prepared to die for what she believed in." His gaze swings over the room. "It's why my father built this compound. To be a sanctuary for carriers, to help us survive, to fight for what's right. That's still what we're here for, what we're working toward. That's what the General is away doing for us right now." His voice rings out with force and conviction, and something prickles to life inside my chest. I'm not the only one watching with admiration. He's easy to admire. I don't know anything about this General—where he is or exactly what he's doing—but somehow I know this place would be fine without him. As long as they have Caden.

Suddenly I feel like I'm toeing the edge of a cliff, so close to falling. If I just let go. If I just step off and let myself plunge. The idea is there that I could put my hand in his and be okay. My heart flutters inside the ache of my chest.

"Pretty words, but what are you going to do about what happened?"

Caden's gaze sharpens on Marcus. "What do you suggest? Get a war party going and kill everyone in sight just on the off chance we get the people responsible?"

"Sounds good to me," Ruben shouts out.

"Moron," Junie mutters.

"Well, I guess that is an excellent plan—for getting us killed. But the idea here is to survive." Caden looks over the room again, his stare resting the longest on Marcus.

When moments pass without anyone else chiming in, Caden adds, "I'm temporarily halting all missions. Patrols are getting too thick out there."

This stirs up some noise in the room, mostly from Marcus's corner. Clearly, his little pack is not happy with the announcement.

"We need to lie low and wait for things to settle down out there. No missions. No convoys. No taking in new carriers." *He means until he ferrets out the spy.* I know this without him saying it, and a warm little feeling hums through me at having this connection with him—this innate knowledge of how he ticks.

Marcus pushes to his feet. "You mean we have to hide like rats in this hole."

A muscle feathers the flesh across Caden's jaw, the only outward sign he gives that he's even heard Marcus. "I've already sent word to our liaison at the cell in Presidio today that we're temporarily not accepting carriers." He nods at Terrence, indicating that he had left and returned today to convey this message. And of course he would have sent Terrence. He's probably the only guy left in this place that Caden trusts completely. Especially now.

"Like hell!" Color mottles Marcus's face. "I didn't sign up to sit on my hands and do nothing!"

Caden finally acknowledges Marcus. "I said this is only temporary. Until I know our position is secure and I'm confident that we're not going to walk into . . ." His voice fades, and I know he's thinking *a trap*. Instead he settles on, "Danger."

"This is because of her." Marcus swings a finger at me, and suddenly I'm the object of all eyes. "This is just an excuse to keep her here when it's obvious she wants to catch the next convoy to Mexico."

My face burns and my breath hitches, my lungs suddenly pinched, unable to take in enough air.

"I won't even dignify that with an answer." Caden's voice is deep and vibrating with suppressed anger.

"He let her go before, you idiot," Junie calls out from

beside me. "Or did he arrange for the entire convoy to be killed except for her?" She snorts, crossing her arms in a huff.

"Good question." Marcus arches an eyebrow at Caden. "Did you?"

My heart stops. You can actually hear gasps at the question, at the implication that Caden arranged for the murder of Tabatha and the others. A long stretch of silence follows. A thousand emotions cross Caden's face before he erupts and charges across the room. "You bastard!"

Marcus comes forward to meet him, a giant grin on his face, eager for the confrontation, and I know this was his hope. He wants this fight. Maybe he even planned to provoke Caden into it. They're cut off, several guys getting between them. Terrence's arms wrap around Caden, holding him back.

"Tabatha was my friend," Caden growls, one arm swiping for Marcus.

I realize I'm standing—that I've vaulted to my feet like so many others in the room. Only their expressions are bewildered as they look back and forth between Caden and Marcus. Clearly they're reconsidering who should be leading them while the General is away, and this makes me feel a little panicky.

Something churns inside me as I watch the torment flicker through Caden's face. The idea that they think he could have arranged the death of all those carriers, of Tabatha, that he could have been behind my own death had I not slipped away from the camp when I did, moves through me like a steamroller. It's not right. I quiver with indignation. The sudden need to protect him, shield him, surges through me. I squeeze my hands into fists, my nails cutting tiny moons into my palms.

"Anyone else think this way?" Caden's gaze sweeps the room, his brown eyes gleaming fire. "Anyone else think I'm up for sabotaging what my own father worked so hard to build? That I would kill one of us in this cell?"

Several eyes dip and study the floor almost guiltily. Marcus stares hard out at the group, his expression one of frustration. Clearly he wants others to step up and take a stand against Caden, but their faith in Caden isn't shaken. At least not to the degree that Marcus wants.

"Then it's settled," Terrence announces, releasing his hold on Caden. "We're in lockdown until it's safe enough to resume activities."

Normalcy slowly returns. People continue eating.

Caden and Terrence leave the room, Marcus and Ruben hot on their heels. Clearly the discussion isn't entirely finished, but apparently the remaining conversation will be held in private. Junie and I exchange looks before following. After those accusations, this involves me now, and I intend to be present.

Marcus's voice can be heard inside the controls room. Junie pushes the door open and stands there with her hands on her hips like she has every right to be a part of this discussion. I hover behind, a little to her right. Caden and Marcus stand nose to nose, ready to go at it.

"This isn't over. They might believe you today, but that

won't last," Marcus is saying. "Not after I convince them that you're letting that girl impair your judgment. They're starting to doubt you. You've lost objectivity. Suddenly she's back here and now you've halted all convoys. Convenient," he says with a sneer, his strong features twisting into something ugly. As ugly as his thoughts.

"You're wrong." I don't even think. My voice just spills out of me in a loud tumble of words, rising over the room. "I've decided to stay. So I'm not the reason we're in lockdown." I twist my fingers together until they feel numb and bloodless and add again, determined for everyone here to understand that Caden is not some evil villain, "I'm staying."

I'm not sure who looks more shocked at my announcement, Caden or Marcus. Caden quickly masks it, though. He lifts a hand to rub at the back of his neck. Only I notice how that hand has the slightest shake to it. His eyebrows draw close together as he looks at me, and I know he's trying to figure out why I did what I just did. The others in this room might not think twice about what I just said, but for Caden it carries meaning. I've given him my trust.

Marcus's expression twists into anger, and he looks like he wants to tear me apart. Nothing new, I guess.

"You're staying?" Junie demands.

I actually let her question roll around in my thoughts, trying to be honest with myself. *What am I saying?* I still have to get to the refuge eventually. My friends are there. And my hope for the future.

Meeting her probing gaze, I nod once, trying not to feel

guilty over the lie. Especially since she's really been the only one I could call a friend here.

"It seems your accusations are unfounded," Terrence smoothly inserts.

Marcus storms off, Ruben close on his heels. Caden's gaze catches mine. He sends me a single nod of acknowledgment. He might not fully understand my reasons—I don't even fully understand them—but he appreciates my help.

Suddenly the dinner I ate moments before tastes like dust in my mouth, and I'm afraid I'm going to be sick. What have I done? Even worse than these feelings is the sudden realization that staying here with Caden doesn't seem like such a bad thing. Still feeling Caden's gaze on me, I murmur something and flee the room. I don't make it far down the hall before a door swings open and Marcus and Ruben step out.

My pulse jumps at my neck. Clearly they were waiting for me. I start to spin around, not too brave to head back into the main room crowded with people to avoid them. Only another one of Marcus's goons stands there. I don't know his name, but I've seen him around Marcus before, hovering at the periphery.

When I turn to face Marcus, he's already moved in front of me. I square my shoulders, convinced that showing fear will only satisfy him.

"You just don't stop, do you?" His nasal voice comes out softly, and my skin reacts with a shiver. He brushes my hair back from my ear, and everything inside me contracts.

I knock his hand aside and try to walk past him, intent on

getting to Junie's room and closing myself inside. Even as I try, I know it won't work. A guy like Marcus is used to getting his way. He's not letting me go until he's done with me.

He grabs my arm and slams me against the wall. I wince. The force sends my teeth rattling inside my head. "I'm talking to you."

I reach for my voice, lost somewhere inside my constricted throat. "And I'm not interested in hearing what you have to say."

He laughs cruelly. "I love how you think you have a choice." He pushes his face closer, and I smell dinner secondhand on his breath, fumes of tomato and garlic. He must have had more than one helping. "I don't know what you have going with Caden, but it's only going to make things worse for you. You're in for a rude awakening if you think staying here is a good plan."

"Yeah, if I were you I'd keep my mouth shut until the next convoy goes across," Ruben chimes in.

" 'Cause you're going to be on it. You're not staying." Marcus taps me on the collarbone with a gentleness that grates and makes me want to take a bite out of his hand. "You don't get to kill one of us, my own cousin, and then park yourself here for the long haul." His eyes fix on me with that dead evenness I've come to recognize among carriers. Not all of them, but enough. At least from the ones always eager to inflict pain.

"Understand?" He steps closer and lifts his arm, angling it against my throat, his forearm grinding into my windpipe. I sputter, pretty certain he doesn't expect me to answer him.

Speech is impossible. Breath is impossible.

And then he's gone. A body rushes past me in a blur, taking him out. I gasp, suck precious air into my lungs. Caden collides into Marcus, crashing them both hard into the ground. They tumble together in the hall, all writhing limbs and smacking fists.

Ruben shouts something and makes a move to separate Marcus and Caden, but Terrence is there, bigger, more intimidating. He places a hand flat on Ruben's chest, holding him back. "Stay out of it. This is their fight."

And it is. Even if Marcus took exception to me for killing his cousin, this has been brewing for a long time between Caden and Marcus.

I watch, still laboring for breath, my hand holding my throat. Terrence stands beside me as the hallway grows more crowded, people attracted to the fight. Apparently the smack of bone meeting bone travels.

Caden overpowers Marcus, straddling him and punching him several times in the face until Marcus quits moving. A few voices call out encouragement, but for the most part everyone holds silent as Caden delivers a final crack to Marcus's mouth.

Blood runs from Caden's nose as he grabs Marcus's shirt by both fists and pulls him up, snarling into his face, "You touch her again and I'll kill you."

A shiver runs through me. Marcus manages a whimpered moan that might have passed for some kind of affirmation.

Caden gives him a small, single shake and drops him back to the floor. Rising, he sweeps everyone a heated look, his gaze lingering on Marcus's friends. "Understand? She's under my protection."

A cold chill skates down my spine even as heat blooms across my flesh. Everything inside me that's strong, that's used to fighting for myself, rebels at the idea that I need his protection. But that other part of me, the part that feels fluttery and breathless in his presence? It revels in the idea that he cares about what happens to me that much.

Caden staggers forward in an unsteady line, his boots echoing in the narrow, overcrowded hall. Suddenly I feel claustrophobic. Too many people. Not enough air. At least I tell myself it's this. It's this and not everything that just happened. Caden stops before me, his chest rising and falling as though he just completed a marathon. Ruben helps Marcus to his feet, but the action must have cost Marcus. He groans.

Caden tears his gaze from me and scans all the faces again. When he sees a wide-eyed Junie, he orders, "Pack up her stuff for her." He looks back to me. "She's moving into my room."

He did *not* just say that. Stamp me as his property. In front of everyone. He's gone too far. My face heats, burning all the way to the tips of my ears. Marcus must have damaged my larynx—I can't quite find my voice as Caden grabs my hand and leads me down the hall. Bodies part for us and still I can't speak. Emotions burn through me, blistering a path too hot, too savage. I might do something I regret. I take small sips of air, trying to cool my simmering emotions.

I want to hit him, lash out, and my anger frightens me a little. Usually I'm in control, but he just bulldozed through my barriers, knocked them to rubble, and now I feel exposed. Naked and vulnerable.

I dam everything up inside and try to patch up the walls as my feet trip after him. We enter the hall leading to his room. Alone in his room will be soon enough for me to unleash on him—

Alone in his room?

Suddenly that doesn't seem like such a good idea, either. Not when I feel this raw and battered. Not when he's acting like a caveman. Everyone has a breaking point. Maybe he's reached his.

I yank back, but his grip only tightens. We're almost to his door. Once inside, it will be harder to break away.

I shake my head, telling myself to stop flipping out. This is Caden of the eternal optimism and too many smiles. *You're thinking of him as a predator. The same way you've learned to think of all carriers.*

But he *is* a carrier. Sometimes I forget that because he seems so good, so blessedly normal in a world that is anything but.

I bring my other hand down on his and claw him. His curse hisses out on the air. His grip loosens for a split second. Enough time for me to slip free. I spin and head back the way we came, not even bothering to think how pointless running is. *Where can I go? Who can help me?* I thought he was the safest thing in this giant tomb beneath the earth.

Of course nothing is safe. I thought I understood that, but then I started to think of him differently. I began to let him stand in a separate category from everyone else. I even lied—put myself at risk—to protect him. *Stupid, stupid, stupid.* He's not the exception to the carrier rule.

A hard arm wraps around my waist.

"Nooooo!"

He lifts me off my feet like I weigh nothing and carries me, legs kicking, arms flailing, the remaining distance to his door. He turns the latch and thrusts me inside.

I guess he's confident I'm not going anywhere, because he releases me. His mistake. He turns partially to shut the door, and when he faces me fully again, I'm ready for him. I unleash.

My hand lashes out and smacks him across the cheek. His head snaps back, an oath bursting from his lips.

You would think I'd be accustomed to violence by now. Especially violence committed by my very own hands. But my stomach instantly knots. I'm going to be sick. My throat constricts, keeping the bile down. My eyes burn.

I press my palm against the outside of my thigh. The sting there rivals the discomfort squeezing my chest.

"What the hell was that for?" he demands.

"How dare you?" My voice quivers, betraying me. I'm not the cool, calculated carrier. When I hurt someone, everything in me hurts, too. *Especially when I hurt him.*

His eyes blaze down at me, more amber-red than brown, and I fight against the shiver threatening to roll through me. Fitting, I suppose, for a carrier to have red eyes. It's a healthy reminder of what he is . . . that he snapped back there when he got into it with Marcus. That I'm in an enclosed space with a dangerous person.

"How dare *me*?" He fingers his cheek where my handprint stands out starkly. "That's the thanks I get for saving your life? What count is this, Davy? I've lost track."

I flinch but refuse to let him play with my head. I don't owe him. I'm on my own. Owing him is like handing him a piece of me, and I have to keep myself intact.

"I could have handled Marcus. You didn't need to rush in. And you really didn't need to haul me in here and announce that I'm staying with you. You don't own me. I'm not your property!"

"I didn't say—"

"You may as well have. What were you thinking?"

"That's the only thing they understand." He waves an arm wide. "I did it to protect you . . . just like you protected me back there when you told everyone you were staying." He cocks an eyebrow, taunting me. "Unless that was true and you had a change of heart?"

"I'm not staying!" I hiss. "I felt sorry for you. Marcus was going to turn everyone against you."

That wipes the smile from his face. "What did you just tell me? You can handle yourself? Well, ditto, baby."

"Don't worry. I won't get involved again. I'm only here until the next crossing—"

"Yeah. You've only told me that a hundred times." He moves in, stalking me, no more the smiling Caden who left me so bewildered in the beginning. Now he looks every bit the menacing carrier. This I know. This I understand.

I back away, my feet shuffling, veering away from the bed. I collide with the wall. Maybe not the softest destination but safer.

Wall at my back, Caden at my front, I hold myself still and meet his stare.

"So you lied for me because you felt *sorry* for me?"

I nod, maybe too quickly.

"Interesting." The word is uttered calmly, but he looks far from calm. He looks furious.

"They need you here." I shake my head. "*You*. Not Marcus."

He angles his head, the anger draining from his expression. "You care about everyone in this compound so much then?" His gaze roams my face, but he looks skeptical. "Why don't you just admit you care about me?"

I swallow, wishing I had somewhere to go—that there wasn't a wall at my back. "I just wanted to undermine Marcus. He wants everyone to doubt you . . . and apparently that means convincing them this lockdown is your attempt to keep me here." I shrug. "Which is really a stupid, far-fetched idea anyway, but whatever."

He lifts a short, butchered wisp of hair from beside my ear and rubs it between his fingers like he's testing the texture. "Is it so far-fetched for someone to want to keep you around?"

A lump the size of a golf ball forms in my throat.

"No one keeps me. I'm not a pet."

He inclines his head but still holds on to my hair like it's something too precious to let go. "No. You're like some wild bird, aren't you? Batting its wings and flying against the cage door. Even if it hurts you. Even if it kills you. You won't stop. Even if no one is out to hurt you, you won't stop." He tucks that strand of hair behind my ear, and I flinch at the brush of his fingers on my skin.

I shrug, slap at his hand. "So what? You just described everyone in here. All of us."

"No, the rest of us will keep to this cage. It's protection from the dangers outside. In here, we have shelter. Freedom. Each other. We wait for the door to open, and when it's safe, only then do we go out. You? You don't care as long as you're gone. Away from the rest of us. From everyone. Me."

My eyes flare at his whispered *me*. Can he know how hard I have to fight myself around him? I stare at him, at those flecks of red-gold in his brown eyes. Everything he says is too close, too real, and the rawness that I felt before he carried me in this room is ten times worse.

"But you care." His eyes glow hotly. "I know you do."

"Why? Because I told one little lie for you? Get over yourself. It's not about caring. It's about doing the right thing."

"Such a little machine, aren't you?" he taunts. "With no feeling? No heart?" The words fly fast, his teeth a snap of white in his tanned face. "That's what you want me to think, isn't it?"

"I don't know what you're talking about. I'm not trying to *be* anything with you—"

"Yes, you are." His voice rises, deep and hard like bullets flying. "You're so busy trying to survive and not get hurt that you've built all these walls around you. You want to get to your friends, this Sean guy . . . but what happens when you find them? When you're with them? I bet you can't be around them, either. I bet you don't let even this Sean touch you—"

"Don't! Please!" I hate how close to the truth he is. He's right. *God.*

I've been lying to myself. It's not about feeling uncomfortable here at the compound or among these new carriers. I'm uncomfortable anywhere with anyone. With everyone. *I can't be around people because the girl who could relax and laugh and sing died the moment she took her first life.*

But then I realize that's not entirely true. Because Caden makes me feel alive again. Being around him actually makes me happy. As much as I don't want to admit it, I enjoy life around him.

He keeps going as though I didn't beg him to stop. "So you reunite with them, then what? You think you'll be okay? Will you relax then and be able to forget that you're a carrier? Will that giant chip on your shoulder disappear?" He's squared me in, his arms on either side of my head, palms flat on the wall. "You think running from here, from me, like a scared little girl will fix what's broken in you?"

Words form on my lips. I choke on them and try to shove past him. Tears burn my eyes, and this is maybe the most humiliating thing of all. More humiliating than knowing he knows I'm broken and scared. Now he knows how weak I am, too.

He doesn't let me move an inch past him. He stands before me like an unbreakable wall. I knot my hands into fists and beat against his chest.

"Davy." His voice comes out soothing, and that's worse than his caustic, mocking tone of before.

"No! No!" I slap his chest at each word. "I don't care what you say. I am leaving here and finding my friends and I am going to be okay. I'll find . . . I'll be me again . . . normal."

I gasp as this confession flies from my mouth. Even he looks stunned.

Then he does the unthinkable. He laughs. "You think you can go back to before? That you can be normal?"

God, did I just say that? Did I really think normal could ever happen for me again? I guess I did. I do. I think it's out there still, waiting for me. And the first step to finding it is getting away from here and reaching the refuge. I'd built it up in my mind as a place where I could begin again, and it had to be.

But the look on his face, and especially his laughter, wakes me to the fact that I'm delusional. That's never going to happen. Running from here, I might as well keep running. Because I'm never going to find normal. I'm never even going to find something better. I can find my friends, but even they can't give me that.

His hands close on my shoulders. He gives me a small

shake until I'm looking into his eyes. "I'm sorry. I shouldn't have laughed. The last thing I want to do is hurt you. So you can't be normal. Screw it. Normal is overrated. You can make a new life, Davy, as someone who fights and demands change. It can be a good life. A life of purpose."

I'm panting and my cheeks are wet. *God. I'm actually crying.*

"It can be good. It can be," he says softly, closing the distance between us, the half inch separating our faces vanishing as he brushes his lips with mine, murmuring those soft words.

I gasp. He pulls back. My hand flies to my lips, touching there.

He holds my gaze, looking at me questioningly, waiting a moment before coming down again and claiming my mouth.

He leans into me, his chest pressing flush against me, and I can feel every inch of him as his lips slant over mine. The solidness of his body, his narrow hips settling against me. His hands move from the wall, fingers tunneling into my hair.

He nibbles at my bottom lip. "Kiss me, Davy. Kiss me back."

The plea works. Crushes the last of my resolve to dust. He's been under my skin from the start. Pushing me from my self-imposed cage.

My hands creep up his chest and wrap around his neck. The hair at the back of his head is soft and ticklish against my palm. I grab a fistful and deepen the kiss, surrender to the pull I've been fighting.

With a moan, his arms wrap around my waist like steel

bands, and he lifts me off my feet. Without breaking his mouth from mine, he turns us in a circle and walks us across the room.

We lower ourselves side to side on the mattress. He lifts his mouth and we simply stare at each other, our breaths mingling. He combs his fingers through my hair, brushing it back from my cheeks, his expression intent on me. He tugs the end of one lock. "So you're really a blonde, huh?"

"Yeah." My hand flies to the top of my head, where my roots show. "I was going for inconspicuous."

His thumb brushes my jaw, and he murmurs against my lips, "You want to know a secret?" I nod dumbly. "I've always had a thing for blondes."

I laugh lightly, a giddy sensation pulsing through me. "Lucky me."

"I never thought I'd have you like this."

"Like what?" I push back a dark wave of hair from his forehead.

"So soft and sweet, full of laughter . . . letting me kiss you."

I feel the smile he's talking about and try not to let it slip away even when his words give me a small taste of panic. Part of me wants to bolt, but I force myself to stay. I can enjoy this. *Him.* It doesn't mean I'm weak. It doesn't mean I'm going to get hurt.

His voice continues like a deep purr, dragging shivers across my skin. "The last time I kissed you I figured I had nothing to lose. You were leaving anyway." His liquid dark eyes with their fire underneath the surface suck me in. "I didn't think I'd see you again."

I hear something in his voice then. An echo of the same thing that tremors through me. "Me too," I whisper.

Then I'm kissing him, my hand cupping his cheek. It's a heady and dangerous thing, but maybe it's worth it. It feels good to feel again. To let emotion in.

I unbutton his shirt and slip my hands inside, hungry for the feel of him. He pulls back and slides it all the way off. He comes down on me all warm skin and lean muscle. Life. Vitality. I don't even recognize the sounds breaking loose from my lips. Sharp inhalations, contented sighs.

He kisses my neck, my shoulders. His hand moves under my shirt and curves around my waist. I dig my nails into his back, revel in the flex of sinew under my fingers.

I arch, putty in his hands as he works the buttons open on my shirt. The fabric drops with a whisper. Long fingers round my shoulder and caress my stitches.

I wince.

"Did I hurt you?"

"No. It's just not . . . pretty."

"Everything about you is beautiful." His dark eyes melt me, but his words . . . his words undo me.

I smile, feeling shy. Except my hands can't stop moving, stroking his warm skin.

He pushes the hair back from my forehead. "You know you have to stay here with me."

My smile slips and my hands still against him. I don't like those words no matter the sound of them in his velvet voice.

He brushes a hand over my lips as if he can erase my sudden frown. "Don't. You're not a prisoner, and I'm not trying to trick you into staying with me—even though I want you to. I think I've dreamed of you here, like this, ever since you brained me with that rock." He smiles, and I feel my face heat.

I swat his chest. "Be serious."

He catches my hand and holds it over his heart. "I love that you can still blush."

Because I'm a carrier. Someone who's seen it all, done it all, and can still blush. I guess that is a rarity.

He sobers. Looks at me intently. "Claiming you . . . you staying in my cell. It's the only thing Marcus and his crew understand. That you're mine."

That you're mine.

Pressed against him, his heart beating beneath my hand, it's a far too tempting thought. That I'm his. *That he's mine.*

"Please, Davy, this way you'll be safe as long as you're here."

Stay here every night with him until the next crossing? In his bed. Wrapped up in his warmth and arms. Could I do that? And still leave? Without splintering apart?

I sit up and push him back down with a hand on his chest. Leaning over him, I ask, "Does that work both ways?"

"What do you mean?"

"Does that mean you're mine, too?" I try to keep my expression serious, but can't help smiling.

He looks startled for a second, but then he sits up suddenly on an elbow, sliding one hand to cup my cheek, fingers burrowing into my hair. Only he's not smiling back at me. His expression is deadly serious as he utters, "I am yours. Completely."

And it's my turn to be shocked. Peering into his face, what I see there robs me of breath. His eyes are deep and luminous, open and so full of life, so ready to embrace me. *Love me.* If I just let him. If I just let myself. It's everything I've been running so hard from, and I feel so stupid to think I never wanted this again.

I watch him, wondering at these feelings. He makes me feel like I can do this. That HTS didn't end my life. For the first time I see that. I believe it. I believe I can still be someone. Not the girl I used to be, but someone else.

Maybe even someone better.

I pull a hard, bracing breath into my lungs. Maybe I'm eventually leaving this place—I don't know anymore—but that doesn't mean I can't have this while I'm here.

Sliding my hands around his neck, I bring my mouth back down to his.

Conversation between the president and the chief of staff

PITT: Who's in charge of the Resistance?

SWITZER: Uh. I don't understand, sir . . . I don't know that any one specific person is.

PITT: This isn't happening without someone taking control and directing movements. They have to have a leader. Someone they all respect. I want to know who . . . Find him.

TWENTY-ONE

WE KISS THROUGH HALF THE NIGHT. FEVERISH kisses that leave me aching. He always pulls back just before things get too carried away, and that's a peculiar thing. For a guy. It hasn't been so long that I don't remember that much. Zac had been a master at persuading and cajoling, getting in my head and twisting me around his finger. I just didn't know it then. Manipulating me, wanting to possess me. I thought that was love. I wouldn't have resisted him much longer. If my DNA hadn't turned up positive for HTS when it did, I would have given him what he wanted, thinking it was what I wanted, too. And I guess my heartbreak would have been that much more crushing, because there would have been even more regret wrapped up in the crumbling bits of my life.

It had never felt like this with Sean, either. Never so real. Sure, there had been butterflies in the stomach and heady kisses, but it had been me running from life, terrified and looking to hang on to something. With Caden I'm not running from life. I'm running *toward* it.

My whole world turned on its axis when Caden dragged me into this room. I discovered that I can't run from emotions, from feelings. It's like hiding from the sun. And Caden is the sun to me. Warm and bright, he seeps into every pore.

And since I can't hide from the sun—or him—I might as well embrace it. I'll hold him close for as long as I can. I may never get another chance. In this world, I may not even get another tomorrow.

"Davy." Caden says my name, but I hardly hear him. I'm kissing his jaw, his neck, the smell and taste of him making my heart race faster. The good kind of adrenaline. Not like getting shot or choked, which is all the experience I've had lately.

"Davy," he groans, his hands flexing on me. "Davy," he repeats, his voice more insistent. He tries to sit up, but I push him back down.

I hold his face in both hands and kiss his mouth again, silencing him that way. Kissing him is addictive. Like a drug. When my hands drift lower and brush his waistband, he seizes my wrists.

"Davy." He bites my name in a strangled voice, his chest quivering under me. "This isn't a race. We have time."

I shake my head. Time? That's the last thing any of us have. "Nothing lasts, Caden." Everything I've ever cared about leaves. And then I'm alone. If I have this time with him, this experience, at least it's one good memory to take with me.

He brings my hands back up his chest. His heart thumps strong and steady beneath my palms. "I'm not going anywhere."

"Everyone thinks that." I search the hard lines and shadowed hollows of his face. No one thinks they're going to lose everything. That when they wake up they'll learn that they have a genetic mutation and *poof!* Everything and everyone that matters will vanish.

He pulls me down and tucks me against him. "We're going to take our time, because we have time." His words gust against my ear, and it's tempting to believe that deep, velvety voice. I know he means it. Somehow in the cesspit that's become our world, he has clung to his optimism, his faith in mankind, in a world that's good.

I know better.

Still, I cuddle against his chest and let his arms hold me close, listening to the thump of his heart and his warm exhales against my cheek.

"Tell me more about who you were," I say.

"What do you mean?" His voice rumbles beneath my ear.

I grimace. I made it sound like I was asking who he was for Halloween or something. "Before this," I qualify. He was someone else. Just like I was someone else. No one plans for this. This just falls on you. Like a ten-story building.

"I'm the same. Pretty much."

I tense, thinking about this . . . that he could be the same, that he thinks he is.

"I mean, I guess I didn't go to West Point like I probably would have. Assuming I got in, but I was a legacy. My dad and grandfather went there, so my chances were good."

"What about music? Singing? You gave that up, right?"

"Nothing would have come of that anyway. I did it for me then, and I still do. No one stops me from singing or playing on my guitar when I want to."

I tap my fingers lightly on his chest. "You have a unique sound. You would have changed your mind once you started performing." Once he saw how he could reach people . . . at his first standing ovation.

He nods to his guitar in the corner. "It's not anything I lost."

Lucky him. I wish music still lived inside me. "Sing," I whisper. "Sing to me." Like before.

He's silent for a long moment and I think he's not going to, but then his chest purrs deeply beneath me as lyrics float over the air above my head. I press my lips to his skin, so grateful . . . even happy.

It's been too long since I let music inside my soul. Not since the last time I heard him sing.

Caden is right about having time. A week passes while in lockdown, and it does seem like we have all the time in the world together. There was a brief hint of awkwardness the first morning we emerged from his room. Hand in hand we entered the main room. All noise died as everyone swung to stare at us.

I might have fled if Caden didn't pull me forward, his hand wrapped snugly around mine, his thumb drawing soothing circles inside my palm. We stepped into the line for breakfast, and soon activity resumed.

For the first time people actually smiled at me. Maybe even better than that, Marcus didn't look at me at all. No more threatening scowls from him or his goons.

The only thing marring the misleading haze of perfect coloring our world is the fact that a traitor lurks in the compound. The moment we leave the safety of Caden's room each morning, the tension is there, lining Caden's jaw, guarding his eyes. I notice it because I know what he's like at night with the door shut. The gentle smiles, the teasing, the easy sighs between our touches and kisses.

He keeps me with him throughout the day. At first, I simply think this is because things have changed between us and he can't get enough of me in the same way I can't get enough of him. But it's more than that, I soon realize.

One afternoon, as Caden, Junie, and Boyce pore over maps and discuss the next supply raid after the lockdown is lifted, Terrence waves for me to follow him. Stepping from the room, he offers to show me the inner workings of the controls room.

"Taking pity on me?" I ask.

"You look bored."

In the controls room, Terrence gives a cursory nod to

another carrier listening intently to whatever he's hearing from his headphones while simultaneously scribbling on a notepad. Terrence gestures at the row of computers and equipment like a proud papa. "This is all military issue . . . we *borrowed* it when we first set up operation here. I've got it wired to connect to most of the US information networks," Terrence explains.

"Wow," I murmur. "How . . ."

"I worked on a system like this when I was in the military. That's where I first met Caden's father and the General. We're able to collect intel and use it to help carriers, gather supplies, prevent raids."

But it can't protect from everything. They didn't hear anything to help save Tabatha and the others.

I point to one of the headphones. "Can I listen?"

Nodding, he helps me get set up, punching a few keys on a keyboard and securing the headphones on me. I'm listening to gibberish that I don't entirely understand, most often coordinates being rattled out by patrols and agents alike, when Caden finds me half an hour later. His face is white and his mouth bracketed with stark lines.

"What's wrong?" I demand, rising up from the chair where I was listening to the various snippets of conversations broadcasting between patrols in the area. I pull the headphones off my ears and hand them to Terrence.

Caden doesn't answer, just shoots Terrence a dark look and hauls me off to his room. Once inside, he releases my hand and faces me. "I didn't know where you were." His voice, his intense gaze, remind me instantly that there's a killer out there. Not just a carrier who *could* kill or *might* kill. There's no supposition to this. And now I understand why he kept me so close. It's not simply my scintillating company. Necessary or not, he's trying to protect me.

He motions with his hand. "He's locked in here with us."

I nod, sobering.

"Until we capture him, you're not leaving my side. I promised you nothing was going to happen to us . . . that we have time . . ." He pauses, his throat working as he swallows. "That you can have something good with me, something that lasts for once. I'm going to prove that to you." His voice fades then and I step forward, touching his cheek and ignoring the pinch near my heart.

"I get it. Okay?" I smooth a hand over his face, brushing his lips that have become so familiar to me, hoping to get rid of his frown. When that doesn't work, I kiss him, hating seeing him so scared for me. I prefer him mad to that, and that's when I realize his happiness has become as important as my own.

I should have known Caden would come up with a plan. He's not a leader by default. Sure, his father got the ship up and running, but Caden's not the kind of guy to stand by and watch as the world moves past him.

My father always used to complain about my brother's lack of ambition. Especially after he dropped out of college. He said there were doers in life, and Mitchell wasn't one of them.

Not that I agree with Dad's low opinion of my brother, but the categorization always stuck in my mind.

Well, Caden is, unquestionably, a doer.

When Terrence knocks on our door one night after dinner, I can tell this is no random visit.

"We're all set," Terrence says.

Caden nods. I rise from the bed, where I had been reading one of his books.

"Hey," I greet, looking between the two of them, my familiar wariness quick to grab me. I trust Caden, but that doesn't mean I trust the reality we live in. I cross my arms and look between the two of them. "What's up?"

"We came up with a plan to catch our rat," Caden explains.

A plan only he and Terrence know. And now me. I warm inside. He's known Terrence for a long time. To be trusted alongside him makes me happier than I should probably feel.

"Let's hear it," I prompt.

"I'm lifting the lockdown next week and sending out a group for supplies."

"You're setting a trap," I state, knowing there's no way he would lift the lockdown and risk the mole getting out to relay information to the enemy.

"That's right." Caden nods at Terrence. The former soldier says nothing, simply crosses arms over a chest that any wrestler would envy. "Terrence is going to stand watch at the exit through the next several nights."

"You think he'll try to sneak out."

He shrugs. "Maybe. We've been in lockdown for over

a week. He's probably anxious to get out and communicate with his Agency contact."

I nod slowly. "It sounds like it could work."

Caden flashes me a grin. "Of course it will. Where's your faith? I'll make the announcement in the morning."

He opens the door for Terrence. "Get a good night's sleep, T. You're going to need it starting tomorrow."

He closes the door and pulls me into his arms. I step forward willingly, loving the way his hands move on my back, his fingers skimming each tiny bump of my vertebrae over my shirt.

"Thanks for telling me," I say.

"Are you so surprised to know your opinion matters to me?"

I stand on my toes and kiss him, letting that serve as my answer as I marvel that I ever thought I could resist this. Emotions. Feelings. *Him.* All the things that separate the living from the dead.

No more hiding from that. No more Cage.

Conversation between President Pitt and General Dumont
Undisclosed location:

PRESIDENT PITT: General, pleasure to finally meet you. Your reputation precedes you.

GENERAL DUMONT: I'll let you begin, Mr. President. You wanted this meeting.

PRESIDENT PITT: I want this all to end.

GENERAL DUMONT: I had nothing to do with the attack on Agency headquarters.

PRESIDENT PITT: Be that as it may, you are a recognized leader among the Resistance. You are much respected. Your lead is followed. If we can reach a peaceful accord . . . let's just say I want this country to live another century without imploding.

GENERAL DUMONT: Then start by getting rid of Wainwright, the Wainwright Act, and the camps.

PRESIDENT PITT: (laughs lightly) Is that all?

GENERAL DUMONT: It's a start. We'll talk about restitution once that happens.

TWENTY-TWO

NEWS THAT A GROUP WILL BE GOING OUT FOR SUP-
plies next week lifts spirits. It might be that everyone is simply
tired of eating spaghetti and looks forward to getting some
new staples. More than likely, it's just the promise of getting
back to normal again. A return to routine. The lockdown
frightened everyone and put them on edge and everyone only
wants things to go back to the way they were before. When
there was at least an illusion of safety.

Days pass as Terrence stands watch as agreed, but so far no
one has attempted to leave the compound. We see him in the
mornings at breakfast, after his watch each night. We don't

expect anyone to slip away during the day when they can be observed leaving. It's disappointing. Especially for Caden. These people, this compound. He sees them all as his responsibility.

Some nights, the worry and anxiety get to him, and I have to convince him not to leave our cell and go check on Terrence himself. He listens to me. Mostly he doesn't want to risk the traitor catching him patrolling the halls. And because he enjoys my methods of distraction. Kissing him has become as natural and necessary as breathing.

There's still that clock ticking in my mind, warning me that this could all be gone, vanishing in an instant. So maybe I'm selfish and I want to distract him. For me, I want his full attention for myself.

All I know is that we barely step inside the room after dinner every night before we're in each other's arms. We kiss until I can't feel my lips. Wild and desperate, soul-consuming kisses. We keep our clothes on, because we know taking them off means more. Everything. I haven't pushed to go further. Not since our first night together. He wants to take things slow to prove to me that we have all the time in the world. I still don't know if I agree with that, but I'm not spending time arguing the point. Not when we could be kissing.

"Do you ever think of leaving? Finding someplace else far away?" I whisper this question. Snuggled in the dark beside him, the scent of his warm skin is a heady thing. This holding each other has come to mean nearly as much as everything else. More than the kissing. Talking, listening, connecting with another soul . . . *being* together.

"And go where?" His voice rumbles beneath my ear. I trace patterns on his skin.

"I don't know. Away. Mexico. One of the refuges or someplace else. Anywhere."

"Where can we hide?" His hand strokes my neck, raising goose bumps on my flesh. "We have this." His thumb rubs where I know the H marks my flesh. "Kind of makes hiding impossible."

"I don't know. A cottage up on some mountaintop maybe?"

"Oh. A little hermit's hut? Would you be there with me?" There's a smile in his voice as he continues stroking my neck.

"Maybe," I tease. He likes it when I do that. He likes me playful. He likes my smiles. And I like me this way, too. I've missed it. I thought I lost this side of me with everything else.

He rolls me on my back and pins my wrists beside my head. His eyes gleam darkly at me in the shadows of the room. "I think I could be convinced to go almost anywhere with you, Davy." And then he kisses me long and deep until my toes curl.

Maybe not everything is lost.

On the fifth morning, Terrence doesn't show up at breakfast after his nightly watch. Caden and I get our food and sit down with Junie. I watch Caden play with his meal, flipping his toast over and over in his long fingers, his cheek feathering with tension. After several more minutes, he finally stands. "Wait here."

Junie looks up, appearing annoyed at the interruption to her story of how she broke the nose of a boy twice her size when he decided he wanted to take on a carrier.

I grab his hand and mouth the words to him, *I'm going with you.*

With a curt nod, he leads the way. We check Terrence's room first. Then Caden checks the showers. We search everywhere, all the while trying not to look as though we're hunting for anything in particular.

After we've searched every possible inch of the compound, Caden's gaze drifts up to the stairs that lead aboveground. There's only one place left to look. Caden starts up the stairs. I follow, feeling everyone's curious gazes on us as we ascend.

Caden's worried for his friend enough to draw the attention of the others, including the traitor, to us. He races over the iron grate, swinging right into the tunnel. His tread clangs loudly, shaking the floor under us. His shape disappears as the tunnel darkens. I follow, my hands stretched out in front of me as I run blindly after him.

The faint blue glow alerts me to the chamber ahead. He reaches it first.

His cry of anguish echoes down the tunnel. When I catch up, he's on his knees, his body a darker shadow in the gloom. My blood runs hot and cold all at once. He crouches over something I can't quite identify that's spread out on the floor before him. A big shape. Big as a man. I gulp a breath, my heart thumping hard.

"Cade . . ." My voice is so soft. Like I'm afraid to give any real power to it. Afraid of the response I'll hear.

I shuffle numbly on my feet and peer over his shoulder, seeing for myself what the sick churning inside me already knows.

Caden makes no sound beyond that initial cry. He gathers Terrence close, lifting the big man in his arms like he's a child. I set my shaking hand to his shoulder and move closer. Which only permits me to see better. A sob strangles me, hot as tar rising up my windpipe.

Terrence's throat is cut. The bloody grin gapes open grotesquely.

My fingers clench on Caden's shoulder, and he flinches. I pull away only for a moment before lowering my hand down again, determined for him to know I'm here. He's not alone. "I'm so sorry. . . ."

"I did this."

"No, you—"

"I did this!" he shouts. "It was my plan, my idea!"

There's nothing I can say. I know what it's like to live with blood on your hands. Still, I hold on to his shoulder as if I can take away some of his guilt. As if I can ease his pain.

"Terrence! T! T!" Junie pushes past me and drops down beside Caden, her face bloodless. Even in the dim blue haze, I can see that all the color has been leached from her skin. "Oh! God! What, how— Caden, what happened?"

Others crowd the space. I'm shoved to the side as voices overlap, expressing their horror, demanding an explanation, and in the middle of it all is Caden. Looking lost and broken in a way I've never seen him before, and something shrinks and curls up inside me. The hope and faith that he has so painstakingly brought to life inside me begins to die.

The day passes in a blur. Caden addresses the compound. No one says much. Not even Marcus. Everyone is in shock. One of the captains is dead. Not by any outside threat. One of their own did it. Someone penned up in here with us. This place that is supposed to be a haven, a shelter . . . it's not.

It's no secret anymore. A traitor is among us, and everyone looks around at his and her neighbors with unease. Caden commands everyone to operate in groups. For the first time, he closets himself with Marcus and a few others, leaving me with Junie and Boyce.

Before he went, he pressed a kiss to my forehead and then looked sharply at Junie. "Don't let her out of your sight. Go nowhere. Stay out here in the main room."

Junie nods. Some of the color is back in her cheeks. "Nothing's going to happen to her. Don't worry."

After several moments of silence, Boyce murmurs, "What do you think he's going to do?"

Junie shakes her head. "I don't know. What can he do?"

"He'll catch him." I nod doggedly. "Caden is smart."

"He might be smart, but he's not God." Boyce shoots me a look like I'm an idiot thinking with my girly parts.

"Hey, have some faith." Junie slaps his arm.

"We need the General," Boyce mumbles, fingering the scar bisecting his cheek.

I stare at the door Caden and the others disappeared through. After an hour, the three of us move on to other tasks. I decide to help in the kitchen washing dishes. Mind-numbing work that can be done in relative silence, and I'm still technically in the main room in plain view.

Everyone is quieter than usual, eyeing one another warily. It's one thing to know we all possess a kill gene. We're all unified in that. But this upsets the balance. There's someone among us actually killing, and we don't know who he is. Suddenly we're all hunted.

An hour slides into two, and Caden and the others don't emerge for dinner. My heart races as the minutes tick by with no sight of him.

"I'm sure they're fine in there," Junie offers as she eats. She's trying to be a comfort, but that hardly helps. For all I know, Marcus is the killer and he's in there with Caden. Not a consoling thought.

Then I spot him. I half rise from my seat, waving him over. He doesn't even glance my way. Just walks in a straight line past the main room. I frown, sinking back down. I glance from my half-eaten food to Junie, Boyce, and the others.

"Oh, go after him. You know you're dying inside." Junie makes a shooing motion with her hand, urging me to go.

I look up again at Caden's retreating back heading down the corridor to his room.

"C'mon." She stands and starts pulling me along, even though I'm taller and outweigh her by a good twenty pounds.

"We won't break his rules. I'll keep an eye on you until you get inside the room." True to her word, she stands at the end of the hall, watching me. The door isn't locked, so I enter without knocking, wondering if I should have. Oddly, in this moment, I feel uncertain around him. He's lost one of his best friends, his closest ally. He probably doesn't want to see anyone right now. Even me.

And yet I can't stay away.

"Caden?" My gaze lands on him on sitting on the edge of the bed, his head buried in his hands. I cross the room and sit beside him. "Are you okay?" I place a hand on his shoulder, not surprised to feel the tightly corded muscles there. He feels like he's ready to snap apart.

His response is a heavy sigh. I smooth my hand over his shoulder in small circles. "I'm so sorry, Caden." I hesitate and wet my lips. "Did you and Marcus come to a decision?" As the remaining two captains, it's up to them where to go from here.

His hands tighten in his hair, and I wince, convinced he's hurting himself. "There's someone in here killing and plotting with our enemies on the outside. I don't even know if they slipped out after killing Terrence and liaised with anyone and then slipped back inside." He lifts his head and stares at me with anguished eyes. "I've promised to keep you safe here. You must not have a lot of faith in me at this point."

My heart bleeds at the torment in his expression. "Caden, don't—"

His body turns into me, his hand sliding to cup my face. "No. I've watched you for days pretending with me."

I blink. "W-what?"

"You kiss me, touch me, let me talk about us having a future like it's something you want, too, but I see the truth in your eyes every single time." He nods his head as though willing me to admit it. Both his hands thread through my hair, holding my head in place, forcing me to hold his gaze. Not that I could look away. "You're biding your time. You've never planned on being with me beyond the moment."

My heart races and I feel like a cornered rabbit, caught, nowhere to run. He sees right through me. I open my mouth and gape, trying to come up with something to say, to deny the truth that he flays me with like a whip.

"Caden, you don't—"

"Oh, shut up," he whispers, bringing his lips crashing over mine.

I know instantly this kiss is different. Every other time he kissed me, there was a level of restraint. He always claimed we had time. That we didn't need to rush. He always held back, pulling away a little whenever things got too heated, whenever I kissed him a little too hard. Now he's kissing me hard, heedless of clanging teeth.

His hands roam my body, make quick work of buttons. He hesitates at nothing, and neither do I. Trembling, he stretches out beside me, and it's like he's something from a dream. If I blink, he'll vanish.

His mouth follows his hands, the contact searing. Skin on skin. Hands, lips, warm whispers on every curve, every hollow.

His face returns to me, staring deeply, one hand cupping

my cheek, the other molded to my hip. His amber eyes gleam
darkly at me.

I nod and then swallow, overcome, the taste and scent of
him swirling all around me, reminding me that I'm still alive.

Looking into his eyes, I can see today echoed there, and
I know he's not that confident anymore. He's seizing this—
me—because he's not convinced we have the time he always
promised.

His lips curve in a grin, but the haunted look is still there
in the shadows of his eyes. It tears at me, so I wrap my arms
around his shoulders and hug him close, hold him like I'll
never let go.

His hands stroke my arms and slide down my sides, trail-
ing over me. "Your skin is so soft."

I smile against the tantalizing warmth of his shoulder,
feeling slightly drunk, giddy with sensation and the rumble
of his voice.

"Davy." He breathes my name, tastes it like it's something
delicious. I kiss him again, lose myself in the pressure of his
mouth on mine. His hands. His body. Whispered words and
sighs. I savor the moment and wonder how I ever thought I
could have him—all *this*—and walk away.

Gentle snores wake me. I smile and prop myself up on one
elbow. Caden sleeps with one arm flung above his head and
his other hand resting on his ridged abdomen. I shake my
head. He really is beautiful. I watch him sleep for several more
minutes, my fingers curled against my lips. I can feel my idiot

grin against the backs of my fingers.

Sighing happily, I reach for his shirt and pull it over my head. I'm not going to fall back asleep any time soon. I slide off the edge of the bed and move to his desk, thinking I'll find something to read. Reading always helped loosen my thoughts. Maybe I can help Caden come up with a new plan to catch our traitor. *Our.* Yeah. Because I'm in this.

My fingers trail the surface of the desk. I skim over his military history books. No light reading there. I open a drawer. My hand falls on a picture of a man in uniform with a young boy. It must be Caden with his dad. His father has the same amber eyes. Caden grins, adorable with one of his front teeth missing. His father's hand covers Caden's smaller shoulder, and there's something so loving, so accepting in that pose that it makes my heart squeeze in longing for my own family.

Lowering the photo to the desk, I notice a paper with a LabCo insignia in the drawer. At first I don't even understand what I'm looking at. I start to look away from it, but a single word, a sentence really, stops me. *Subject HTS negative . . .* I read it again, fully, starting at the top of the document, a lab report, absorbing it all with a terrible clenching in my stomach.

As comprehension settles, everything inside me wilts. The clenching in my stomach turns into a violent twist, and I think I'm going to be sick. All the euphoria of earlier evaporates, lifting from me like a melting fog. I turn. Still clutching the document, I gaze at him on the bed, still so beautiful, his face innocent, guileless. *It's the face of a liar.*

Dropping the paper, I grab for my clothes on the floor and

quickly dress myself, tossing his shirt off me like it's poison on my skin.

I'm lacing up my boots with shaking fingers when his voice rumbles on the air. "Davy? What time is it? Come back to bed."

I cringe, closing my eyes in a pained blink. I fumble with my laces and start over.

"Davy?"

Turning, I whirl around, my face hot with fury.

He props himself up on one elbow and scrubs at his eyes. "What are you doing, baby?"

"Don't call me that."

He focuses on my expression and frowns. He sits up, and the sheet pools around his waist. A distracting sight, the way the muscles in his abdomen ripple. "What happened? What's wrong?"

"You lied to me." The words scream inside me for all that I whisper them.

"What are you talking about?"

"You. Lied. You told me to trust you."

He drags a hand through his dark hair. "Davy, I don't get it. What are you saying?"

I laugh brokenly at his bewildered expression. "I knew I was taking a risk. What did I really know about you, after all? Just that you're a leader, a captain of the resistance. And a carrier. But nothing I couldn't handle. I left a place surrounded with people who would rather slit my throat than lift a hand to help. But gradually, you made me believe this place was different. You showed me proof that carriers don't have to be violent. They could be good. *You* were that proof. I began to think a carrier could be good because you were. But that's not true. You're not even a carrier. You're just a normal guy."

A normal guy. *Normal.* Something I can never be. Even he told me that—to stop longing for normal. And yet he's just that. The gulf between us never seemed wider.

I grab the paper off his desk and wad it up and fling it at him. It hits him in the chest and drops to the bed. He picks it up, his face bleeding of color. He rubs a hand over his jaw. "Guess I shouldn't have kept this."

"Yeah. Not so smart. But I have to wonder why you were hanging on to it. Did you think it might save you someday if the Agency ever caught up with you?" I laugh thinly. "You could show them you're not a carrier." I shake my head slowly side to side, the betrayal hot and acrid in my mouth. "Why? Why would you want anyone to think you're a carrier when you're not?"

He drags a hand through his hair again. "My father didn't want me to join the Resistance. He wanted me safe. With my mother. My sister. But I just didn't see it that way. So I went ahead and got the imprint." A faint smile hugs his lips. "Dad was so pissed."

"Stupid," I snarl, and come at him, hitting him in the chest with both fists. He pulls me down on the bed and flips me on my back, looming over me. "You could have been safe," I rage into his face. "But you chose this? This life!" And ended up with me. "Stupid, stupid! You made me think we're the same."

"We are," he insists. "We can be together."

"No." I hit him harder. "We don't even belong to the same species! How could you do it? You shouldn't even be here." Then I would never have met him. Never have fallen for him.

He lets me beat him for a moment before grabbing both wrists and pinning them on either side of my head. "We're not different species. We're the same. We're both people."

"No!"

"I believed in the cause—"

"Why? Why?" I'm not sure what I'm even asking. Why did he choose this life? *Why did he break down my walls and make me love him?*

I'm sobbing now, and I realize it's been a while since I gave in to serious deep-from-the-chest tears. They're not like when Phelps dug a bullet out of my shoulder. Or when Caden found me in the desert. Or that other time in his room. Fine. I might have cried around him before, but these tears feel different. Because they feel like the last he will ever see. The last I will ever permit myself to shed in his presence. They feel like tears of mourning.

"No one would listen to me, no carriers . . . they wouldn't let me lead them if they knew I didn't have HTS. I had to do this if I was going to be of any use."

I try to pull away, but he still clings to my wrists, pinning them to the mattress.

"Let. Me. Go."

His eyes sweep my face, a nearly physical touch. Finally he

releases me, but even as he does, he says, "I'm not letting you go, Davy. Ever."

The determination with which he utters those words sends a ripple of sensation through me that makes me remember everything we did, everything we shared together in this bed. My cheeks flame hot at the memory. I scoot to the edge, dropping my legs over the side as I rub my wrists like I can rid myself of his touch.

"This was a mistake." I moisten my lips. "I knew it. I knew I shouldn't have let myself—"

"No." He closes the distance between us again and takes hold of my shoulders, his voice a harsh growl. "Don't say that. You and I are not a mistake. We are fate."

I shake my head with a snort, tempted to cover my ears. I can't do this with him. Can't hear any of this.

"I thought that we were alike, that we were coming from the same place, that we faced the same future, the same struggles." I'm babbling now. Tears burning at the backs of my eyes. This is what I didn't want to happen. What I refused to let happen. To love and die from pain when it all fell apart. When I end up alone. Again.

I realize now that I had been contemplating forever with him.

His hands tighten and he hauls me against him, lifting me onto his lap. "We are! You don't see that? You don't know?" His eyes lock on me, looking deep, seeking something, everything. He takes my hand and forces it over the steady thump of his heart. "Don't you feel it between us? You're a part of me now, Davy. I'm a part of you. I'm not letting you go."

I choke on a sob. "Don't do this—"

He kisses me then. Not like the other kisses. This one is tender, pleading, soft and tormented. It breaks me. Or would. If I wasn't already broken.

I wedge my hand between us and tear free. "No!" Standing, I jab a finger in his direction. "Don't touch me again."

Spinning around, I charge from the room.

"Davy! Stop!"

The door slams after me, muffling his cries. I don't look back, just push ahead blindly, not thinking about where I'm going. About the fact that there's nowhere *to* go. I'm trapped in this tomb, and the one person I loved, who I thought could love me back, doesn't exist. He never did.

Conversation between the United States chief of staff and Dr. Louis Wainwright:

SWITZER: The camps are finished. The president is ordering them disbanded.

WAINWRIGHT: You can't do that! Where will we put the carriers? Where will—

SWITZER: It's not really your concern anymore. Congress is opening a special investigation into your research data behind HTS. And Wainwright . . . you might want to start polishing up your résumé.

TWENTY-THREE

THE COMPOUND IS STILL AND SILENT. EVERYONE sleeps. I don't think about where I'm running—that there is nowhere *to* run—just that I have to get away from Caden.

He's not like me. *He's not a carrier.*

Everything inside me shudders. I press a hand to my stomach. It hurts to breathe.

"Davy! Davy!" I turn at the hiss of my name. Junie stands in the doorway of her room to my left, blinking like she's surprised to see me.

Behind me, Caden bellows my name, and there's a ring of panic to his voice that tempts me—makes me want to turn and run back into his arms like that's where I belong. I can see him in my mind, struggling into his clothes, his movements fierce and desperate.

But not as desperate as me.

He'll be out in the hall after me any second, and that terrifies me. The idea of coming face-to-face with him makes breathing even harder. To see him now, knowing he's normal, he's *good* . . . someone I shouldn't even be in the same room with. *God*. I can't do this. *I can't!*

Junie follows my gaze. "You two have a fight?"

I nod. A fight? Yeah. You could call it that.

She steps back into her room. "C'mon. You can hide in here," she offers with a small jerk of her head, her twin braids loose and unraveling over each shoulder.

I plunge into her room. She shuts the door. We press our ears to it, listening together. Moments later Caden's feet charge down the hall, loudest the second they come flush with our door; then they grow faint as they recede.

He's gone.

"Thanks." I sigh, staring into Junie's probing gaze so close to mine. She smiles slightly and moves away from the door.

"Want to talk about it?"

I rub the center of my forehead. Do I want to talk about what a fool I was to trust someone again? To let someone inside?

I open my mouth, then close it with a snap, feeling suddenly so very tired. Drained, depleted. What am I supposed to do? Tell her Caden's secret? That he's not like us? As betrayed as I feel, I can't do that. I can't reveal that about him. Because I still care enough about him to protect him.

"Must have been pretty bad for you to run out on him in the middle of the night." She moves to the table and unscrews the cap on a water bottle, takes a long swig. "Especially 'cause we're talking about Caden. I've seen him without his shirt." Her eyes widen meaningfully. "It's impressive, you know?"

Yeah. I know. "Well, I guess it's been an all-around crappy day." I move to the bed, ready to sink onto the bottom bunk and wait for morning.

And then leave. Take what supplies they'll give me, a map—with a scout or not—and just go.

"Are you so surprised that you've had a crappy day?"

I stop and turn, looking at her curiously. Usually Junie is the upbeat one.

"I mean, do you think you're immune to crappy days or something? You're a carrier no one wants in a place full of carriers . . . that kind of sets you up for misery."

I angle my head. "Excuse me?"

She fiddles with the electric lantern sitting on the table, making the room a little brighter. "Well, I guess Caden wants you. Or wanted? Which is it?" She arches a fine eyebrow, waiting, hoping I'll elaborate more about why I ran out of his room. I compress my lips. At my silence, she laughs harshly, staring straight ahead as she brings the bottle back up to her lips for another drink. "He always had shit taste in women."

I hold my hands out in the air, shaking my head at this girl

I'm suddenly not sure I like anymore. "What are you talking about?"

"First Tabatha. Then you."

The air rushes from my mouth as understanding sinks in. I take a step back until the back of my skull bumps against the top bunk, feeling sucker punched. "You're in love with Caden."

She snorts. "Ding, ding, ding! Give the girl a prize." Her gaze swings to me. "I'm not the first girl. But I'll be the last. Once he sees how good I am for him. How suited we are."

She faces me fully. "I thought Tabatha was the problem. That if she wasn't around, he'd be more willing to move on. But her body wasn't even cold before he started looking at you. You wove some kind of spell over him."

"You don't have to worry. I'm leaving," I whisper, my fingers digging into my palms. *He's yours,* I start to say, but can't. Even if he isn't mine, I don't want her to have him. Besides, he's not some toy I can give away because I'm done playing with him. He's Caden. And he's better than all of us. Than everyone here. I don't deserve him, but neither does she.

"You *keep* saying that." Her lip curls up over her teeth. "Sorry if I don't believe it. Tabatha told me she and Caden were finished, too, but that didn't keep her from throwing herself at him every chance she got."

I push away from the bunk. "I'm not having this conversation with you." I cross the room for the door, but pain bursts through my head. I blink up at the ceiling, unsure what happened or how I even ended up on the floor.

A loud ringing blares in my ears. I lift a hand to my head and pull back my arm. Blood coats my fingers.

Light spins, shadows dancing on the walls. The electric lantern rocks on the floor beside me. Junie wraps her hands around it and carefully sets it back on the table.

I open my mouth, but words won't come. A sick, withered little moan escapes me.

"You're right. Talk is overrated. I'm more of an action person myself." She steps over me, her boots squared on each side of my body. She grips a knife. "I got rid of Tabatha. I can get rid of you, too."

Junie's the traitor? The thought chugs through my throbbing head. That means she killed Terrence, too?

"Why? Why did you kill Terrence?"

"I'm sick of this place! Everything . . . everyone in it . . . keeps getting in the way of me and Caden being together. It's too much pressure on Caden. If this place falls, then he can be free. We can slip away and be together."

I stare up at her, one eye blinded by the blood running from the pulsing gash in my head, only one thought pumping through me. *She's crazy!*

Rap! Rap!

The beat of knuckles on the door sends Junie's head popping back up. Her wild eyes fasten hard to the left as Caden's deep voice drifts into the room. "Junie, sorry to wake you . . . is Davy in there with you?"

I open my lips wide, but Junie pounces on me, slams a hand over my mouth. I scream against her moist palm, manage to get out some sound before she digs the knife into my throat. The sharp point pricks my flesh, and I feel the warm ribbon of blood trail down my skin.

"Junie?" The door starts swinging open. My eyes strain from the door to her face. She does the same. I feel her panic. Getting caught red-handed by Caden isn't part of her plan.

"Don't come in," she commands. "I'm not dressed."

The door halts its progress, hangs open a half foot.

"Sorry, Junie. Have you seen Davy?"

"No." Her gaze flicks to me, darts over my face in warning as she pushes the blade in deeper. More blood runs, a pulsing chug, hot on my skin. "No, I haven't."

The door starts to close again, and with it my hope dries up. Once he's gone, she'll finish me. Stick my body somewhere else. He'll never know she's the one. Life in the compound will continue with her by his side. She'll keep trying to infiltrate her way into his heart. Nausea rolls through me. Temporarily. Because resolve sweeps in then, hardening in my veins. My hands curl into fists at my sides. I won't leave him to her.

She's going to kill me anyway. Either now or later. At least I can make sure Caden knows who did it.

Opening my mouth, I bite down on the inside of her hand until the metallic taste of blood runs over my teeth. She cries out. Her hand flies off my mouth and I scream.

The door flings open and slams back against the wall. I catch a glimpse of Caden's horrified expression as I jerk to the side, trying to roll away as she pushes down on the knife. I knew it would come. The blade rips my flesh. Blood gushes.

That's the cost. The price I'm willing to pay. I know that, but it doesn't stop the pain and terror.

I see the satisfaction light her eyes a second before Caden tackles her.

Her weight flies off me and I slap a hand over my neck, trying to stall the blood, frantically trying to force the skin and tissue back together. A wasted effort. It pours steady as a stream between my fingers.

I watch them wrestle, my body growing cold. So cold as I lie on the floor. It doesn't take long for Caden to gain the upper hand. He twists the knife from her, not even flinching at her cry of distress.

He slaps her when she lunges for it again, a madwoman, desperate to win. The slap spins her back to the ground. "Enough, Junie!" he shouts, wielding the knife.

Panting, she curls up on her side on the floor. "Caden," she whimpers. "It's for you. For us."

Shaking his head, he scrambles over to me. "Davy, Davy, baby." He carefully lifts me against his chest. "Let me see." He peels back my fingers from my neck and his face goes white.

"Bad?" I rasp between my labored breaths, no longer cold. Just numb.

His eyes lock on mine, and the anguish there is all I need to know. "No, not bad. Nothing Doc can't handle." He places my hand back over my neck. "Push down for a sec." He pulls his shirt off and carefully wraps it around my neck, removing my hands and tying off the fabric, assessing my face. "Not too tight?"

I murmur some form of assent. I can still breathe.

"Caden!" Junie is standing now, holding another knife. It's her room. I guess she would know where to get one. She cocks her head, looking at him with wounded eyes. "I only wanted you to want me. I did it all. For you."

He sweeps me into his arms and stands, holding me close, his body wired tight, ready to react. "Get out of the way, Junie."

Her gaze travels over me in his arms and then darts back to his face. "Why? Why wouldn't you let me love you? That's all I ever wanted."

"Let us pass. Now, Junie."

The angle of her head sharpens, and her eyes cloud like she can't quite believe he doesn't understand . . . doesn't care. With a small whimper, she lifts her chin and turns the blade so that it points to her chest. With a cry, she plunges it into her body, defiance bright in her gaze.

Caden turns away before her body even hits the floor. Bellowing for Phelps, he races me toward the infirmary.

Phelps is up, standing in the doorway as we arrive.

"Hang on, Davy. You're going to be fine," Caden says as he lowers me to an exam table. He clings to my hand as Phelps comes over, snapping commands to Rhiannon. I don't look at them, though. My eyes stay on Caden, darting, memorizing, loving his face, the angles and hollows, the slope of his dark eyebrows over his deeply set eyes.

He's still too pale, and his eyes are bloodshot. Moisture gleams in the agonized depths. "It's not so bad," he assures me.

I choke a little on a weak laugh. "Still a liar."

My hand slips from my neck, no longer able to hold on.

I always thought death would be something blissful, but it's not. It hurts.

A piercing ringing stabs me in the ears. My body is one giant wound, every nerve expanding and contracting in agony. And then there's my neck. It burns fire, and each time I turn my head the barest fraction it feels like someone is taking a hacksaw to my throat.

A moan slips past my lips, and I frown. That's not right. Should I be making sounds? Moaning? Should I be feeling pain? Feeling anything at all? I inhale thinly, dragging air through my nostrils as I take in the aroma of astringent.

Should I be able to smell when I'm dead?

"Davy, Davy. Come back to me, Davy."

Now that whisper, that voice, should definitely *not* be floating around in the land of the dead. I whimper, my head rolling to the side, and then gasp at the burst of wildfire that shoots lancing, blistering heat through my neck. The reason I'm dead at all is because I let Junie stab me. And I did that so he would be safe from her. Caden shouldn't be dead.

And if he's here, then he's not dead . . . I'm not dead.

My eyes pop open and I gasp.

"Davy!"

My gaze flies around, squinting at the bright light, at the face above mine, his midnight-dark hair haloed in so much yellow. And that voice, saying my name.

I lift a hand to shield my eyes from the light and focus on his features. He looks gaunt, pale beneath the tan of his skin. A smile cracks his face. "You came back to me, Davy."

I work my lips before managing to get out, "I'm not dead."

He laughs hoarsely, the sound laden with relief. He smooths a hand over my forehead. His fingers catch on something prickly and sharp, and I wince.

"Oh, sorry, those are your stitches. Are you okay?"

I gingerly touch the one-inch row of stitches on my forehead.

"Might leave a scar," Phelps volunteers, peering around Caden at me.

Caden shoots him a brief glance. "Doc?"

"Hm?" Phelps sends him a mild look.

"Can you give us a minute?"

Caden's attention turns back to me as Phelps shuffles from the room. The door clicks after him.

He leans down, propping his elbow on the mattress, his eyes scanning my face, staring at me like he can't believe it's really me he's looking at. "I'm so sorry, Davy."

For what? Lying to me? Being someone I can't possibly have in my life? Or does he mean the almost dying thing?

He presses his mouth to mine. I close my eyes at the warm texture of his lips. My mouth moves slightly in response. I can't help myself. I cling to his bottom lip, savoring him, reveling in the taste that's so innately him, something I know I would recognize in the dark—crisp, clean, faintly salty—even years from now.

I turn away, severing our kiss, even though the movement makes me hiss in pain. He stares down at me, searching my eyes, reaching, looking for something in me that isn't there. Not anymore.

I work my throat and find some words. "How long have I been out?"

"Since yesterday."

"I thought she cut my throat." I cringe, remembering. Junie pressed over me. That knife arching high, bearing down, slicking through my flesh like butter . . .

"She did. Missed the artery. Doc stitched you up. You need to be careful. Stay in bed. No ripping those stitches."

I do have a tendency to do that.

He takes my hand and brings it to his mouth. "So cold." His warm lips move against my knuckles. He chafes my hand between his, working heat into my bloodless fingers. Suddenly he stops and closes his eyes. "I thought I lost you."

You did. The words whisper through my mind, but I don't say them. They seem cruel. And even though they're true, I don't want to hurt him. But it's like he hears them anyway. He looks up from my hands, his amber gaze hot with intensity. He shakes his head at me, conveying what he thinks of this.

"I have to go." I manage to get the words out, even as impossibly thick as they feel in my throat.

"No," he says, still shaking his head. "We can send word to

your friends that you're staying—"

"Caden, I can't stay with you." *I can't be with you.* "You and me . . . we don't fit." Me, a carrier. Him, passing for a carrier.

He moves so suddenly I think he's going to climb up on the bed with me. Our noses almost touch as he thrusts his face closer, planting both hands on either side of me and looming so close I can count those flecks of gold in his eyes. "How can you look at me and *lie* like that?"

"*Me?* I'm not the one who lies." My voice falls hard as flint.

"This is all because of a piece of paper you found?"

"It's what it means."

"What about what *we* mean?"

Forgetting about my neck, I shake my head and then freeze in pain.

"You're still running, throwing up your walls," he accuses. He takes my face between his hands, his thumb grazing my cheeks in small, roving circles. "You're grabbing on to this because it's the excuse you need to run. I love you, Davy. Nothing about that scares me. Nothing, you hear me?"

But it scares me.

And it's not just an excuse. What would I do the day he wakes up, regretting sentencing himself to the life of a carrier? He has a choice. He doesn't have to live this way. He has a mother and sister out there waiting for him. He can embrace normal. College. Marriage. Kids of his own someday. What happens when he realizes that being with me is just too hard? What happens when he turns his back on me? I won't survive that.

I moisten my lips. "Your traitor is dead. No reason you can't let me go now."

He shakes his head, his expression bleak, and something shudders inside me at the sight of it. "You're not going to listen to me, are you?" He inhales, his chest swelling.

"This isn't my world here." I brush a hand over his cheek. "It's not my life to live." *It's yours. Your lie you're living. At least until you decide not to live the life of a carrier anymore.* I don't say the words, but he hears them nonetheless.

"You want me to go out there and tell everyone the truth? Is that what you want? I'll do it. Right now." His voice softens. "For you, I'll do it, Davy."

I shake my head. "No. It doesn't matter what any of them know. I know." *I'm the broken one. Not you. You deserve more. Everything.*

Moisture brims in his eyes. "You can't go. I won't let you, Davy."

"Yes. You will. Because it's the right thing to do. And you always do the right thing."

He stares at me for a long moment, silent. Some of Phelps's equipment hums in the corner, but that's the only sound.

In the quiet, there's just his searching eyes and the steady pain thrumming through my body. The pain will fade. My body will heal like it always has. My heart is another matter.

It is with a heavy heart that I address you today. Recent events have proven to me that this country needs me more than ever now. I firmly believe that things will not improve. And yet I stand before you no longer with the support of this administration . . . the Wainwright Agency is closing its doors. God help us all.

—Dr. Louis Wainwright in a press conference upon the termination of the Wainwright Agency

TWENTY-FOUR

IT TAKES A WEEK AND A HALF FOR PHELPS TO PRO-
nounce me well enough to travel, and four more days for
Caden to make all the arrangements for the crossing.

Caden didn't ask any of the other scouts to escort me to
the border. He did it himself.

It would have been easier in the company of Boyce or someone else. Anyone. No tension. No uncomfortable silences. No
staring at the hard, strong back moving in front of me, leading
me away from the compound and his life, remembering the
texture of his skin beneath my fingers. No stopping heart and

seizing breath when he accidentally brushes against me. And the worst is when we actually look at each other. When my eyes meet his and the connection sparks between us. When that thing that's been there from the start flares up, reminding me that what I feel for him isn't something that's going to be forgotten or replaced in a month.

But he isn't interested in making it easy for me. Our final good-bye is torture. Misery in a way I could not have anticipated. I made my choice. My decision. It shouldn't hurt so much.

The dark pull of his eyes, the deep velvet of his voice is my new ghost. I know he'll haunt me. "Stay, Davy," he asks so simply, his gaze stark. "Come back with me. You don't have to go."

He doesn't give up easily. Anger radiates off him. He wants to shake me. I can tell, can feel the urge seeping from him. I moisten my chapped lips.

"If I could force you to stay," he adds, "I would, but I know you'd hate me."

I nod even though it's not true. I could never hate him, but it's better he doesn't know that. No sense revealing the power he has over me.

My feelings for him, the love I feel . . . it terrifies me. It's not something I can trust.

It's more than him lying to me. *He's not a carrier.* Such a simple distinction, and yet it weighs heavily. I'm scared enough. Almost every waking moment for so long now I can't remember any other feeling. I can't choose a fate where that fear has no hope of fading. With him, each day, there would be fear. Fear of disappointing him. Losing him. Fear of just being who I am—what I am—around him.

So I smile at him and stamp down on the impulse to touch him, caress his face. "You'll be glad someday—"

"Stop telling me what I feel. You have no idea. If you understood how I felt, you wouldn't go. You'd believe in us."

I stop talking for good then, sealing my lips tightly shut. Our farewells are done.

There's nothing left to say.

My guide in Mexico is an old man not much taller than me. If he speaks English, he keeps that fact to himself. All communication is conducted in nods and gestures. No sound passes his withered lips. Not even a grunt rises up from his frail-looking chest. His face is as weathered and lined as the brown earth taking each hit of my boots. His cheeks are sunken like the many ravines and gullies rutting the broken landscape. His black eyes remind me of an animal, staring out with some manner of prescience.

Before we parted ways, Caden assured me he was the best. "Mauricio is smart. Do as he says."

I nodded, holding silent. That was enough recommendation for me. Caden would never leave me in the hands of someone unqualified to get me safely to refuge number four. *Caden would never leave me....*

I squashed the thought. *I* forced this on him. Well. Short of putting a gun to his head. I made him turn and walk away from me.

He adjusted my straps on my shoulders. "That comfortable?"

He still cared, still worried about me even though I was leaving him.

I nodded my answer . . . my thanks. Even if I wanted to talk, the golf ball–size lump in my throat made that impossible.

His hands stilled, gripping my straps. His gaze flickered over my face like he was memorizing it. "Be careful, Davy. I hope you find what you're looking for."

I watched him go, trying to remember what that even was.

Oddly, I feel comforted by my guide's presence—this quiet old man who seems a part of the land. Small talk isn't necessary. He got me across the river with none of the drama of my first crossing, and I'm confident he'll get me the rest of the way, where I need to be. *Where I need to be.* I worry such a place doesn't exist for me.

At night, he directs me to smooth the ground of rocks before unrolling my sleeping bag. As I stare up at the stars flung across the immense sky, I'm convinced I'll never be able to sleep out here in the open with a stranger only a few feet away from me. I keep seeing Caden's back walking away from me, his long strides taking him farther and farther away, his figure growing smaller on the horizon until Mauricio made me start walking.

But then suddenly it's morning again. We pack up and get moving, drinking from our water bottles and eating power bars as we head out, walking hard through the day.

It's dusk when we arrive there. Refuge number four emerges almost magically out of the land. We crest a ravine and it lies below like some village of old except with modern conveniences. Vehicles are scattered through the assortment of buildings. Mostly small houses, a few trailers, but there's a large metal-sided building. The closer we inch, the more I can see of the hangar and the nose of an airplane inside it.

When I'm finally standing in the middle of the bustling camp, a dog trots up to me and sniffs at my legs, tail wagging in greeting. I pat its head, feeling like the new kid on the first day of school. Anxious and uneasy—like I might be sick any moment and puke all over my shoes. In this case, not expensive leather but my well-abused hiking boots.

Mauricio motions me forward now. Like a parent shooing their child into the classroom. I made it here. I just need to walk. Step forward, left foot, right foot, and find my friends, and everything I set out to do will be done. I get some curious looks as I pass through the refuge, but no one seems overly concerned at my presence. A small group of women sit beneath a tree, shelling beans into bowls. I feel their eyes on me. One waves, and a quick glance over my shoulder reveals Mauricio waving back. Of course they would recognize him. He probably brought a lot of them here, too.

I spot Sabine first. Her chestnut hair shines with gold highlights in the sun as she walks out of a flimsy-looking building balanced on cinder blocks. She's wearing a blue sundress. It's casual and a bit faded, the hem frayed at her tan calves. The sight of her gives me a start. I've never seen her in a dress before.

It shows off her shoulders. She has lovely shoulders, slim and smooth, slightly toned. She seems more grown-up somehow. Not that girl who shadowed me at Mount Haven. Those days suddenly feel so long ago.

She's carrying a box, propping it on her hip for support. I stand frozen. I glance down at my grimy clothing. The green cargo pants and the ill-fitting, long-sleeved button-down shirt. I've been wearing button-downs ever since I was shot. I'm covered in dust and grit from the journey. I touch my cheek, certain I look a mess. Stitches mar my forehead. My neck is covered in gauze that must be more brown than white. Phelps insisted I keep it on and only change it out once I got here, so the wound stays as clean as possible.

I stand motionless, my voice locked in my throat. She spots me then. Her gaze passes over me and then jerks back.

Then she moves. Drops her box and races toward me, crying my name. She grabs me and hugs me, squeezing so tightly I have to wince—I'm still pretty much one giant walking bruise.

She pulls back, both hands gripping my arms. "You made it! They said you were alive, but that was, like, over a month ago. We were beginning to doubt it!" Her smile is huge, probably the brightest I've ever seen from her.

"I'm here now," I say dumbly.

Her gaze strays to my forehead and neck, and she frowns. "What happened to you?"

"Nothing that won't heal."

Except my heart. That won't ever heal. That still feels like a twisting, crushed mass in my chest. Or an empty ache right dead center because it's gone. Left behind.

"Well, come on. Sean and Gil will be so happy to see you." She loops her arm through mine and God help me . . . but I feel the impulse to pull away.

Curious stares follow us as we pass through the camp. I look around and spot my guide. He's sitting in the shade under that tree with the women shelling peas into bowls. Someone has given him a beer. He tilts his head back and drinks deeply. A pair of boys race past, tossing a football to each other. It's such a normal scene.

We move between two buildings and Sabine chatters on, so unlike that solemn, watchful girl I first met. She's comfortable here. I smell meat cooking over charcoal somewhere nearby, and my stomach rumbles.

"Are you hungry?" Sabine squeezes my arm. "We'll find the guys and then go get something to eat. I'm sure you're exhausted, too. I think I slept twenty-four hours straight when we first got here."

I spot Sean first. He's hard to miss. I'd forgotten how big he was. He and Gil and another guy bend beneath the open hood of a truck that doesn't look like it's started for the better part of the century. Sabine doesn't call out, but it's like he knows. His smoky-blue eyes lift up and lock on her. A slow smile spreads across his face. Then his gaze drifts, evidently catching the movement of me beside her. His hand stills, stops turning whatever it is he was rotating inside the engine.

His gaze scans me, head to toe, missing nothing, not the wounds on my neck or forehead. Even though we haven't been apart so very long, it feels like forever since I felt his eyes on me. We're different. Him. *Me.* I know it instantly. Even further apart than the last time we were together.

I appreciate him almost clinically. His dyed hair is longer, some of his blond already showing at the roots. He's pulled it back into a short ponytail. The tat on his bicep dances with his movements as he hands off his wrench to the guy beside him and edges around the truck toward us.

He approaches me with his long-legged stride, and I start to hyperventilate. Not really, but it feels that way. As good as he looks coming toward me, there's another face there, filling my mind. Maybe part of me thought that when I clapped eyes on Sean I wouldn't think about Caden again. I wouldn't compare his lean ranginess to Sean's muscular bulk. That I would remember the way that Sean used to make my pulse stutter, and that's what I would feel around him again. It would be all that mattered once more. But no. Nothing.

Nothing familiar stirs my blood. If anything, the ache in my chest that's been there ever since I found that piece of paper in Caden's desk, ever since I woke up from near death on that exam table, intensifies.

Sean reaches me and hauls me into his arms without a word. He wraps me up, engulfs me in the immenseness of his body, and . . . there's nothing. His touch doesn't *bother* me. It just doesn't affect me, either.

I break down. Tears spring from my eyes, and noisy, angry sobs burst from my lips.

"Shhh," he soothes, and I shudder at this first sound from

him. His voice used to get beneath my skin. "You're safe." I cry
harder. Because I don't feel safe.

I don't feel anything.

I thought the moment I saw him and Sabine and Gil everything would be right again. Or at least as right as anything
could be. Certainly, I'd at least feel *better* than I did when I
left the compound. Like I had finally arrived at the place I'm
supposed to be—with the people I'm supposed to be with.

"You're home. You're home, Davy," he assures me.

Home?

Caden's face fills my mind, his eyes, his voice telling me
that we're a part of each other.

No. It can't be. He can't have been right about that. The
tears come harder, faster, as I face the truth. I can't have been
wrong, but I know. The knowledge swims through my blood,
settling into every particle of me.

This place is not my home.

The rooms are more comfortable than I expected. Behind the
small houses and trailers stretches a clapboard building that
sleeps eight. It's reminiscent of military barracks I've seen on
TV. No air-conditioning, but a fan whirs noisily on top of
a table, stirring the warm air well enough. The showers are
outside, enclosed by a tent. Sabine pointed them out to me
after we grabbed a sandwich from the mess hall. She shares the
cabin with three other females, leaving four empty beds. I'm
grateful for the arrangement. There's no picking up where I
left off with sharing a room with Sean. I'd rather sleep among

strangers than deal with that awkwardness.

Two of her roommates are in the cabin when we enter. She introduces me to them and then sits on the bed beside me, her legs swinging off the side. "We were so worried. Even after the message came through that you were okay, I didn't want to get my hopes up. You still had to get across, after all."

"Yeah." I sink down on the bed across from her. "And I didn't manage that the first time."

She frowns and plucks at the blanket covering her bed. "I think the three of us took turns blaming ourselves for that."

I look at her sharply. "Why? It wasn't anyone's fault. I was shot."

She shrugs. "It's not hard to come up with reasons to blame yourself. We each thought that we could have done something."

"You couldn't have."

She shrugs again. "I don't think anyone felt guiltier than Sean."

And this makes me feel guilty. "How's he . . . been?"

She looks somewhere over my shoulder. As though there's something of interest on the wall behind me. "He likes it here. Likes working on the cars."

I nod, glad that he's found something to do here that he enjoys. "And you? What about you?"

She looks back at me. "I like it here. They let me work in the school with the children. I take a morning shift. I can probably get you on the same shift."

Her eyes shine eagerly at me. I nod my agreement, feeling

a little numb. I can't even wrap my head around being here yet . . . seeing my friends. Working in the school seems like a big jump ahead. It feels so long ago since I last saw them, but I know it hasn't been. Not so long that I should feel this yawning chasm between us.

"It reminds me of my little brothers and sisters. I was always stuck babysitting them." She smiles ruefully. "'Course I always complained about it back then. Never thought I would miss having to do that, but I do. Being around little kids . . . they're so innocent. You can forget everything else, you know . . . all the bad stuff, when you're around them."

I nod, understanding. There are plenty of things I miss. Family. Friends. So why is Caden the only face I can see? The thing I miss the most?

Why is he the one person who blocks out all the bad stuff for me?

I inhale and look around the cabin, studying its bare walls as though I might give away some of my thoughts if I keep looking Sabine in the face. "So. What else do you do here? When you're not helping with the school?"

"Oh. Sometimes we ride out in one of the cars Sean works on." She stops to giggle. "Last week, the car died. We had to walk five miles back to camp. Turns out the thing ran out of gas! Sean was so embarrassed. The guys made fun of him." She laughs again, rocking back on the bed a little. "He hasn't quite lived that one down yet."

She's happy. I see that. And Sean's part of that happiness. Does that mean he's happy, too? I hope so. Desperately. I need him to be. I need his happiness to not be wrapped up in me.

"I feel gross." I pluck at my shirt. "I think I'd like to take a shower."

"No problem." She hops up from the bed, that eager light still in her eyes. "You have something else to wear?"

"Yes." I gather my spare change of clothes from my pack. Maybe someday I'll possess a wardrobe again. Not as big as the one I once owned, but something beyond a couple of shirts and pants.

She leads me across the grounds. I blink against the sunlight, still acclimating, it seems, to being aboveground again. I had gotten used to life in the compound. The hum of the artificial air pumping through the vents. The low drone of voices. Out here it's just openness.

And no Caden. I'm not sure I'll ever get used to that.

It's time for this country to heal its wounds, and the re-enfranchisement of carriers into the population is the first step in that process. That said, I've assigned a special committee to oversee the formation of protected areas for carriers should they want to live in communities together. The choice will be theirs. Not only is this their right, but it is my administration's act of restitution for their recent treatment. This nation has lost its way, and our only hope for survival is by remembering our legacy and coming together in a spirit of camaraderie and tolerance. Let us all recall the founding principle of our justice system: Any accused person is innocent until proven guilty. Judgment should not be passed without evidence of a crime. . . .

—Presidential address, July 30, 2021

TWENTY-FIVE

THE NEWS IS SEVERAL DAYS OLD BY THE TIME IT reaches us.

US detention camps have been dismantled. The president has discharged the Wainwright Agency and formed a new committee consisting of a mix of high-level officials and HTS resistance leaders. I think of Caden's General Dumont and assume he had a hand in this. Maybe he'll be on the committee. As one of the leaders in the resistance, and with his former position in the military, it makes sense. It also makes sense considering his recent absence from the compound and Caden's explanation that he was away on important business.

As for us, we only need to wait. The tide has turned. If we want to, we can return to the States with no fear of persecution. At least of sanctioned, lawful persecution. Prejudice will always exist. For that reason, most everyone chooses to stay. For now at least.

Only I don't feel a part of this place. I wait it out. Tell myself to give it time, but two weeks pass, and I'm still not part of the "us" that is Sean, Sabine, and Gil. It's no one's fault. It simply is.

It's not a bad place to be. I've started helping in the school, at meals. There's plenty to do to keep the refuge running. I could have purpose here. Companionship. Friends. Sean, Sabine, and Gil go out of their way to include me, but it feels different. Like I'm an outsider to their threesome, even though I've been here awhile now. Long enough to start fitting in.

The news from the United States is met with celebration. The populace of refuge number four mingles around a bonfire and roasts *cabrito* like it's the Fourth of July. And maybe in a way it is. A new independence day. Someone drags out a guitar and plays.

"You should sing," Sean encourages me at the picnic table where we sit. I give a swift shake of my head.

"You can sing?" Isaac, the guy who was working on the truck with Sean the first day, asks.

I shrug. "A little."

"She's amazing," Sean insists, giving me a nudge.

Isaac holds up both hands in mock offense. "You mean better than my rendition of 'Sweet Child of Mine'?"

At this Sabine, Sean, and Gil bust out laughing. Sabine wipes at her eyes. "Oh, that killed me."

I look from them to the bonfire's nest of dancing flames, uncomfortable. Yet another inside joke I've missed since arriving here.

"Yeah, you had to be there, Davy, but I've never seen a guy sing and dance *simultaneously* like that."

There's been a lot of this. Laughter. Stories I don't get. While I was with Caden, they had carved a place for themselves here. A life where they can be free. Free to laugh. Free to live. Beneath my lashes, I see Sabine hand the barbecue sauce to Sean. Their fingers brush, linger.

Free to love.

It's not the first touch I've noticed between them. Not the first long glance. They're trying to hide it. From me. Maybe from themselves, too. But it's there. While I was away, falling in love with Caden, they were falling for each other.

A whimsical smile plays on Sabine's lips, and the color deepens in her cheeks. I search inside myself, probing for anger, jealousy. Nothing. There's nothing there except envy that they've found this in each other, despite everything. And then I feel a stab of loss that I walked away from a chance for the same thing with Caden.

Suddenly I hear myself speak. Over their laughter and conversation, over the clink of beer bottles and scrape of silverware, I say what I've known for weeks now, even before the news from the States. "I'm going back."

The smile slips from Sean's face. The laughter dies. The clinking stops.

"What are you talking about, Davy?" Sabine demands, leaning across her plate.

My fingers tear at my bread, shredding it into bits. "I'm going back."

"Home? To your family?" Gil asks. "Shouldn't you send word first? It can't be totally safe yet."

"No," I say. "Not home."

"To that resistance group." Sabine states this more than she asks, and I realize then that she knew something had happened to me there. That I had changed.

"To that underground bunker?" Gil asks, looking bewildered. "What for? They'll be disbanding. We've won, Davy."

I don't feel like I've won. Not here. Not without Caden.

Then what he says sinks in. *They'll be disbanding.* Of course. If they're free to go anywhere, why would they stay hiding underground?

"I need to go," I say faster, feeling slightly panicked. What if he's gone when I get there? How will I find him?

"What are you talking about?" Gil shakes his head. "This is your home now."

"No," I say, pushing up from the table. "It's yours. And Sabine's and Sean's. My home is there." I swallow, looking down at all of them. "With him."

The three of them fall silent, staring at me like I've sprouted a second head, and I guess this is some shock. Sabine might have realized something happened there, but I haven't shared much about my time with the resistance group. I never mentioned any people. Nothing about Caden.

Sean is the first to speak. "You're in love with someone."

My gaze jerks between him and Sabine. "And you're in love with Sabine."

A gasp slips from her mouth. I smile at her and reach down for her hand, cover it with my own. "It's okay."

Her gaze darts to Sean. She looks almost afraid. Like he might say he doesn't care about her. He smiles at her reassuringly and then looks back at me. "Let's walk." He pushes up to his feet, dropping a hand to her shoulder for a gentle squeeze. "We'll be back."

With a nod, she smiles, crossing her arms and hugging herself.

We leave the revelry behind, slipping into shadows as we move out of the bonfire's glow. Our steps fall in a steady rhythm, crunching over the gravel path between temporary buildings.

"Guess a lot happened when we were apart," he murmurs, breaking the silence.

"A lot happened when we were together." At Mount Haven. The moment I shot that man. Everything turned in that instant.

"True." He runs a hand through his shoulder-length hair. Stopping, he faces me. "I didn't . . . Sabine and I were together so much. We didn't mean for—"

"Sean, you don't owe me any explanation." *Really.* He doesn't.

He drags his hand down around his jaw. "Yeah. Okay. But Davy, you're sure? You really want to go? We still care about you. *I* care about you."

"I know you do." He stares down at me with his eyes so full of emotion, mute appeal for me to be more like the Davy he first met months ago. Months that feel like years. That Davy wouldn't walk away from him. Not willingly. And if that Davy had been ripped from his arms, he would have waited for her. No female on earth would have tempted him. Not if I had given him something to wait for. His heart is loyal like that.

He reaches out and slides his knuckles down my cheek. "Is he worth it?"

My lips twitch ruefully. "It's more like am I worthy of him?"

"I don't have to know the guy to know you are." He pulls me in for a hug, his hand tight around the back of my neck. "I'm going to miss you."

I flatten my hands against his broad back. "I'm going to miss you, too." One of my few friends through all of this, through everything. I bury my face in his chest, muffling the sob that cracks my voice.

He pulls back and drapes an arm over my shoulder. "C'mon. Let's go eat some barbecue, and you can tell me about this guy." His voice rings with humor, but there's still that undercurrent of regret to it. I understand it. I feel a bit of it myself. A bit of sadness to leave my friends. But there are other feelings, too. Strange feelings. Excitement, determination, and anxiety to get to that place I was so desperate to leave.

"Hey," Sean says near my ear like he can read my mind. "Life is a series of hellos and good-byes, right?"

I nod. That's one way to look at it. "The guy who brought me here—"

"You mean Mauricio?"

"Yeah. Is he still around?" Because over the noisy thoughts and feelings crowding around inside me—there's something else. Another sound in the background. A ticking clock.

It's over. I'll be there soon . . . and then we can all go home now.

—Message from General Dumont to Caden

TWENTY-SIX

THERE'S COMFORT IN MAKING THE RETURN JOUR-
ney with Mauricio. Comfort in the familiarity of his company.
I don't have to wonder at his silence. I understand his gestures.
I fall in with his steady pace, remembering it well. It's easier
to keep up this time, even hours into our trek, and I'm sure it
has to do with my eagerness to make the crossing and get to
Caden before he leaves.

Sweat dampens my flesh. My shirt sticks to my back, but
I push on, my gaze sweeping over the jagged landscape. Heat
ripples on the air almost in tempo to the droning cicadas. We
walk headlong into them. I adjust the hat on my head, keeping

the brim low. Ahead a dark smudge grows, breaking through the heat waves.

I squint and shoot a quick glance at my guide. "Hey, Mauricio, do you see—"

He nods, his expression tight and alert, his rifle ready in his hands.

I glance back at the figure. It grows and lengthens, drawing closer. I don't let myself panic. The war against carriers is over. And it's just one man. Mauricio seems more than capable of dealing with one man. Even I've proven myself against such odds.

As we get closer, something about the figure makes me increase my pace. I can't see his face, but I begin to think, to suspect . . .

I know that poncho. The tall frame and loose stride. A hat covers his head and hides most of his face from me, but I know. I know it.

I know him.

I break into a run, leaving Mauricio behind. I'm not moving fast enough, so I lose my pack, send it flying to the ground.

"Caden!" I shout, my hat falling back from my head, hitting the baking earth. Nearly tripping, I catch myself and keep running, moving, the sun soaking my bare head.

He came for me. I came for him.

We came for each other. Because he's right. We're part of each other now.

Our bodies meet, collide. We nearly fall, but he catches us, staggering as our arms wrap around each other. He lifts me up, feet dangling above the earth as he twirls me in a circle.

"Davy, Davy . . . Davy." His deep, lyrical voice whispers into my ear, mingling with the rush of wind and chattering cicadas. His voice. The world in general. It all feels clean and fresh. Bright and hopeful.

And I can hear it. Music. Warbling at first, and then gaining rhythm, strength, power. And it's not just in his voice. It's not just coming from him. It's inside me.

I hear music again.

Dear Davy,

Your email almost had me packing my bags. I can't believe you get snow in May. I've never even seen snow. Well, real snow. Snow that sticks longer than one hour before melting. You know what I'm talking about. It's always been a fantasy. I used to dream about going to college up north. When I dreamed about things like college.

Sabine's father visited us last week. It was really nice. He cried. She cried. I think Sean and I might have cried, too. It really made me think of my mom. I'm ready to visit her. Sean might come with me. And Sabine, of course. Sean wants to see his foster brothers. Travel has gotten easier for carriers. At least for those of us without imprints. Sean might still want to wear a scarf. Ha!

We just have to figure out a good time to get away from here. Sabine is the lead teacher in the preschool, and Sean has more work than he can handle in the garage. We're still getting carriers here every day. The camp has doubled in size even though we're all free now. They can't (or won't) stay in their old homes, and the protected areas set up by the government are already crowded.

But at least we have a choice. It's funny how things work out. A year ago, I never would have thought we could go home. I never thought you wouldn't be with us. But change isn't always bad, I guess. We each have to follow our own path. At least we're all free to do so now.

I know we'll meet again, Davy. Friends don't forget each other. Stay happy and tell Caden to keep treating you right. If he doesn't, he better watch his back.

I gotta go now. The guy next to me just crashed his computer. Opening half a dozen programs at once. Idiot. Some people just shouldn't go near a computer.

Build a snowman for me.

Love, Gil

—Email sent from Gil Ruiz to Davy Hamilton, May 2022

EPILOGUE

Alaska, September 2022

I SLIP ON MY HEAVY PARKA, PULL MY KNIT CAP
snug over my blonde, shoulder-length hair, and step outside
into cutting wind. At forty degrees it's one of the coldest Sep-
tembers on record for this area. This high in the mountains,
the cold bites pebble-sharp against my face. For me it feels
arctic. Caden has adapted better, walking around in nothing
more than long sleeves.

Carefully holding a steaming mug of coffee in my hands,
I follow the sounds of whacks to the back of the cabin where
he's cutting wood. Making a decent cup of coffee has become
one of the many tasks I've mastered since moving here. It's not

the end of civilization. At least I've determined it won't be. It might be a far cry from a city with its malls and Starbucks on every corner, but we have neighbors and a small town at the base of the mountain with mail service and a pretty good pizzeria.

I smile, thinking about how everything I have here is better than any future I imagined for myself . . . how *I'm* better than that girl I used to think I wanted to be. Caden and I have found a new community here. People. A life where we can live without looking over our shoulders. Several times a week we perform at the local pool hall in town. Occasionally, we get other gigs, too. Parties, weddings. I just signed a fourth student for music lessons. It's everything I thought I could never have. I stop and gaze at Caden as he hefts the ax and swings at the log he positioned just so.

And love. I've found that, too.

No longer do I fear. No longer do I let others define me. I know what I am. What I'm capable of. That I'm a girl . . . a woman who will fight to survive. Which makes me not that much different from anyone else.

I'm human, with or without HTS.

The majority of carriers have taken to reservations, feeling safer in large numbers. Some returned to families and homes and tried to pick up the pieces of their old lives. Others float, nomads on the fringes of society. And then some are like us. Existing in remote locations, finding their own definition of normalcy.

Caden must feel my stare. He looks up, and a brilliant smile breaks out across his face. I melt inside, and it does wonders for warming me.

"Hey." He sets down the ax and comes toward me.

"I brought you some coffee."

He takes the cup with one hand and wraps his other arm around my waist. "I don't need that." He doesn't even take a sip before giving me a long kiss. Lifting his head, his amber eyes glow at me. "Just you."

I glance at the pile of wood he's cut. "How long until you're finished?"

"I could stop right now." He smiles that smile that's only his—that's made just for me.

Grinning up at him, I wrap both arms around his lean waist and hug him. "I don't want to be a distraction."

He chuckles. "Yes, you do."

Suddenly a distant shout from the front of the cabin rings out.

I tear myself from him. His hand slides down my forearm, fingers lacing with mine as we walk together to the front. Neighbors stop by often. Even though we're apart by miles, there's a strong sense of community among the people out here. Some are carriers. Some aren't, but there's no judgment. Not like back home. The laws might have changed, but a great deal of persecution lingers back home. The world can't change overnight. Not even in a year.

But here, where everyone forges their way, for the most

part judgment is reserved for actions. Not words. Not what we're reputed to be or have done, but who we really are. How we live is what matters.

As we clear the cabin, my gaze lands on our visitor. I don't recognize him at first as he shuts the door of a beat-up truck. Then it clicks. He's thinner than I've ever seen him, his hair long, brushing his shoulders. I break free from Caden and run across the yard, screaming his name. "Mitchell!"

Laughing, my brother hauls me close. "Hey, little sister . . . long time no see."

My laughter twists into a sob. "Only forever."

Pulling back, my brother fondly cups my face. His sharp eyes are as bright and shrewd as I remembered, looking into me, *seeing* me, but then he's always been able to do that. See me even when my parents couldn't. "We got a lot of catching up to do."

I nod jerkily, feeling so ridiculously happy. "I didn't know you were coming."

"Did you think I wouldn't after getting your email? I wanted to surprise you." His gaze slides to Caden, who has come to stand beside me, waiting patiently through our reunion. Mitchell unwraps one arm from around me and stretches a hand out to shake Caden's hand. "I had to meet this guy in your life."

"Mitchell, this is Caden." I take a breath. "My fiancé."

Mitchell stares back and forth between us with wide eyes. "Yeah. You must have missed the email I sent you last week. The good news is that you'll be here for the wedding." I watch my brother's face, suddenly nervous at how he'll react. "It's next week."

He pulls me into a hard hug. "Then I guess I'll be giving you away."

I bury my face against his chest, my smile so wide it hurts my cheeks now. My words are muffled against him. "I'd love that."

I come up for air and look between my brother and Caden, emotion overflowing inside me as I wonder just how I arrived at this moment. Where everything feels right. Still smiling, I lift my face to the wind, to the open sky. I don't even feel the cold.

BEFORE DAVY WAS UNLEASHED— SHE WAS UNINVITED.

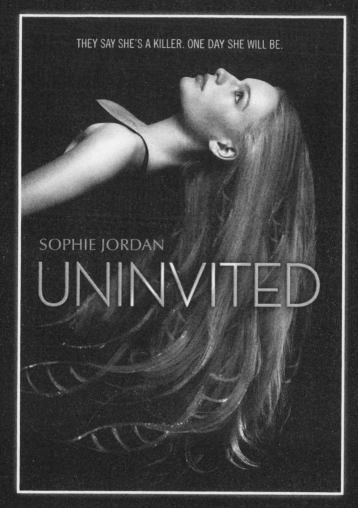

THEY SAY SHE'S A KILLER. ONE DAY SHE WILL BE.

SOPHIE JORDAN

UNINVITED

Don't miss the first book in the *Uninvited* series.

JOIN THE
Epic Reads
COMMUNITY